Gospel

By Bill James in Foul Play Press

GOSPEL

Bill James

A Foul Play Press Book

W. W. Norton & Company
New York   London

First published 1992 by Macmillan London Limited
Copyright © 1992 by Bill James

First American Edition 1997
First published 1997 by Foul Play Press, a division of
W. W. Norton & Company, New York

Printed in the United States of America

A complete catalogue record for this book can be obtained
from the British Library on request.

The right of Bill James to be identified as the author of
this work has been asserted by him in accordance with the
Copyright, Designs and Patents Act, 1988.

Library of Congress Cataloging-in-Publication Data
James, Bill, 1929–
Gospel/Bill James.—1st American ed.
p. cm.
ISBN 0-88150-383-5
1. Harpur, Colin (Fictitious character)—Fiction.
2. Police—England—Fiction. I. Title.
PR6070.U23G67   1997
823'.914—dc21   96-53090
                                                  CIP

W. W. Norton & Company, Inc.
500 Fifth Avenue, New York, NY 10110
http://web.wwnorton.com

W. W. Norton & Company Ltd.
10 Coptic Street, London WC1A 1PU

1 2 3 4 5 6 7 8 9 0

Chapter One

He should not be here. At Harpur's rank you led from the Control Room, did it by radio. Instead, he had turned out again, late thirties, kerb level, waiting in a plain car with three sound lads, conscious of the Walther's weight in a shoulder pouch, loathing its hard presence.

'This them?' Inchiver muttered, staring ahead into the traffic.

'Could be,' Harpur said.

So why was he tooth-and-clawing once more, mutton dressed as wolf, deeply downtown in this street behind Valencia Esplanade? The hand-gun was crammed to his heart and he breathed the sweat odours of four, the nicotine odours of two, and whatever else was going. Set up something like this after a direct whisper, a whisper to you only, and Harpur reckoned you had to join the outing. Part, it was ego, saying the job was his, right through. On top, if he sent men to possible grief on the private word of a grass, he put his body where the grass's mouth was. Harpur did well for private words from a grass, which helped get him fast to Detective Chief Superintendent. It also meant he often sat, pulse up, waiting in ambushes, treating himself to squeamish thoughts about guns, and bloody thankful he had one. You did not dress to kill but you matched the forecast, and the forecast said possible firearms.

Harpur had queried it hard. Such a cheapskate target – a sub-post office in a dismally mini mini-market. Worth gunplay? But the grass again whispered 'possible firearms', and, the grass being Jack Lamb, you listened. Doubts kept their head above water, all the same. What might be available here was at most twenty-five thousand, more likely twenty or fifteen – say four maximum around the mini-market tills, the rest in the post office on pensions and allowances day – to be split three ways, if Jack had the raid party right, and Jack would. They'd risk shots in anger for seven or eight grand each? 'Possible firearms, Col,' came the chorus. 'I wouldn't be talking to you otherwise.' Probably it was quaint these days to think of guns as big stuff.

Yes, this could be them now, a driver plus two in the back of a dark green Audi Quattro, current registration, approaching at a nice unshowy pace. If you stole, steal class, and the car was probably worth more than the purse. But they would not be keeping the Audi. In any case, a lot of people lived a year on much less than eight thousand. He ought to stop thinking in hundreds of grand: vanity – dread that handling nobodies sent you to a nobody career.

'Tinker Bell driving,' Garland said from behind him in the Senator. 'Webb and Venton in the back.'

All as Lamb had promised: three bits of malign trivia – trivia to date – none over thirty, no gun histories, but possibly keen to flower before old age sucked out their sap and sent them back to jemmying gas meters. These boys could fret about careers, too.

Harpur put a hand inside his jacket and touched the Walther, just checking. The weight of it and the tug of the harness around his chest gave nothing but comfort now. Weaponry could be addictive, one reason Harpur dreaded it. There were other reasons – better, sharper: even rubbish like these three could squeeze a trigger and make a decent hole. The Audi had turned in from the main road, officially still Valencia Esplanade, though since its social slide 'Esplanade' sounded comic or cruel, and most knew the area of tarts, thuggery, drug commerce and poverty as just the Valencia. Or may I call you Inner-city?

Martin Webb he could have done without, and he had prayed Lamb was wrong, at least on that. Harpur did pray now and then, an impulse from childhood, and the response was not always so utterly null. Webb had uncles, a father, cousins, grandparents, aunties, brothers, half-brothers, all into crime or thereabouts, a really warm, extended, villain family, lawless in-laws, too, and any of the kin liable to come settling up later, if one of theirs was hurt on duty. Above all, you worried about his father, Doug Webb, known generally as Webby, or as a number when on one of his times away. Today's meeting could be the start, not the wrapping up, of something. That you could say about so many jobs, though.

Harpur glimpsed Martin Webb's delicate straight nose behind Bell in the Audi now before they masked up. Somehow, Martin had collected almost noble features from the wide, underclass lineage, along with a brain that went a little too slowly: not quite retarded, but close. Webb wore his fair hair long and always put Harpur in mind of pictures he saw years ago of that First War poet Rupert Brooke, another childhood recollection. *If he should die think only this of him/ That he was set up cold at Link Street Post Office.* Link Street might not be a foreign field but was highly multi-racial. Among flyposters on a wall near where they waited, Harpur saw news of a show by 'Nigeria's brightest comic, Papa Ajasco and Boy Alingo – pre-London appearance, tickets here'. Could be a good night.

For a moment then, Harpur thought Webb had spotted him. Alongside Harpur, Chris, the driver, seemed to feel the same. 'That's wrecked it,' he muttered. Webb appeared to be staring right at them, and even from so far Harpur could see the bright blueness of his eyes: not so much Rupert Brooke now as a handsome, imperturbable colonel of the old school in that same war, getting his dawn view of the Boche across no-man's-land. Four men in a Senator, three of them bulky, none genial-looking, were always going to be conspicuous, even half-obscured by other vehicles in the mini-market's car-park. Maybe they should have waited on foot with the rest of the ambush in Jailhouse Frock dress shop. But Harpur had wanted a manned vehicle like the Senator ready, in case these people abandoned at the last moment. That could happen with the fourth-rate. He also had an Escort around the corner in Anchor Drive.

Webb's grand features seemed to remain still. As far as Harpur could make out, he was not yelling what he had seen, or even speaking at all. Maybe that unmoving stare came with short-ration marbles. Webb turned away now and looked towards the target, as if just recalling why they were there. The Audi pulled in. These jobs scared anyone, even Francis Garland, but at least they had clarity: take men while they were taking and you side-stepped the chewy problems of manufacturing a tight case. There were hunters and hunted, no grey area stuff, no need to beef up truth for trial.

The rear doors swung open hard together, so Webb could after all act fast when the moment came. He was out first, on the pavement side, the stocking already over his head, bending and blurring that radiant profile. He held an automatic pistol in one hand and a green rucksack in the other, their modest collecting bag. Even they did not seem to expect much. As always, stocking masks brought unreality, a boon to the wearers. Confronted by a nyloned face, some people lost their thinking power, like kids frightened by TV monsters. The real would break through, though: once Harpur had seen a bank robber shot in the mouth through a stocking mask, a chubby old pro called Ernest Lattie – bad police marksmanship, chest being the designated area. That day, a bullet split the stocking sideways in a neat line, and he remembered the difference between the eyes, rosy cheeks and nose, still vague and distorted under their intact, covering film, and the sad actuality of the shattered lips, false teeth and tongue oozing out through the gash. Hard to imagine that the stocking might have previously held only a delightful leg. Harpur heard Ernie's

7

family put 'Blessed are the meek' on his gravestone, all-round debatable.

'Christ, what's that?' Inchiver said.

'Bernardelli Parabellum?' Garland replied – a question so he would not sound too know-all, the know-all, pushy sod. Quite late in life – about thirty-two – Garland seemed to learn the rudiments of tact. 'Nine millimetre, sixteen-round. Used to be called Combat Line.'

'I thought maybe imitation,' Inchiver said.

'Nice for you,' Garland replied.

After a minute, Inchiver muttered: 'Jesus, sixteen rounds in Martin's hand.'

'And Hal's,' Garland said.

Venton, also stockinged, was out on the other side of the Audi and running around the rear to join Webb. He was darker and squatter, not a bit like Rupert Brooke, but he held what could be the same kind of automatic. There had been some choosy buying. Both wore standard British Post Office-doing gear – jeans, denim jackets, oldish-looking trainers. They and the stockings would all burn easily afterwards, not that this time they would get an afterwards. Trainers were expensive, with modes fluctuating non-stop, and people like this kept obsolete pairs for work.

Martin Webb was elegantly lean and athletic looking – altogether the kind of beautiful, flawed baby a mother would think should be given understanding rather than blazed away at by butcher cops, even after duly shouted warnings. If matters went like that, the family would be searching for the grass as well as the police crew, and the grass more, for breaching silence. Plus there were what were called 'the grasses' grasses' – people who brought little tips and rumours to the informant for sorting and possible onward transmission. They could be at peril, too. It had struck Harpur lately, and horrified him, that Denise Prior might easily be mistaken for one of those. Christ, yes, Denise. He would have to think very carefully, very selflessly, very sexlessly, if he could, about her. Naturally, he had mentioned most of these worries to Lamb – though not the ones about Denise – and Lamb replied, 'Noted, Col. Thank you,' just as if he had not agonised over them fifty times already himself. You would not find a politer grass than Jack.

Harpur spoke to the rest on the radio. 'Not yet. Let them get inside.'

It was the old, crucial conundrum, which Harpur had grown brilliant at shutting his eyes to. Did you try to grab them before they hit the shop and Post Office, minimising risk to the customers and veg, or wait until they filled the bag, so a jury had less room and inclination to doubt that men carrying sixteen-round automatics, masked up and with a flight car waiting, engine unswitched-off, definitely had criminal intent, despite what their battling, progressive-minded QC said? For himself, Harpur liked there to be something the exhibits officer could label Swag. Although he obviously wanted no old-age pensioners or nursing mothers felled by ricochets or taken hostage, if you were bringing in robbers you wanted to see them rob. Mark Lane, the Chief, had come to hate such reasoning, though in his detective days he would have lived by it, like everyone else. Promotion brought people down. But Lane could not win that argument – not until some pensioner or mother really was shot or held.

Webb and Hal Venton ran hard and together towards the double doors. Who said Webb was slow? Keeping a fraction ahead, he seemed to have promised himself, maybe promised his dad, that he woud be in first, unscared, dominating, at last a late developer. But for the mask his golden hair would have streamed behind like a Greek god's, but this but was a real but – the stocking made his head look shaved, angled and evil. They would both be yelling threats and orders pretty soon, though the sound might not reach the Senator.

'Move,' Harpur said to Chris and to the radio.

The car jumped forward and Harpur brought his Walther from its holster. Chris had to block in the Audi and three people from Erogynous Jones' Jailhouse Frock party would deal with Bell who had stayed at the wheel, unmasked but crouched down to hide his face, not really managing much of a sentry job. What could a sentry do, anyway? The Audi's hazard lights were flashing – standard signal near a bank or Post Office that a hit proceeded inside. Timothy Bell was the youngest at twenty-four, a father of three, including twin girls, and a genuine family man by all accounts, with regular leisure centre visits, teaching the infants to swim early, and tea in the cafeteria afterwards. Eight grand would look after quite a bit of blancmange. The dossier did not say anything special about his driving, but perhaps he fancied himself. Slight, bald, still unstintingly acned and with an education including A-level biology, he had been a civil servant for a while in Transport and wore what looked like a suit and a collar and tie today, giving the raid tone.

Chris slipped the Senator nicely across the Audi's bow and the Escort came in hard behind. The pavement was wide here, with a string of black bollards along the road edge to prevent cars mounting to park. Planners had put some zestful environmental thought in and prescribed mock cobbles for the pavement which, with the bollards, gave a continental port flavour. Well, it *was* the Valencia. The bollards, the Escort and the Senator sweetly boxed Tinker in. That made three cars with hazard lights on the go, like a street festival. As Harpur left the Senator he glimpsed Bell's head come up suddenly, his face full of fright, eyes puzzled and injured: why were they expected? All he wanted to be was a provider, wasn't it?

Had they given him a Bernardelli, too? Sometimes drivers were drivers because they refused to arm, but don't count on it, and two of the three boys for Tinker had Brownings and instructions to forget his children if he turned explosive.

Harpur, Garland and Inchiver sprinted towards the mini-market, Harpur already making his invitation: 'Put down your guns. Armed police.' Webb and Venton would not hear it yet through the closed doors, but people in the street would, and that might be useful in an inquiry, if you could get any of the buggers to speak. Harpur's legs felt fine. One day, age and cumulative fear over the years might take the core out of them on a job like this, but not today, thank God. His voice was good – strong and persuasive and clear despite a tension wheeze.

He pushed the doors open. Three men were to come in from the back and four more from the Jailhouse Frock contingent had joined him, Garland and Inchiver. Once in a while, numbers favoured the law. The odds might frighten these two into quick surrender, or into a shit-or-bust blast-off: psychology rated with Harpur as only an approximate science, especially when one of the psychologies was Marty Webb's. Harpur saw him now at the Post Office parcel counter, wagging the automatic to terrorise three Asian women working there and screaming: 'The money, the money, the money.' He must have rehearsed. One woman had started filling the bag. This was timing.

Hal Venton had four or five of the customers and assistants herded near the mushrooms, grapes and cucumbers: innocent bystanders were called mushrooms, so mushrooms near the mushrooms. Venton wanted the rest there as well, and was waving the pistol and yelling commands and menace. People did not realise how noisy and verbal a hold-up was. Until those two arrived there had not been a man on the premises and nobody under forty. Most of the women, white and black and brown, gazed calmly at the two, and then at Harpur and his people, as if in these parts armed robbery interceptions came as part of normal shopping. The Chief would have noticed that and felt guilty in his soft way. 'We can't offer safety?' he would grieve. No, we couldn't. Harpur howled two warnings again and raised the Walther so Webb and Venton knew it was all factual.

Venton lurched around when he heard Harpur, forgetting his captives for a second, and near him a thin black woman wearing a brilliant floral dress, her face impassive, suddenly swung her loaded shopping bag and knocked his pistol hand to the side. He swore and would have turned abruptly back to her but Garland, his own Walther still holstered, flung himself at Venton, part wrestling, part rugby and pulled him down to the floor. Immediately, Inchiver kicked twice at Venton's wrist with his red Doc Martens, the second time sending the gun scuttling across the shop. Inchiver gave Venton's arm and hand another couple of careful stamps, guarding against recovery. Foresight figured in his appraisal papers.

The rear door at the side of the Post Office section swung violently open and Erogynous and two others burst in, all fucking wrong. Webb, back to his usual laboured style, looked from the rucksack on the counter to Harpur then to Jones and back to the quarter-filled rucksack, and for his own cloudy reasons decided that since Erogynous led he must be the danger man, though armed only with a truncheon. Deliberately, Webb brought the automatic around to point at him. Jones's gun ticket had lapsed. Both men behind him carried pistols but were obscured. Shambolic: Erogynous – Jeremy Stanislaus – Jones had a long-service award, and was still the world's finest tail, but not always a thinker.

Harpur fired twice from about three yards, without more warnings. Webb's gun went off as he half-spun and fell and the 9 mm piece of lead smacked into a magnificent pyramid of shining green apples, shattering a few and bringing the whole thing tumbling to the ground as Webb tumbled, too – a torrent of minor thuds and then the heavy, helpless one and a clatter when Webb's fingers gave up the gun and ghost. He lay on his side. A couple of apples rolled against Webb's chest and were gradually encompassed by spreading blood, bulbous islands in a bright lake. And, staring at them, for a moment Harpur was capable of only one thought: thank God the Bernardelli had been real and loaded. Even Garland could be wrong.

'Nice one, madam,' Francis told the black woman. 'The Chief Constable will certainly write a letter of thanks on my personal recommendation, if you'll kindly give me your name and address. You might wish to frame it. And possibly the Post Office will want to reward you.' He and Gordon Inchiver had Venton standing between them now, manacled to Inchiver. Garland briskly pulled the stocking up off Venton's face. 'Just a little turd, you see, lady, negligible son of a ponce, but you weren't to know that, were you?' The woman did not respond and resumed her shopping. Race immaterial, not many Link Street people talked or listened to police, or

11

gave names and addresses, or volunteered for perilous media notice, or publicly accepted money for fouling up an enterprise.

Harpur bent to feel for a pulse on Webb. 'You must be joking, sir,' Garland remarked. 'Gorgeous shooting. Necessary shooting. In his numb fashion, young Marty would understand.' Garland crouched down also and peered at Webb's shrouded face. 'Yes, he's looking entirely resigned.' Harpur straightened.

Erogynous said: 'What else could you do, sir? And thanks. Was I hasty there?'

Three men brought Bell in to the shop, his wrists handcuffed behind him. Bell gazed at Martin Webb, heavy tears sliding down and dripping from his pimples. 'I don't think we'll be letting you out for the funeral, Tinker,' Garland said.

And so, on the way back to headquarters in the Senator, Harpur began to worry about Denise Prior, worry more than before, wonder more than before whether he was putting her in peril. Denise had made her irresistible way into his life a few months ago, at a period when he had just begun to feel the hunger for moral certainties which did get to him from time to time. This yearning he regarded as forgivable and even natural: a reaction to spending so much of his professional life in realms where moral certainties got only a short-term visitor's pass, and where Truth, as the Assistant Chief used to say, was not Beauty but what the jury believes. Then, while Harpur felt really into this kind of clean-up, reformist mood, along might come a girl like Denise Prior aged, what, nineteen? True, she was not married, but he still was. As a matter of fact, things between Megan and him had seemed pretty tolerable this last year or so.

Well, there was no 'along might come' and no 'what, nineteen?' about it – no uncertainty at all. She *did* come along and she was just nineteen, a university student here from the Midlands, but without a fume-dried complexion or accent like the death of thought. Instead, Denise was academically as bright as high summer, apparently, yet not bright enough to see, or, at least, not wise enough to care, that contact with him put her at hazard – even before Link Street, and additionally now.

As to complexion, she had glorious skin and features that lived up to it, which he could not help occasionally visualising cut about and wrecked. Worse he could visualise, too, after today. Garland's words stuck in his head and he could imagine himself watching Denise's funeral from the corner of a street in her home town, simply as a bypasser, which is all he would be then.

'Feel all right, sir? Chris asked.

12

'Never better.'

'It was a good outing.'

'I think so.'

Might it be humane, selfless and noble to drop Denise, considering Webb's death and the probable sequel? Harpur tried to console himself with the idea that no matter what he decided now, she would refuse to be dropped. In any case, Harpur recognised that he was humane and selfless only once in a while, and only once in a very long while noble. Other powers generally ran him, some not noble in the least, though maybe none outright evil. None?

He had bought Denise a birthday present last month, some junk jewellery bracelet which she chose herself and alleged she loved. Well, she wore it all the time, all the time she was with him, at any rate. Kids could be surprisingly sensitive, even the highly educated. There were moments when he thanked God she either did not spot the dangers of being tied to him – linked, you could say after this – or did not worry about them enough to say, Thanks and goodbye, Colin Harpur. That is, did not drop him, either. Well, of course, of course, there were such moments: for instance when they were walking on some remote bit of the foreshore or arguing about the Gulf – she had been fiercely pro-war – or Woody Allen or Madonna – she, fiercely anti both – or making love in a hotel bed, or the back or front of a car, or among cement splinters, glass and mortar on the floor of a derelict house, often in the Valencia, as it happened.

And then came the other moments, when this throwback urge to do things right and decently and in keeping hit him hard: nobility raising its thin, bitchy little voice for a second or two. In keeping? That meant suitable for a husband and a father of two daughters, and for a head of the Criminal Investigation Department: once, in fact, a veritable whizz-kid but now the agonising lover of a potential whizz-kid, if kids could whizz anywhere much on Literature and French, her subjects. Denise had a brother and sisters and parents in what sounded like a prime suburb away in Stafford. God knew what they would think of it if they knew. People who named a daughter Denise probably had very wholesome, enthusiastic hopes for her, and sending the girl here to study would be part of those. They certainly would not want her giggling and then sex-groaning in a university town with some thirty-six-year-old heavy, wearing, but half not-wearing, a three-piece suit, on the rotten floorboards of a previously fine sea-view villa, marked for obliteration immediately the slump eased. He had actually gone to H. H. Seabrook's and bought himself a classier outfit than he usually wore – off-the-peg, but a genuine muted country-style tweed job – as if this might make his behaviour sweeter. He adored her, but was not entitled to. No tailoring could put that right.

As to the perils, then: through evening ballet classes in the town hall Denise was friendly with Jack Lamb's live-in bird, Helen Surtees. Harpur had first met Denise more or less by accident in a record shop, when trying to pick a rap disc for his younger daughter, who had come second in a judo tournament. He asked Denise for advice: probably he would not have, had she been less pretty, which was why he thought of it as only more or less an accident. Denise had been unable to help. It was not her sort of music, either. Things developed from there, though. Only later, and *too* late, did Harpur discover the link to Helen, and so to Lamb.

Jack and Harpur took endless care over security, but evidence grew that some folk suspected Lamb leaked, and had done it for Link Street. He lived with risk, like any grass, big or small. He also lived with this once-punk kid, Helen, who would definitely qualify for some of the reprisal package, too, if the word seriously spread about Jack and Harpur.

But for her connection with him, Denise would probably have been safe – not really close to Jack, only to Helen, which was remote enough. Now, though, it would look as if she were tied up with Lamb and with the prime killing cop, as well. She might appear a go-between: one of those skint students earning a bit extra carrying the tales from informant to executioner. She was not, but that's how it might seem, and this would be enough. These people did not need perfect proof, did not have to persuade a jury. To get Jack himself, or Harpur himself, might be difficult, though not impossible. They did know something about protecting themselves, and protecting those who lived with them, like Harpur's family or Jack's Helen. It meant that if the Webb mourners wanted to make a point and return some agony they might pick the supposed messenger. Harpur recalled another girlfriend of Helen, who finished dead inside a rolled Wilton carpet on the foreshore, though not the stretch where Harpur and Denise sometimes strolled and argued and talked love in what he hoped was secret.

'You saved a police life this morning, Col,' the Assistant Chief said. 'No worries. The inquiry will be fine. Some are appointed to see filth shall not swamp the earth, and at times the only way is plug the orifice.'

'*Psalms*, sir? A word for all situations.' They were in Iles's big immaculate room at headquarters, the ACC cleaning his nails.

14

'Lane wonders if you should think about being counselled. As a killer,' he said. 'Well, the creepy Mick jerk would, wouldn't he?'

'I might. I hear it's often effective.'

'The Chief's wholly into the caring dimension. I certainly don't say it's a total write-off.'

'I'll think about it, sir.'

'That Webb rabble – when they hear!' the ACC whooped. For a while he went into a rich chuckle, sitting back radiant at the desk. He examined his hands and put the nail-file away in his top pocket. There was a copy of what looked like a novel on the desk called *The Sun Also* something-or-other, title and book part-hidden by papers: Iles hated it to be known he read. 'Perhaps they've had the news by now. Oh, boy, I'd love to be the one who broke it. Bit by bit we'll force that rotten dynasty down. Well, you've cut a few corners today. Another suggestion from the Chief is armed protection for a while, you and the family. You *are* still with them, Col? Obviously, we won't be publicising who actually let daylight into Martin, not till the trial, at any rate, but there were a fair number of people watching. These things do get out. You're not an anonymous figure.' Iles stood suddenly and bent his thin silver-grey head forward a little, to watch whether the creases fell out of his suit, as the tailor must have told him they would for that money. It, also, was silver-grey, double-breasted, built for him, certainly in London. Almost slight and almost refined looking, Iles in plain clothes was not always recognised by strangers as a policeman, one of his several assets. He sat down again, apparently content.

'I don't want men at the house, sir. I can look after myself and the family.'

'I told Mark Lane how you would feel. But you know him. Everyone's nanny, lovable old biscuit. And the student girl? You're still enraptured there?'

'The Webb menace is exaggerated.'

'Will you tell this youngster to keep her eyes open, Harpur, and to walk with care? Around that age people can be very casual, especially the clever ones. They assume life's running only their way, whereas it could be something diabolically different. Really, what the Chief would not want, and neither do I, is a kid like that, on our patch from elsewhere as an undergraduate guest, given heavy and messy hammer by the Webb culture. I'd feel we had failed her. We do not do that. You hear? Col, sometimes I wonder if you see beyond the end of your hormones.'

Harpur tried to leave the subject: 'Sir, about Erogynous –'

'Gagadom setting in there? Time he took a pub?'

'Erogynous has so much courage and pride, sir. It would be instinct for him to come first through that Post Office door.'

'Holding a twig. What's he think he's doing, water divining? Naturally, I'm not wholly displeased to see Marty wiped out before he can grow into something heavier – probably a sawn-off next time – but not wiped out in that sort of scramble. And I am able to view matters from your point of view, Harpur – the shock. It's a feature of top leadership, known as empathy. I shouldn't think it will ever come your way, but I've plenty: they called me Empathy Iles at Staff College. I can see this was a shooting forced on you, and you're sensitive. Yes, that's one word for what you are. How's Megan?'

'Great. We're all supposed to be going out to dinner tonight. It's one of my daughters' birthday.'

'Lovely. Why not?'

'Sir, after this morning I suppose I'm feeling—'

'Unbearably success-thrilled. They'll put up with that. It might humanise you a bit and bring a spark. The lads from your Link Street project will be having a little celebratory drink-up, too, I suppose. Where? The club here?'

'No, Ralphy Ember's place, the Monty, sir.'

Iles beamed. 'Great. Take the fight to the enemy. Let them see who's in charge. Well, have your nice family occasion and then go on to the Monty, yes. I might look in there myself. I'm fond of old Panicking Ralph. Which daughter?'

'Hazel. Fifteen.'

'Already? My best wishes to the child. I mean your daughter, not the undergraduate. And to Megan, obviously.' He opened a drawer in his desk and brought out a twenty-pound note. 'Give that to the girl – your daughter, that is. Oh, say from Uncle Des.'

'That's not necessary, sir, really.'

Iles sat up very straight and spoke fiercely. 'I don't want this kid dead or mutilated on my ground, Harpur – that's the one who's not your daughter. Well, I don't want your daughter hurt, either, naturally – either of your daughters, or your wife. In her own way, Megan's a gem. But give some powerful thought to the other.'

'This is most generous of you, sir,' Harpur replied, putting the money away for Hazel.

'She the snooty one – Hazel? Doesn't think much of police? Especially doesn't think much of myself? They develop good taste very early, some children today. If you suspect she won't want to take the gift from me, say it's out of the slush fund, Col. She'd believe that, I expect.'

'Neither of them thinks much of police. Nor Megan.'

16

'They don't understand, Col. That's all. You mustn't feel harsh or injured. We're surrounded by the worthy who believe good might prevail. Once in a while it does – Link Street. Then we dance on the grave. It's a therapy, and you need a therapy, Col. It's an aid for the future.'

At the restaurant in the evening he found himself for a moment arguing with Franco over the table reserved for them. Harpur wanted to sit where he could watch the door.

'What's the matter, Colin, for heaven's sake?' Megan asked. 'This one's fine, Franco.'

Jill, Harpur's younger daughter, said: 'To do with Link Street, dad? The thing on TV news? You were there?'

Harpur dropped the objection and they took the original table. When he handed Hazel the ACC's gift she asked: 'Has he finally flipped, I mean, completely?'

'I think Mr Iles must have a hidden, lovely side to him,' Jill said.

'You what?' Megan replied.

'He does what he can,' Harpur said. 'He's fighting a war.'

'But is it a just war?' Megan asked.

'God, Mummy, what a slab of trite piety,' Hazel replied.

'Well, thanks, Hazel,' Harpur said.

'Just this once,' she replied. 'Not a permanent alliance.'

'Of course not,' he said.

After dinner, Megan took the children home and Harpur went out to the Monty, Ralphy Ember's place in Shield Terrace. It had been Garland's idea to come here. Occasionally, after a good operation people wanted to celebrate in public, not on home ground – even wanted to celebrate in somewhere like the Monty, where half the membership was on bail and most of the other half away, locked up. As Iles had said, to come here in strength after Link Street was a victory fanfare, a lap of honour on the other team's ground. Harpur would not have minded missing it, but you did not miss an outing like this. Leadership brought its own fierce set of rules.

Iles and the others were already there. 'We'll get Ralphy over,' the ACC said, beckoning to Ember behind the bar. 'Bring some of that connoisseur's Kressmann Armagnac, there's a saint, Ralph.'

Ember came to their table carrying two black-labelled bottles.

'We mean to be properly behaved tonight, Ralph,' Iles said. 'Well, what else in such a decorous spot? These boys have done exceptionally well today. You know Erogynous? Excelled himself. Bob Cotton? Sid Synott? Chris? Gordon Inchiver? And so on. All lovely fellows. And, of course, Col Harpur, himself, always our sombre star.'

'I heard there'd been activity,' Ember replied.

'Exactly that.'

Ember poured.

'Have one yourself, Ralph,' Iles told him. 'Me, I'll stick to the usual – the old tart's drink, port and lemon. And Col will have gin and cider, I expect. Ever the prole.'

Ember went back to the bar for the drinks and to fetch himself a glass. Harpur saw he met the eyes of no other customer. The ancient long knife scar along his jaw seemed to have grown pale with stress. People said he looked like Charlton Heston without the money, but tonight haggardness had taken over, and he stooped slightly. Iles could always have that kind of effect on him just by walking in the door. Being forced to drink with a bloodstained ambush crew would not bring him relaxation, either. He sat down and took some Armagnac, all the same, and Iles grew quiet for a while, gazing at Ember as at a dear friend just returned after long absence.

Then the ACC said: 'Enough about us, and our little achievements, Ralph. How about you, your wife, Margaret, and the children? Erogynous will have their names, I'm sure of it. He's a walking dossier.'

'Venetia, Fay,' Erogynous said.

'Spot on,' Iles remarked. 'These names are redolent.'

'All fine,' Ember said.

'They're going to be ladies, worthy of you and the Monty, Ralph,' Iles told him. 'I'm certain of it. That fine school, and the gymkhanas.'

'I ought to get back to the bar,' Ember said.

'Ought you?' Iles replied.

'It's a busy night for him, sir,' Harpur said.

'Always the placator, is dear old Harpur. But you're right, Col. Crowds. They're all out drinking to Link Street, aren't they?' the ACC shouted. 'We'll have a toast, too, yes, Ralph? Here's to – well, life?' They all sipped.

'Shall I leave the Kressmann's?' Ember said.

Chapter Two

Jack Lamb liked to give a big summer ball every year, mostly when his mother was over on holiday from the States. After Link Street he wondered if he should forget it this year and focus on health. Almost anyone could sneak in and out again when the house and grounds were open for the ball. Helen wanted to invite that friend, Denise Prior, who was into a warm relationship with Harpur. Lamb worried a bit about this but thought it would be harsh to object: they had become quite close, the two girls. Lamb liked Denise. She seemed bright, so must see the dangers, surely.

His doubts over the ball did not last, anyway. Could he let rubbish like the Webbs chill his life, for God's sake? Physically huge, Lamb hated any notion of small-mindedness or nerves. What could the Webbs know? They weren't organised for information, or for anything else except strong-arm and thieving. Besides, Helen would be really distressed if the party was shelved, and he had an idea his mother would be, too. He could not let himself look troubled, and it would be measly and ungracious to own a manor house like Darien with its big lawns and flower-beds and fail to put on some hosting, this year or any other. The Lamb summer party was in the calendar and must stay there.

He liked his mother to see he knew people of all sorts, many of them entirely decent, despite everything. At the ball there would be not only other art dealers and important collectors, but genuine county figures and the very seriously rich, some with money and land stretching right back.

'If only we could get the Lord Lieutenant, Jack,' Helen said.

'Tricky.'

'We had the Lord Mayor last year.'

'He was in scrap metal. The Lord Lieutenant is Her Majesty's representative in the county, love.'

'Why it would be great.'

'Perhaps I'll work on it,' Lamb replied.

'He might feel hurt he's never been asked.'

'I don't bump into him much to find out.'

Helen was a very rare kid – although still not twenty, able to run one of these parties as if she had been doing it for decades, arranging the catering, the marquees, a lot of the guest list, the bands and the security with no trouble at all, and on the night making sure the social mix never led to unpleasantness. If after something like this Post Office botch it ever came to the darkest – though, pray God, with Helen getting out of it unhurt – he had left her comfortable. Helen understood about cash, wouldn't blue it, and was learning picture dealing very quickly. On *l'art fang* she knew more than he did already. She had wisdom, despite being so young.

Obviously, she could not be told everything, and did not expect it – not the full details of how the business worked, the reciprocals with Harpur, and where some of the pictures came from, and so on – yet he knew she sensed the general situation. She could even give him sound advice. And she had real control of herself. In her punk period – over now, thank Christ – she had looked as wild as any kid could, but only looked. Always, this solid dignity.

'But Denise, definitely?' Helen asked.

'Of course.'

More than once he had tried to speak to Harpur about this girl, and every time Colin instantly killed the subject, in that way of his. Lamb understood. Some situations would not stand much examination. The curtains had to stay shut.

Chapter Three

Denise Prior drove home to Stafford for a couple of days to bring back an evening frock for Jack Lamb's summer ball. She had a Katharine Hamnett pink sequin flower shift there which would do a treat on a warm evening, a nineteenth-birthday present from her father that had cost a real packet: sixties look – very short, very seeming-simple – which was what had won him: nostalgia for his own student days, silly old generous jerk. Denise's feelings lately were a jumble, adding up mainly to brilliant, happy, slightly nervous excitement. These last couple of months her life seemed really to have taken off, and this occasion at Jack Lamb's would be a soaring part of that. Admittedly, there were other parts: the filthy floor of some abandoned dump in the Valencia would not rate with everyone as magic, for instance, but it could be. Afterwards, she would have a giggle watching the brick dust swill from her hair across the shower floor, like a march of pink insects. With the shift dress, she could wear the grand lumpy fun jewellery she had from Colin for her nineteenth, another lovely present.

Things did look great: the good weather had come, her first-year examinations were finished and probably all right, and the invitation to Jack's big night brought notions of May Ball glamour at Oxbridge, which as a kid she had raptured over in magazines – all that privileged gaiety, beauty, noise, excess, fashion. Although she had always half hoped her university would come up with something like this, too, she now feared it probably wouldn't. Deconstruction and *Fleurs du Mal* you got by the truck-load, plus plenty of gayness, but little gaiety. Excess she fancied, also. She had chosen not to go to Oxford, so felt obliged to make the best of where she was. The shindig at Jack's might help. Lavish was a word Helen used a lot about it.

Denise had a pretty good idea from hints Helen gave, plus from what she had seen herself of Jack and his place on a couple of visits, that there might be something not quite publishable about how Lamb earned his money. Just to look at the pictures he had on his walls made her thrilled and uneasy. Even if the market was shaky at the moment, you still had to be talking about hundreds of grand and sometimes many hundreds. She had seen what Jack told her were Whistlers, a Tissot, two Sisleys and a Hockney there, and she did not think he would lie. Anyway, she would have identified the Tissot and Hockney herself. The pictures at Darien changed frequently – like at the Odeon, Helen said. That could be all right. Jack called himself a dealer and dealers bought and sold. Denise wondered if all those transactions were above board, though, to use one of her father's honest-John phrases.

In fact, Denise thought this function at Darien might be less like a May Ball than one of those oddly peopled get-togethers run by the crook-hero of *The Great Gatsby*, a book you got through because it was there, on the 20th Century Fiction course, and which made her deeply ratty with its wispy prose. Robert Redford had played Gatsby in the film, gorgeous and wholesome-looking, but still a jumped-up hood. If Jack Lamb had been as pretty as Redford then it would not stop her wondering, either. Of course, genuine notables would attend: Helen said she was trying for the Lord Lieutenant, who would be such a catch, apparently. Denise thought his pictures in the local paper made him look a right little prat, all chin and graciousness. However, it was his cachet Helen wanted, not his sex-appeal.

At home in Stafford, Denise gave a breathless preview of the ball and told how she had met Helen at dance classes.

'Outside the college?' her father asked.

It was hard to know which answer he wanted but she said: 'Oh, yes.'

'I like that,' he replied. 'Ballet. Not narrow and campus-locked.'

'Helen's into a really various life.'

'Well, it sounds good, as long as— And this party is given by her boyfriend?'

'Long-established. Art dealer. Jack Lamb. A manor house.'

'Really?' her mother said. 'Denise is seeing the world, Andrew.' She sounded jumpy.

'It's only one event in a whole year.'

Denise thought that as well as the Lord Lieutenant, if he came, there would be other, rougher, sorts present at the ball, too. It was intriguing, irresistible, her chance to know something of a different world, see some social cheek-by-jowling; her chance to grow up faster than almost any kid on her courses. A bit scared, she felt she could handle things, all the same. Didn't everyone say she had a brain? Anyway, how could she turn it down without hurting Helen?

Obviously she would be careful how she described Helen and Jack and the prospect of the party to her parents, and she would not be describing or mentioning Colin Harpur to them at all. They were liberal enough – both students themselves in those tearaway sixties, and both briefly involved with all sorts before they married – yet now awash with Aids angst, in the nagging, worthy way their sort of middle-aged set could be about offspring. It would bother them to hear more than a tactful account of Helen and Jack Lamb, and especially Helen. Or especially Jack. It was not just sex that worried them. Denise's father had begun to grow obsessive about what he called 'the new common currency of violence', and fussed over where Denise found her friends. He could be a pain, despite the dress.

'It's real art this Jack Lamb has in his home?' he asked.

'Entirely.'

'This is grand,' he muttered.

'A lot of interesting bohemians at a do like this?' her mother asked.

'I should think so.'

'They can be fun,' her father said.

'And you'll look so lovely, I know it,' her mother said. 'You look lovely, anyway, doesn't she, Andrew? There's a boyfriend? Boyfriends? I mean, who will you go with? It's the sort of thing where you'll need to go with someone, I should think, isn't it, I mean?'

'I see some people,' Denise replied. 'Off and on. You know how it is in college.'

'Consider yourself silenced, Sybil.'

'Oh, sorry. Am I being nosy?' her mother said.

They worried about all the usual things, her mother and father, yet also as a relic of their sixties pot and student-revo bilge, they were not pro-police, and certainly not pro thirty-six-year-old married police for one of their daughters. Well, this daugther wanted him, and, if she had been asked, could have listed twenty-five positive reasons, none HIV, and knew it would probably turn out a bad, sad and agonising thing eventually. A few times most days she told herself eventually could be quite a way off yet, and this thought kept her reasonably content.

She had asked Colin about Jack Lamb. Colin said he knew him and the house and the business, though not well. And that was nearly all on the subject – lips zipped, so naturally she did not believe him. Quite often she could not believe Colin. For instance, she had asked him whether he was involved in the Post Office shooting in Link Street. He told her people of his rank did not go on ambushes. She still wondered though. Secretiveness was a minus factor, but perhaps it was bound to happen if you loved a gifted cop. He was. She did.

As a topic, Jack Lamb had been more or less dropped a long time back, except that, without actually warning her off, Colin said enough to show he'd prefer she missed the ball. 'You'll meet some rare ones there, Denise.'

'I hope so. How come you're not asked? You're rare.'

'My breeding's not up to it.'

She had put his objections down to possessiveness, liked that, and still decided to go.

At home, Denise's younger sister, Jane, asked: 'Marquees on the lawn – lawns?'

'The lot. The Lord Lieutenant.'

'It all sounds very select,' Sybil Prior said, meaning that it all sounded to her like horribly grey-area stuff. 'Art dealer', manor house, live-in dancing kid – what was Denise playing with? The whole thing reminded her of that gorgeous American novel she read years ago as a student, *The Great Gatsby*, with its marvellous lacy writing and sad scale. She had seen something like it in the sixties – that 'fun thing' mentality, when people liked to behave as if the gaps between right and wrong, legal and illegal, rich and poor, class and no-class could be so casually bridged. Life was there to be lived, et cetera. She had done some of it herself, of course. It really frightened her now to hear Denise talk so cheerfully, so innocently, about what might be a re-run of all that twenty-five years later. People could get hurt, and worse. She had seen some of that, too.

'Art?' she said. 'Dealing with museums, collectors or what?'

'Collectors mainly, I think.'

'And the buying? It fascinates me, the whole business. Where do the pictures come from?'

'Well, collectors, too, I suppose. People raising the wind, hit by recession? Or looking for a change on the wall of their drawing-room? They'd be the kind to have drawing-rooms.'

Sybil laughed with her, knowing she would not rest properly until she found out more about this successful businessman, Jack Lamb, and his dancing popsy, Helen. But where did you start? Andrew was right – you could not badger Denise, and, in any case, she might not know the half of it, the tenth of it. Denise was a child – a smart child, an adult child, but a child. As they talked now, Sybil found herself planning a day trip in that direction and asking a question or two about the manor house and the expensive culture it contained. She might tell Andrew she was going, she might not. She could see he was worried, but he would say a visit was useless. Probably he was right. Where did you ask the questions? What did you say: *Excuse me, is Mr Jack Lamb of Bigtime Manor a crook? Is my daughter in danger because of him?* All the same, Sybil felt she had to try. Every few months she went to London on a shopping trip alone. Possibly she could skip London and use one of those days.

'No special boyfriend yet?' she asked.

'They're all special – in their own eyes.'

'Our daughter's growing worldly wise, Sybil,' her husband said.

Sybil doubted it. 'I always said university was an education,' she replied.

Chapter Four

Ralph Ember felt pressure. Those bastards, parading in his Monty – flaunting, crowing, making him look like a pot-boy before his customers, sucking him into a toast which, although even they would not say so, was a blaze-of-glory toast to the end of a simple boy, Marty Webb. Everyone there would know it and talk about it. That was just like Iles. He loved bringing people right down. Of course, he would realise Ember was rated more or less Number One in the business community now. And to Iles and some of the others with him, such as that Garland, all this meant was, Destroy him, humble him, turn him feeble in public. It was probably one of these who cooked up the saying, years ago, that he looked like Charlton Heston without the money. Well, fuck them. He still looked like Charlton Heston, and he had the money now, plus status, plus a great house almost in the Jack Lamb class. People watching what happened the other night in the Monty would expect him to hit back, and would tell him to hit back if he did not do it soon. And so, yes, he had pressure.

Not right at this moment but never far away. At this moment, he was in a dormobile double-bed with the wife of its owner and as comfortable as anyone needed to be. At this moment, this exact moment, the only pressure was of an acceptable, downward, physical sort, since Christine Tranter was fond of doing glorious spells on top and had just sat up straight backed, her fingers laced behind her head and elbows out like delta wings, with him, naturally, enclosed below. She regarded sex as being what she called 'totally reciprocal' and this signified among other things not spending all the time on her back.

He had no objections and Christine seemed happy now and had a good smile on, her tan eyes open and gazing up at the interior light, which flickered occasionally, meaning the dormobile battery might be last-legging. That would be just like her damned uneven husband, Leslie, so obsessed with his work, yet slapdash on vehicle maintenance.

26

Ember knew Christine had read somewhere – possibly an article by Germaine Greer – that any woman could be good just taking and relishing underneath, but the riding position required zappy commitment. Challenges interested Christine – one of the most fascinating things about her in Ember's opinion, though there were others. She read a tremendous amount and believed that much of what was written could have an important bearing on life, and should not necessarily be regarded as just print and pages. Ember always listened when she talked of things she had found in books or journals. Christine was a girl he thought extremely seriously about and might have been ready to consider permanence with, if the two of them had not been already heavily settled where they were, what with kids, property, possessions and marriage. Christine meant so much to him that for weeks he had entirely cut out interest in all other spare. She deserved dedication.

He gave her that now, yet part of his consciousness stayed focused on the messages he had been getting lately, sometimes only hints, sometimes very direct. Whichever style they took, they said the same: that sod Jack Lamb, up there with his bird and art in a manor house with art, behind a wall and gates, had become too much and could not be allowed to continue – that is, had to be silenced, especially after Link Street. If he did not do it, someone else would, and probably a Webb. That could make Ember look a discarded thing of the past, not at all like Number One.

Of course, none of those leaning on him offered ideas on how to finish Lamb. Using the finger-on-the-trigger argument, some wanted Harpur as well, though you could argue he had only done what he had to. A cop was a cop, unless you could purchase, and Harpur you could not. In any case, it was not totally established who fired.

Arranging anyone's death was a foul and solemn matter, definitely no formality. With Jack Lamb it was especially tough. He was too big – not just his body, though Jack was like the rock of ages, uncleft. There were also his position, his wealth, his land and Darien, his pictures, his pull, his friends. Obviously, his pull and his friends were the same item: police. This was now the standard view on Jack and, even if Link Street had not happened, because of him there would be lads from other betrayed jobs living three in a cell and exercising under guard for as far ahead as it was worth thinking about. Ember saw why people were enraged: relatives, friends, women. But those who grassed to police the police looked after. The Latin for it came out as *quid pro quo*, Latin had words for anything. This bastard Lamb had a Latin motto of some sort on his gates, as a matter of fact, though not that: what was Latin for grassing?

27

So, stress. The Lamb situation had started turning into a test. Ember sometimes thought you could regard it as like single combat, modern gladiators or knights, if you did not know what Lamb had behind him as concealed back-up. Although, in his time, Ember had managed one or two superb triumphs – clearly, or he would not be still around, and around at the summit – taking on Jack Lamb, with or without his allies, would be mighty. Ember liked non-violence, even civilisation, unless pushed. Now, he was being pushed hard. His own feelings of duty saw to that, as well as the rumour and angry pleas. He wondered if it might be more convenient to do someone close to Lamb – his girl, or a tipster who fed him – and make the point that way.

The interior light dimmed, went out, came back on, then went out again, finally. Christine giggled. She leaned forward so that her breasts brushed his face, a sensation she had learned he loved. 'Like manna from heaven but bonnier,' he had told her not long ago: Christine knew Religious Knowledge figured as one of the first-year subjects Ralph took in his degree course as a live-at-home mature student in the university up the road, and he could come out with some extraordinary phrases, including from the Koran. Christine found it great that he should study while still running the Monty, and running whatever else it was he did on the darker side, the business he kept curtained. When she originally met him he would sometimes talk like a sick dictionary, using such words as 'untoward' and 'deleterious'. What she loved in him was that he had come to realise he sounded puffed up and quaint, and bravely decided on a late-life change – decided to complete an education, which had stopped at school. That place was doing things for him.

To suggest contentment, Ember poked out his tongue to meet her breasts as they caressed him. And, normally, contentment was what he would genuinely have felt. But the failure of the interior light troubled him, though not the darkness, or any symbolic aspect in the on, off, on, off again, like the switches of fortune in life itself: no, only the practical fear that this vehicle might fail to start. What he did not want at this stage in his career was exposure to hazard through the patchy doziness of bloody Leslie George Tranter.

Ember and Christine were on the fourth floor of a multi-storey carpark in the middle of the city, the curtains of the dormobile decently closed, naturally. They often came here, which was what troubled Ember now. People spotted habits, and multi-storeys could be no-man's-land without the stretcher bearers. It was not Christine's husband he feared. Leslie was unquestionably in Cumbria or Wales or the Isle of Wight selling his automatic feeding machine for cats and dogs, which by all accounts could not be bettered. Apparently, it was a boon to families where nobody was at home all day, or where they liked to flit off to the country cottage for a few days without pets. Possibly Leslie would go international subsequently and be absent marketing even longer: the Continentals were very keen on the weekend out of town.

No, no worries over Leslie, but Ember fretted instead about other lads – hard and evil lads like some of the Webbs, who might decide he was showing soft on Link Street, and even think he was part of the system that shopped Martin. The stories about drinking with Iles and Harpur would spread. Iles had made a big show of paying for everything, even the Armagnac – to tell the world the treat was on him and that Ember had earned a part of it. Iles contained authentic evil. And then, of course, to get an insult in as well, he and Harpur make out the Monty's top Armagnac is nothing much and prefer their own rubbish mixtures.

Even before Link Street Ember had felt exposed. Envy went deep with some. Since his success, or successes, really, all sorts would be happy to find him immobilised and unprotected in a concrete corner of one of the modern urban world's big shadowy hutches. His career had been bound to produce an enemy or two. They heard of profit nicely garnered and wondered why it was not theirs and how it might get to be. The multi-storey was Christine's idea. He would have preferred countryside, but she needed to return home quickly to her children. Of course, a woman like Christine, with a nice background and Church connections, did not think about the grim potential of these buildings, though, God knew, they were used as thuggery sites in enough telly dramas. He gave no argument, not wishing her alarmed. Ember had always believed that consideration for a woman was vital, especially one as lovely and warm as Christine, willing to bring in a short-spell baby-sitter so she could see him. At least nerves did not get to Ember where it mattered, not immediately, anyway, and he gently rolled Christine on to her back now and eased himself on to her.

All the same, Christine sensed at once that something was wrong, but had no idea what it might be, and knew it would be pointless to ask. With Ralph, these sudden disastrous changes could happen, splintering even the best moments. They gave her heavy pain, because she felt so incapable of helping him. His complexities saddened and intrigued her. She wrapped her arms and legs around Ralph and murmured in his ear the extent of her love, yet knew she was failing to reach him. His whole body had grown tense, and not from sexual power. Her fingers traced a line of sweat forming across his shoulder blades, and he ran his own hand caringly over the strange scar along his jaw, almost as if expecting it to open spontaneously through worry.

She had heard that some called him 'Panicking Ralph' and wondered at times like these if she was getting a glimpse of why. It made her love Ember more. She yearned to understand. Did his wife Margaret excel at dealing with these agonies? Was this why they stayed together, despite everything? Basically, he needed her, only her? Christine could feel intolerable jealousy at that.

When she tried to start the dormobile the engine turned over once and died. 'Don't worry,' Ralph said. 'I'll push it to the ramp and you can jump start.' But his voice was hoarse and weak. He glanced about, as if looking for help.

'We can wait until some volunteers show up,' she said.

'Volunteers?' Dread clothed the word. 'No. I'll manage. You're late home already. The sitter will cost the earth.'

'It's heavy, Ralph. The stove and other fittings.' He was not young. A heart attack or hernia in a spot like this would be awful.

'I'll manage. Let's get out of here.' Ralph glanced around again and this time she realised that he was checking for trouble, not seeking aid.

Once he had the vehicle moving things were easier. At the top of the ramp she waited and he climbed in. The engine started at her first try. He smiled: 'Nothing to it.' Now his voice was fine, the voice of a dear lover and a man who could always cope. As they drove out into the street she turned to look at him for a moment and he smiled. The skin over the scar tightened and shone, becoming yellow-grey and almost transparent under the street lights, like an envelope's address window, though he was hard to read. Ralph himself seemed to have forgotten all about the scar now.

'Should we find somewhere else, Ralph?'

'How do you mean?'

'Not the multi-storey. It seemed to – well, to upset you.'

'Upset? Why on earth should it? I don't think so. The multi-storey's fine.'

He wondered what chance he had of dealing with someone of Jack Lamb's calibre when a bit of engine trouble gave him terror. Ember put his hand on Christine's thigh as she drove and summoned a vision of two, perhaps three, bullets smacking Lamb in the left-eye area, and that huge lumpy body folding up with a single groan to finish finished at his feet. It would be in some nice secluded spot from which a swift, untraceable exit should be simple, and from which the legend of his achievement could then trickle out to the initiated, though no hard, usable evidence. *That Ember – some operator. Remember they used to call him 'Panicking'? What a laugh.*

Christine sighed and gasped a little with pleasure at the tightened grip above her suspender buckle. He radiated sex and affection and she had never known anyone comparable. 'That scar, Ralph?'

'Fading, isn't it?'

'Oh, yes, but how did—?'

'Don't let the engine die until you get home,' he replied. 'The lights are probably taking as much out of the battery as we're putting in.'

'Soon again?' she muttered. Presumably his sodding wife knew the full story of the scar, though. That's what marriage was about, inventorying your husband's wounds.

'Next Tuesday?'

'Before if you like.'

'Of course I like. Friday.'

'Friday.'

Visions of brilliant coups, like the one of Lamb he had just enjoyed, came easily to Ember. Good ideas could result that way, and he always dreamed in full detail: it was specifically Lamb's left-eye region where Ember imagined the bullets banging home, and he had visualised which of his pairs of shoes Lamb would tumble down on to. Getting the ideas into practice was where he could be poor, though. Ember knew himself to be exceptionally frail at moving from planning to doing. He was someone who had charted his being pretty thoroughly and disliked most of what he found, even though he generally kept up a superb, brassy show. With Winston Churchill he believed the greatest human quality to be courage, and hoped always that one day he would acquire more. Time was slipping along, however.

She put him down near his own car, parked in a side street. He could probably have left it in the multi-storey, but something from far, far back said two vehicles standing close to each other were more than twice as conspicuous as one. Old instincts you listened to. They formed part of your very self, and it did not matter how much you suspected this very self was candy floss. You had nothing else, nothing.

When he left the dormobile and they kissed goodnight, Christine could see he still felt uneasy and restless and might plan to go somewhere else, do something else, before returning home or to the club. Again she knew, though, that it would be useless to ask him. He was smiling, but very drawn, as if some weight dragged at his spirits and he had determined to fight back. That gameness was like

31

him, and she admired it. 'Wonderful,' she said. 'It was wonderful, Ralph.'

'Yes, wonderful.'

What he had decided was to drive up to Lamb's big place, Darien, just outside the town, take a look at his spread – the bloody wall, the tall gates and Latin tablet and what you could see of the house behind the drive of trees – but that was all, at this stage: remind himself he had a target, brush up on hate. If you were Number One and wanted to stay there you never really stopped work. Leadership brought its terrible, endless compulsions.

Chapter Five

Always, as her car passed through the tall gates of Darien, she felt a marvellous surge of pleasure and excitement. 'This is the life, kid!' she muttered to herself today. So, was she growing snobby? That idea troubled Denise, troubled her a lot, yet she still adored the rich sound her tyres made on the curved, beech-bordered drive: a steady, gentle, but all-conquering crackle over the golden gravel: how a lovely, Georgian house, with its genuine sixteenth-century core, ought to be approached. It made her think of Jane Austen, if they'd had Fiat Pandas then.

Darien stood encircled by a fine high grey-stone wall and had the elegant black-painted wrought-iron gates, with their slab of Latin at the top, *Omnes Eodem Cogimur*. At school she did engineering drawing instead of Latin, for a lark, really, but Helen had told her the words came from Horace and meant, basically, No choices. Poor Horace, if he really went for that. She had chosen Colin Harpur, and he had sort of chosen her. Hadn't he? Yes, he was married, but Denise could make herself believe she was now the one he really wanted. Must believe it. As to choices, she also opted to pop out here whenever she could to see Helen and Jack, even though she wondered sometimes if this was bright. She had an idea Colin thought it dodgy, and that the summer ball would be especially unsafe, though, of course, he would never spell out why.

How different from arriving on the Heritage Park Estate, Stafford, so dinky and small-scale prosperous, so mock-weathered cement brick: an expensive, cut-price Shangri-La. Mostly a dutiful and sensitive daughter, she felt ashamed such a thought could come to her – ashamed, disloyal to her parents, and juvenile. The thought was there, all the same, and she never made a meal of guilt: all right then, she was snobbish. All right, she loved big houses and fine grounds, trees, seclusion, real pictures, real history, stone walls, space, a heavy front door like something from a castle, not the ginger would-be timber job they had at home.

When she arrived today, Darien seemed as busy as ever. A couple of big cars, one a Mercedes estate wagon, stood alongside Helen's Maestro and Jack's Lancia. All sorts were in and out of Lamb's house. This was another part of the excitement – meeting his friends or business acquaintances, being introduced to them by Jack as if she were his equal, their equal. Jack was so brilliant like that. After all, some of these people must be plump money if they could buy the art he kept here – even the kind on show; and Denise had an idea there was other, more special still, that she hadn't seen and never would. Very early on she had sensed it better not to talk to Colin Harpur about the paintings moving in and out of Darien. And very early on she had also sensed that Colin knew more about all that than he said. Yes, a lovable, sexy, crafty police prince. Did his wife, Megan – Megan, for heaven's sake! – ever break right through the curtains to him? The thought upset her, caused her miserable jealousy. Oh, God, to be older – to have seen Colin first and have a right to him.

Denise parked close to the Mercedes and had a long stare into it. This was the sort of car someone bringing or taking costly paintings might use, but she saw nothing there now. Well, was it likely works like that would be left unattended, even in the privacy of Jack's grounds?

She looked about for a moment before leaving the car. Somehow she always felt it necessary to do that when arriving here. The outer door in the porch at Darien, like the gates, almost invariably stood wide open, even at night. That was another thing she admired about the place and about Helen and Jack – they were warm and welcoming, and did not seem to fret over all the modern perils, and imagined perils, which bothered people on Heritage Park Estate: the burglars, the violent, the vandals, the seekers after their prized, slogged-for, minor bits and pieces. There, doors were for keeping closed and chain-guarding. Alarm boxes, red, blue and orange, hung nervy and boastful on almost every gable end. *What we have we hold* – the middle-middle class's gospel. Well, it was her father, now one of the middle-middle class, who had bought the Panda for her, so perhaps she shouldn't be such a daft and sniffy bitch about them.

She got out of the car and found herself about to lock it, even here. God, that was just the kind of piddling small-mindedness she disliked in her parents and their neighbours. Instead of bringing keys from her bag, she switched quickly, took out her compact and had a formal check over in the mirror. Fair to middling. Then she walked towards the porch.

At Darien, there were no alarms as far as she could see, and Jack always seemed untroubled and cheerful, despite all the incredibly valuable works he had on his walls. Despite, too, the enemies she somehow knew he had collected. Why did she? Was it that anyone so obviously successful must have savaged his way up? Or maybe there had been hints from Helen, though Denise could not pinpoint anything. Jack himself certainly never spoke of enemies, talking always in his huge voice as if life was a piece of cake, and then another piece. Perhaps she sensed a message in the way Colin Harpur always went suddenly blank or switched subjects when she mentioned Jack and the house, evasive cop swine.

Jack must have heard her car and came to an open window upstairs, smiling, massive, dressed in some quaint sort of eastern thing today, and with a glass in his hand. Jack liked wacky clothes. As she reached the porch he waved and she waved back. Then he turned and Denise heard him shout to Helen elsewhere in the house that she had a visitor. He faced her again. 'Go in, Denise,' he called. 'Grand to see you.'

She entered the wide, stone-flagged hall. Style. And style counted – had to be an indicator, surely. Oh, she thought Jack Lamb probably less than saintly – just as any survivor businessman might be. As Helen once said, ten minutes or a few generations ago half the aristocracy were crooks. Look how fast the Kennedys stepped up to status, and think of that glacial Henry James line: 'the black and merciless things which are behind great riches'. As for Jack, Denise might not say black or merciless, but she had learned many areas in life were grey and not too gentle. Sadly, that was a big part of growing up, like the temptations of snobbishness. God, she could still just about remember when life used to seem simple. Less than a year ago she was a sixth former – very sharp, though she said it herself – but also very schoolgirl. *'Nous avons changé tout ça.'*

In the upstairs den – a sort of combined study, gallery, store, darts and snooker refuge and bar – Tony Towler said: 'All these strangers around the place, Jack. I had no idea.' Towler kept away from the window and whispered.

Lamb thought it early in the day for tension but was used to Towler's edginess. He didn't hold it against him. 'Got some information for me? Don't fret. She's just a kid. A good kid. Helen needs friends her own age.'

'Well, I dare say.' Towler hummed something, barely loud enough for Lamb to hear – one of those exercises people did to quell uneasiness or rage. They were both drinking Coke.

'She sees and hears nothing beyond what I decide's OK, Tony. Same as Helen. This kid won't get a look at you. Go out down the rear stairs. You don't object to the tradesman's entrance?

'Me? I *am* a tradesman. Tipster. Apprentice, anyway. Jack, you're beautifully relaxed – your thing, always has been, and I admire you – but all the same. What I've got to think, Jack, is I fed you the Link Street stuff, to feed wherever you feed it, as is your right. And, then, bad luck, a death. I don't find it so easy to, well, take it easy.'

'We're all right, Tony.'

'Maybe.' But Towler did not mind dealing with Lamb, despite this eternal, carefree, stupid lord-of-the-manor performance. Jack never failed to pay.

'Dancing,' Lamb replied. 'That's ballet, not the other. This is what brought Helen and Denise together. City hall evening classes? They're gifted. I've almost become a fan.' He thought of pirouetting, but saw Towler remained too taut for jokes so came and sat down on a stool at the bar. He heard Helen yelling a welcome to Denise downstairs and then a lot of giggling and chatter. He was supposed to stop a nice friendship like that?

Towler finally forced himself to offer a brave grin. 'Stressed, Jack, I admit it. First time here. Usually, phones, or meetings down the foreshore – that's different.' He knew his voice was high and trembling.

'We'll stick to that way in future, if you like. So what's the new story, Tony?'

'And then the fat Merc outside. Exactly the kind of motor major business people favour. That almost gave me a seizure, too.'

Lamb laughed. 'None of the Webbs, don't worry. Doug in a Mercedes! My mother always hires a jalopy when she's here from America. Independence. What's come up then, Tone?' Keep asking and there might be an answer. Lamb wondered what it would do for Towler's fibre if he knew Denise and Harpur had something going. You left some items under wraps.

'This is very shadowy so far, Jack,' Towler replied. 'I'm looking at Sanquhar-Perry.'

'Courtney? He's making moves?'

'As I say, very maybe at this stage.'

'Tony, you're a boy to pick out real information even when it's hardly there at all, I know that.'

'Sometimes it turns into a real one, sometimes no, but casual you can't be in my game, or you're left at the post.'

'Which doesn't happen to Anthony Towler.'

'Once or twice.'

'Once, maybe. And a long time ago.'

'Quite a time. We learn.' His father always said, Why undersell

36

yourself? But his father had ended up a school teacher in some nowhere part of Devon, so you wondered what he knew.

Lamb thought of Towler's face as aristocratic. Remarkable how many of the devotedly villainous managed that. Think of Marty Webb. Tony's face was lean, his nose slender and slightly arched, his dark hair brushed very flat, teeth in spanking order. Despite shortness, with his silk trousers, fine jackets and handmade shirts you might easily think class, even landed, if you did not know. Aloof you would have said, as if nothing much would interest him. And yet certain things did – really took his abiding fancy – and he knew how to go deep inquiring, and yet not cause waves. He was an up-and-coming tipster, still in a terrace house somewhere pathetic, but probably due for a little social climb.

'So what's the story, Tony? I've not heard a thing about Sanquhar-Perry, I'll admit.'

Towler was standing by the big grey stone fireplace, under a sunny Hockney pool picture. 'What I love about you, Jack – you never try and con, pull the price down by saying information's third-hand.' That old fireplace and Tony really looked right together, like the squire in his library. The timid little bugger was never going to earn his own Darien, though.

'Who'll operate with Courtney on this I don't know, not to date,' Towler said. 'No regular team there.'

'He's a lad with ideas. He'll attract the talented.'

'In a way, I even like him,' Tony said.

'I do myself. All right, we know about the hair and the hyphen and all that Scottish ancestry stuff, but they're bearable, and he was humane beyond requirement to Liz-Anne – that wild piece he lived with – for months and months, despite at least two serious abdominal rips from her.'

'Three. But information's information, Jack.'

'I think so.'

'I'll need to find out what confeds he's using.'

'Of course.'

'No, not just to have it complete.'

'I know what you mean, Tony.'

'When it comes to information – all right, let's spell it out: when it comes to grassing – I spill to you so you can spill where it matters, but only if I think there are people in it who've done me damage – people where I'm under an absolute duty to hit the bastards in return. Survival. Well, Webby and Tinker Bell I owed something. Both. Not so far as death for Marty, but that's how it went, regrettably. Or, again, I'll shop people to forestall, naturally, if I believe they're dogging me, which can certainly happen. Or, again, people who could and probably will go violent and with guns, especially sawn-offs. Where there's a real danger people could get killed, I mean the innocent. What I'm saying – bystanders in peril, mushrooms. It could be your mother, my father. I won't have it, Jack. It could happen with Courtney. I don't feel evil about putting out the word on something like that. So, Link Street qualified twice.'

'Right,' Lamb replied. 'There's more I keep quiet about than I pass on.'

He had often heard Tony Towler traipse through the informant's gospel. Grassing did lack nobility, and needed some explaining. For himself, Lamb had more or less come to terms with it over the years, though he could still fall into a fever of shame now and then.

Talking things out at full length seemed to give Towler comfort and Lamb always listened tolerantly and joined in. 'Likewise, you've sold me stuff, I've paid you, and it's never gone any further, Tone. I decided I had nothing against the people involved, and that they probably wouldn't do injury. So the curtains stay across.' Towler and other so-called newsboys fed Lamb, for fees. And Lamb fed Harpur, for an understanding.

'I appreciate you sieve stuff, Jack. And I've accepted. Your judgement – I respect it without question. I know you'll make what you will of information. Your mother's down below now? It's a lovely holiday for her here. In such a setting.' Towler wanted to get back to pleasant, harmless topics: it always upset him to analyse the ethics of grassing, though he felt compelled to do it.

'Chopsing with Helen and Denise. We've got a big function coming off soon.'

Towler lit up slightly. 'The Jack Lamb Summer Ball. Well, I hear about that, naturally. Doesn't everyone, for heaven's sake?'

'Tony, I'd like—'

'Jack boy, you mustn't get embarrassed. Please,' Towler raised a hand to quell apologies. 'God, don't I know you can't have me at a do like that? There's wheels within wheels, and some wheels have to stay out of sight or the engine stops.' He laughed, a short, hard, officers' mess sort of laugh, which seemed to Lamb just right for Tony's bold check jacket. 'Oh, let's be reasonable,' Towler said. 'But, look, Jack, what I'd really like—'

'Don't we even send you an invitation for refusal, Tony? This is bloody bad.' Lamb decided to lay it on in full.

'What I was going to say. I'd really cherish one.'

To have to crawl like this really pissed Towler off. Lamb, the sod, would know well enough an invitation never came to him. 'If it could arrive via the mail, Jack. It makes it official? And I'd like the postman to know I'm asked. These are in very high quality envelopes, I believe, recognisable. And RSVP. I know the form. *Mr Anthony Towler greatly regrets that he is unable to accept the kind invitation to the Summer Ball, owing to a long-standing previous commitment.* It's a foolish wish, I suppose, but it would show I counted, Jack.' Towler felt ashamed. Jesus, so slimy, so low, so desperate.

'Count? One of my closest. Yes, I'll ask Helen to send one. Delighted.'

'It's only I know you do that with some other people, Jack – known as SFR: sent for refusal. They get bloody arrogant, flashing the card like a referee. I mean, Tired Ferdinand and Seymour Wiggins, for example. That jerk, Seymour, says to me last year, "Unfortunately I shall be prevented from attending, owing to a diary clash, but it's decent of the old bugger to ask me to his little knees-up, Tony." Extremely unpleasant to listen to, Jack, if you haven't been asked. And naturally you can trust me completely not to accept.'

'It's the principle,' Lamb remarked.

Towler turned and gazed at the Hockney. 'Mellow. He's got such a knack with pink. So, I'll keep an eye, Jack. I mean, Sanquhar-Perry. Plus any vengeance signs after Martin, of course.' Towler finished his Coke with a show of relish. 'At present I don't even know what sort of job, if a job at all. Only some activity around Courtney. That's the extent of it.' You didn't give too much too soon. Draw back the curtains slowly.

When he had gone, Lamb went down to the big living-room at the rear of the house and joined the women. His mother said: 'Jacky, I was just explaining why I always hire a car. It's dangerous to be driven by Jack Lamb, Denise darling, that's my view these last few years.'

'Clean licence, mother.'

'Not that sort of dangerous. And then this child, in and out of your house. Associating.'

'Denise is part of the set-up, almost,' Lamb replied.

'Are you considering her?' her mother said. 'Denise, my second husband – the one I went to the States for – was in pharmaceuticals, not a great man or habit-forming, but he never walked with less than $5,000 on him, cash, as a means of tempering possible trouble. I didn't learn a hell of a lot from Sam, but I learned readiness.'

Denise found it hard to get Mrs Lamb placed. She had on a blue print dress that looked like someone's throw-out, someone not well-off or the same size. And yet there was the hired Mercedes outside, presumably for the whole stay, and a general air of plenty in her voice.

'But you keep your eyes closed a lot, kid, do you?' she asked Denise.

'Nobody dances that well with their eyes shut,' Helen told her.

'Every year I come over here I find Jack's looking older,' Mrs Lamb replied.

Denise laughed and said: 'Well, Mrs Lamb, he —'

'By which I mean older than people he looked younger than last time. This year he looks older than Reagan. Last year he only looked older than Nixon. Jack's not forty-seven. This was a late war-baby. I lived in London, then. I suppose the flying bombs could induce a complex which explains the fucking garb he goes in for. The people he talks to upstairs. Would you give them house room, Denise? What I'd say to you because he won't and she won't is watch your back at all times. Go ready. You noticed any unnecessary figures hanging about? I definitely don't say tell Jack if you do, and, of course, don't tell the police, because who ever knows which way they're pointing?'

'Mother dotes on this Alma-Tadema painting, Denise,' Lamb said, walking to where it hung near the French windows, a framed picture about two feet square of some women, maybe ancient Roman, in long, soft, coloured dresses and gorgeous headbands. To Denise it looked delightfully corny-classical, happy Victorian nostalgia.

'Some of the drapery works OK,' Mrs Lamb remarked. 'And he had a gift for Med elbows.' Denise went over to gaze at the picture more closely. 'Kid, I really wouldn't outline myself against glass doors if I were you.'

Chapter Six

These days, Ralph Ember would not allow formal meetings with off-colour colleagues at his club, the Monty, however closely he was working with them. Ember wanted to think of himself as someone with a civic role – letters to the local Press on environmental topics et cetera, plus an interest in education – and this status could be seriously shaken if known forceful boys like Doug Webb or Courtney Sanquhar-Perry turned up night after night at the club, obviously abrim with schemes. Of course, you couldn't get away from it, the bulk of Monty regulars were total criminal rubbish, bringing the club no actual social esteem; yet small-time rubbish, this was the point: defeated, untargeted, undangerous, non-pushing and non-firearm rubbish – authentic rubbish rubbish, who would never rate the serious interest of Harpur or Iles. Not like Webby and Sanquhar-Perry.

Take conversations about the need and possible ways to wipe out Jack Lamb: undoubtedly, these might have been conducted nicely, with absolute security, in a comfortable upstairs room at the club, but Ember did not want that topic even raised within the Monty. Gross. This club had a solid history. Before Ember's time, it was a meeting place for really well-placed and very genuine professional people – Chamber of Trade members, estate agents, county councillors, Masons, solicitors even. You could still see some of this quality in the mahogany panelling and brass fittings.

He was not going to allow tainted associates into his home, Low Pastures, either, of course, so to work out how to destroy Jack Lamb and possibly Harpur they assembled in Courtney's place at Henry Fielding Crescent on the Ernest Bevin council estate. It was a house, not a flat, and kept quite nicely by Zena, the girl Courtney had living with him now; a really good find, apparently with winning breasts and typing speed, and soft drinks only – quite different from the Pernod and kitchen-knife flair of Liz-Anne, Courtney's previous.

Ember took a taxi to a corner three streets away and walked to Henry Fielding Crescent. It would have been semaphore to park his Rover outside Courtney's house. Police watched the Ernest Bevin almost as much as the Monty. In any case, leaving a decent car for more than three minutes on the Ernest Bevin was an invitation to what one of his university lecturers called 'the inevitable, reactive violences of an aggrieved, congenitally unmonied urban population who feel betrayed by those in power'.

Ember had discovered early that in university politics departments 'urban' meant excusable. They ought to tell Harpur. Ember had moved up only quite recently from his Montego to the Rover: a progress in class, but not ostentatious, like a Jag or BMW, which could bring Harpur sniffing: just more trade savvy.

Courtney said: 'First, Doug, I've got to say a word of deep sorrow and sympathy about Martin. Please accept condolences, and I know I speak for Ralph.'

'Absolutely,' Ember remarked.

'And it's wonderful, in the circumstances, to see you still willing to turn out like this, I mean even before the funeral.'

'It keeps the mind off,' Webb replied. 'But it's pain, pain that calls for a reply.'

'True,' Courtney said. First, though, he wanted to talk about a scheme to feed Jack Lamb dud information about a job and then do one somewhere else at just that time. 'This way, when police turn up at the wrong bank, we prove for sure he's grassing, and we make an uncontested profit also because their posse is stranded miles away,' he said now. Ember could see this idea really delighted Courtney, adding up in his eyes to 'a package'; that is, having more than one element but forming a business unity – one of his specialities. He gave another of them: a great smile, like a child's, warm and cheerful and rich in merry innocence. It could not have been a more convenient kind of smile from a business point of view, particularly for somebody so two-faced. This smile was famous and a few Monty louts used to joke about changing to Sanquhar-Perry's dentist for the secret. 'Look, this is using our heads,' Courtney said, touching his with his finger. He had boyish, curly, fair hair to go a treat with the happy-lad smile.

It almost gave Ember a giggle, really, to hear him now. Courtney talked as if you wouldn't find another working mind in the western hemisphere. True, he had his hyphen and the Sanquhar element, which apparently came from a genuine strain of the family in Scotland, but the fact remained this was some eternal, wasteland rent-payer, wearing the year before the year before last's suit, and even then not up to much. They sat in his tiny front room where things, except the wallpaper, certainly seemed clean enough, but with furniture like evening-class work by a drunk, and a mauve carpet worn so thin you felt callous treading on it – kicking it when it was down. Nothing here said Courtney's brain had actually started producing much for him yet, and he was getting up fast to forty. Sanquhar you pronounced Sanker, to rhyme with wanker, which he was not: Courtney always said it rhymed with banker, which he was not, either – well, a lot less – though he had come into passing contact with one or two.

'This would be cashing in – turning trouble to a plus,' Courtney said.

Webb frowned. 'I don't want any hanging about, no fancy work, Courtney. I want Lamb taken out now. No need to prove he's grassing. We know it. We suffer. Ask your arse if a dog's got teeth. Not just my own lad, Martin.'

'Look I do understand about Martin,' Sanquhar-Perry said, 'I feel he's almost family to me, too, you know.'

'This was a lovely, backward boy,' Webb replied. 'He needed special attention, that's all. So they give it, yes?' He lowered his head for a second. The other two waited. He straightened up: 'And then other relatives locked away – seven, eleven years – because of Lamb. This is a first cousin – I mean, immediate blood again – plus someone very dear and handy, connected to my wife Kay's uncle. Who's next, for God's sake?'

'Well, I know, Doug,' Sanquhar-Perry said. 'We'd still get Lamb later, yes. He has to go, no argument. But let's take what we can first. Maximise. I always look for that.'

'This one, Lamb, he gets to hear all sorts,' Webb replied. 'Obviously. That's his trade. If we wait and mess about he'll pick up an intimation somehow. Then he's ready for us, qui viving.'

'How pick up an intimation, Doug?' Sanquhar-Perry asked. 'There's only us three.' He shook the curls gently, to prove bafflement, like a sweet, slow breeze over harvest fields, so you almost heard the corn ears rustle. Ember supposed that to gays Courtney must look brilliantly succulent though middle-aged, but try anything and they'd get a fist kiss, at least. He could be very butcherous, Sanquhar-Perry.

'How hear things?' Webb answered. 'Who knows? How did he pick up the intimation about Martin and the lads?'

Again Ember almost had a laugh – all this 'intimation' verbiage. People like Webb thought big words were education. Well, Ember realised he had been like that himself once, so he let it ride.

'How's Lamb going to discover what's on the agenda?' Sanquhar-Perry said. 'This is a sealed room.' He waved his hand around to point out the solidity of 1966 Ernest Bevin lath and plaster, like Saddam's bunker. 'Do any of us talk – me, Ralph, you?'

'Well, I know that, Courtney,' Webb said quickly. 'This is not personal. But stuff reaches him. You don't pick up a place like that Darien without special information.'

'So we give him some,' Sanquhar-Perry said, smiling.

Webb shook his head: 'I —'

'What's Darien, anyway?' Sanquhar-Perry asked.

'In Panama,' Ember replied. 'Mentioned in quite a sonnet – "silent upon a peak in Darien".'

'Silent,' Webb said. 'Get Lamb very silent. We think about Harpur after that. *Silence of the Lamb*. That's more literature, yes?'

'*Lambs*,' Ember replied.

'Who's counting?' Webb said.

'Anyway, what do you think, Ralph?' Sanquhar-Perry asked. 'You're the decision maker. I like the way you just listen there, tolerant, but we know you're thinking, always analysing, weighing.' Sanquhar-Perry turned towards Ember, his face attentive and respectful, like a kid and his headmaster. Although the argument was with Webb, Sanquhar-Perry had been getting a glance or two at Ember all through, trying to read him. This was their second meeting lately and to Sanquhar-Perry it grew obvious that Ember felt sick and paralysed at the idea of doing Lamb.

Today Ember's reluctance suited Sanquhar-Perry. Ralph would put up a decent show of hardness, naturally, but anyone could look behind it and see trembling doubts. You never really knew where you were with Ember – why they used to call him 'Panicking Ralph'. Now and then you still heard that name, even though he had collected so much caste, plus unarguably heroic possessions. Gutlessness and this late lust for education could not be the whole personality. Just the same, Sanquhar-Perry sensed Ralph dreaded the idea of going after Lamb, and admittedly it made some sense: people spoke of Lamb as if he had a sort of magic to him – so keep clear.

'Me?' Ember replied. 'I think I'm with Doug on this. Hit Jack Lamb. Hit him now.' Ember knew he had to say it and without hesitation. Webby had lost a son, for God's sake. They must both be wondering if he would crumble, Doug and Sanquhar-Perry, so it was vital to talk resolute. They would have heard of his ups and downs. Who hadn't? He longed to grab at Sanquhar-Perry's idea of a postponement and was wondering how he could bring things around to that in a minute. As an immediate answer, though, he saw little opt-out to manliness.

Webb nodded hard. 'Right.' He had picked up that note of would-be courage in Ralph's voice and saw Ember was trapped by the role and had to go right through with it now. 'Thanks, Ralph,' he said. 'Sorry, Courtney. But, look, we can still put on a job once Lamb's taken out. Well, clearly – even more so. Why else are we dealing with him? It's part cleaning up and revenge, yes, but also the practical matter of needing security, which we lack while he can leak.'

'Fair enough, but there's another way of looking at this, too,' Sanquhar-Perry said.

'Yes?' Ember remarked. Come on Courtney, get spinning.

'If Lamb sends police to the wrong place they start wondering,' Courtney said. 'They ask themselves if he's part of the operation himself, in charge of decoys. They think he's turned. So, Harpur gets irritated, and then he turns, too – turns on Lamb. Police start looking at all the matters they closed their eyes to these last God knows how long – especially the art trade – and Lamb ends up in court with a real sentence. Millions involved, pounds, not dollars.' Delightedly, he punched the arm of his chair, which seemed able to take it.

'It wouldn't ever happen and you've got to know it, Courtney. Couldn't happen.' Webb had a desperate, worried, bleary old face, reminding Ember of some train guard's on TV as he described toilet damage in a football special. Doug must be touching fifty, time for a lot of envy and hatred to mature. He ran two households – one local, one up around Preston way, with hellishly hard kids in both, especially the girls of course, so you could understand not only the evil in him but the terrible, non-stop need for thick earnings. With the big spread of his family connections he was always sure to have some relatives locked away on prolonged ones. All of it added up to an unjoyous outlook. What Ember always felt Webb would not be mistaken for was a *bon viveur*.

'Oh, yes, Doug, believe me the police could turn on Lamb if they were given a bit of an excuse,' Sanquhar-Perry said. 'Look, here's a Chief Constable who thinks grassing's evil – suspects the whole notion. One big cock-up like this and he'd make his move.'

Webb said: 'I want to see Lamb—'

'Dealt with outright and unmistakably by the people he's sold – or their next of kin, such as yourself,' Sanquhar-Perry replied. 'A totally human impulse. After Link Street accounts need to be settled and be seen to be settled. What you've got to think, though, is it's the first motive police would look for. They know who hates Lamb, and why. Harpur would be on your doorstep next day.'

'This is a point,' Ember said.

'Think of Lamb in Long Lartin or Wakefield. We've got real

45

friends there who could give him such an old-scores time,' Sanquhar-Perry added. 'Even a decisive accident. People can have bad falls and so on. And the beauty is, nobody would be looking our way for it. Doug, we have businesses to run in the future. Meanwhile, we're richer from a soft job. Yes, maximise. The modern approach.'

'It wouldn't happen,' Webb replied.

'You keep saying,' Sanquhar-Perry answered.

'Too much shit flying in a trial, liable to stick on others. Harpur would just have to look after him. His soul's bound to Jack Lamb. The bigger they are the harder they fall on you.'

'Maybe,' Sanquhar-Perry said. 'But Harpur doesn't run the shop. It's Mark Lane, the Chief. Plus Iles, of course. You think Iles would sit back smiling if he saw his boys had been cleverly sent wrong? Take it from me, they're both waiting a chance to nail Harpur. For one thing, the story goes Harpur was seeing Iles's wife.'

'I've heard that,' Ember remarked.

For a second then Webb began to yell, really yell, in that crude Northern voice Ember loathed. Christ, anybody could be under-privileged, but to write it in the sky? 'This huge everyone-who's-sodding-anyone party – ball he calls it – he gives in the summer – that's what sickens me to death.' Sanquhar-Perry glanced towards the kitchen where Zena was cooking oatcakes or something else homely. Webb noticed and quietened right away. 'This is the Mayor, Confederation of British Industry, editors, a calf on a spit, Moët and Chandon in the due flute glasses, and every bit of it paid for by Martin and by other prime and wholesome walled-in lads, visitors as and when. This is not just vol au vents, this is expense.'

'What kind of job did you have in mind, Courtney?' Ember said. He made this come out only ten per cent interested, if that, as though, basically, he still wanted it Webb's way, the instant perdition thing with Lamb, but was prepared to listen to Sanquhar-Perry from curiosity and fair's fair.

'I've been getting a signal or two about an opportunity,' Sanquhar-Perry said.

'Oh, yes? Bank, wages or what?' Ember asked – no boil-up of enthusiasm, just casual, sounding like quizzing him automatically, unbelieving. The old hand.

'And manageable by three, that's the beauty,' Sanquhar-Perry replied.

'OK, then, so don't tell us,' Ember said.

'Early stages yet,' Sanquhar-Perry replied.

Webb jumped on it. 'That's what I mean. More delay.'

'I'm not forgetting what we're here for, Ralph, Doug,' Sanquhar-

Perry said. 'Lamb's still on my list, and high. The highest. That needn't mean he's first, time-wise.'

'Reasonable point,' Ember said. There still seemed something half crazy about it all: to be sitting in this downgrade room, in a street named after a major literary creator, where half the people had trouble spelling out the *Sun*, with framed cheapie prints of flowers and leafy streams on the greasy green wallpaper, and over the mantelpiece a picture of what might be Courtney's mother in a hat like an almost-dead badger, with a Scotch-looking rhododendron bush behind – yes, to be sitting here in these no-hope chairs, talking about confidential money signals from the National Westminster or whatever and doing some sensitive measuring of priorities, as if it was General Motors' boardroom.

Webb said: 'I'm talking to myself.' He realised he had blown it by making a noisy song about Jack Lamb's summer do. That had come out sounding like sour vengeance frenzy, something he knew Ember expected from him. People with Ralph's long run would despise rage or envy as childish. Webb saw he had handed Ember a dodge-out.

'But you're going to ask how to get a phoney tip to Lamb so he'll believe it,' Sanquhar-Perry said.

'Too right,' Webb replied. 'This boy – antennae, none better.'

'I've got something in hand,' Sanquhar-Perry replied.

'Well, it might work,' Ember said.

Sanquhar-Perry heard happy thankfulness shoving its way through the show of indifference, and relief seemed to bring a meaty beige glow to that scar along Ember's jaw line.

And Doug Webb saw the satisfaction in them and grew more bitter. They thought they were strategists, was what they thought. He would not let it go, though. 'As a matter of bloody fact, I can give you the connection,' he said.

'What connection, Doug?' Sanquhar-Perry asked.

'The link – Lamb to Harpur. I've got it spotted, logged.'

'Well, easy enough,' Sanquhar-Perry said. 'Whispering grasses have always found a way to whisper. They don't need the satellite.'

'Perhaps. But I've been doing a systematic watch on Jack Lamb. There's a girl,' Webb replied.

Ember sat up straight in the crummy chair: 'Christ, what, Doug? You've been tailing Lamb?'

'Don't worry. I can keep an eye and not get spotted.' He was some clumsy amateur, for God's sake?

'Watch Jack Lamb, so he doesn't know?' Ember replied. 'This is not too good. Well, you said – antennae. He'd be alerted. This throws a new light on things generally.'

'Yes, it does,' Webb replied. 'This girl – in and out of Lamb's place, then seeing Harpur. I mean regular contact with Harpur.'

Sanquhar-Perry smiled and said: 'Oh, the teenager, Denise Prior.' He leaned over and picked off the wall something which Ember would avoid nearness to without a surgeon's mask on. 'We know about her, Doug.'

Webb looked dazed: 'You what?'

'She doesn't make the situation anything more or anything less,' Sanquhar-Perry said. 'They don't need a girl to take messages, do they? Are we back to carrier pigeons? Phones, Doug. Undercover meetings. Phones can be a bit dicey, true, but tapping's all exaggerated – spy books.'

'This is just Harpur having a sweet time with a pretty kid,' Ember said. 'Always been like that. You know Harpur. He and his wife – more than iffy. She's very Seamus Heaney and *Late Show*. Harpur has to express himself elsewhere.'

Webb said: 'But—'

'She's friendly with Lamb's bird, that's all,' Sanquhar-Perry replied. 'Student. Some night-class dancing. Ralph's seen her around the university.'

Webb stared at them. 'I don't believe this – you two being so— This girl knows Lamb, she knows Harpur – I mean, it's got to add up to something. You saw it and didn't tell me?'

Sanquhar-Perry said with a sad shake of his gorgeous curls: 'You know, you should really watch your tone, Doug. This is twice. I know you're disturbed by grief, but what's your suggestion now – we're in on something with Harpur?'

'No, but—'

'That's how it could sound, Doug,' Sanquhar-Perry replied. 'For a second that's definitely what I heard, old comrade. But, all right, we forget it. Look, this girl – what it adds up to is Harpur bowled over by some lovely, uncomplicating student. No husband to worry about, which makes a nice change for him. And that's the total picture. Enviable, yes, but not crisis.'

Ember grew anxious for this kid, and about the kind of Harpur typhoon that would start if his girl was touched. Peace for nobody. And not a chance in hell of doing this job Courtney was talking about. You could never be sure with someone off balance, as Webb seemed after Martin. This girl – around the common rooms at the college, in the corridors – he felt he knew her. Well, he thought of her, really, as more of a colleague than these two, more into the kind of things that interested him these days. 'She's no part of it, Doug.' He needed to say this with total clarity. 'Now, look, we don't want a nobody like this involved.'

'We know Lamb talks, girl or not, and we'll deal with him, in due course,' Sanquhar-Perry said. 'And with those who feed him, and even the one who pulled the trigger. To repeat – maximise.'

'In due course,' Webb sneered. 'Let's think and talk again, yes? I want to be reasonable. Courtney and I could pop into the club one night, Ralph.'

'No, I reckon we've covered it all,' Ember replied. Webb, above all, was the kind of work-associate to keep right out of the Monty: so head-on violent and loud and obsessed. Although Ember and his wife and daughters no longer lived in the flat above, he still thought of the Monty as being like home – much more than just a drink-up, girl-find and pool spot. Webb would be so unsuitable there, except as a punter. Good God, in the old days, before Ember quit the flat for Lower Pastures, Margaret and the children used to walk through the bar area sometimes when she was bringing the girls from school or taking them to their riding, so how could anybody bear the idea of a final job on Jack Lamb being brutally discussed there now?

Ember left Sanquhar-Perry's place first. It would be mad for him and Webb to go out together – how the Intelligence officer down police headquarters put his tales together for Harpur and Iles. Of course, the Intelligence officer might still be writing a tale if he heard of Ember alone strolling Henry Fielding Crescent, and using a taxi, but some risks you had to take or business would die. Mind, police took care about coming on to the Ernest Bevin, and, if they did, were generally spotted, and the alarm went out. Courtney would have had a call if there was surveillance.

Standing at the side of the window, Webb watched Ember walk up Henry Fielding Crescent. From the back, Ember looked very fit, on-top, full of himself, big-boy stride and a Prince of Wales check suit. 'So, he's not up to it, Courtney?'

'Who knows? Doug, Ralphy can be wet as a car wash, yet there's depths you wouldn't think of. We use what we can, as far as we can get him to go.'

Ember turned the corner into Attlee Boulevard, out of Webb's view. He said: 'Well, I respect him, regardless.'

'Ralphy is a mind.'

'A sty is how he sees this place, Courtney.'

'Oh, he's pernickety, yes, has royal values. I keep it in mind for settling up with the sod one day.'

Webb came away from the window and leant gingerly against the sideboard, as it might be called. Something would not let him relax. 'And this lovely mind sees nothing wrong with the girl going from Lamb to Harpur and back? Plus you – you don't see anything wrong, Courtney?'

'Of course I bloody do.'

Webb gave a silent, grateful whistle. At times he thought he might be dim, the same brain line as Martin. 'Thank Christ.'

'We might have to do something grave there. From the start I've thought that. This is a girl who looks so harmless – so harmless you've got to wonder, clearly. I've had a look at her myself and done a survey, as you'd expect. From Stafford way, a genuine student, yes, mother and father et cetera. Just the same, it stinks. Lamb – he's hard to get at, I've got to admit. Also his own girl. This other kid, though? He'd read the parable if she got badly damaged, or worse.'

'It has to be Lamb himself,' Webb said.

'Not easy, Doug. I've looked into that, too, naturally. Often. This girl, though — A doddle. No idea of security. But we don't rush. It's the kind of thing that could really upset Ralphy, to tackle her right away. We don't want to lose him. Not at this stage.'

Webb prepared to leave. 'As long as it's only this stage.'

'Absolutely. What I mentioned – bringing him along as far as possible. He's got a lot we can use.'

'And I'll go on keeping an eye – her and Lamb?'

'I don't see why not. I don't know anyone who could do it better, Doug.'

At the door, Webb waited a second and turned. 'Listen, you're not just saying it, making out you agree, bringing me along, like you call it, like with Ember?'

'Don't make me laugh, Doug. You'd see through that in half a second.'

'You said it.'

Chapter Seven

Crouched in his armchair early at the office, Harpur decided he had to end it with Denise, and wept for a couple of seconds. Christ, a blubbing copper, and on the senior management floor. Who'd believe that? Real tears. She was a girl like nobody he knew: some innocence, some growing worldliness, much sense, much devotion. He wiped his face with the back of his hand. When had he last wept? The big effort of memory helped him get some control again. He knew when it was: as a young teenager, he awoke one night sure Christ's Second Coming was imminent and that he was not ready, not 'saved' as the Gospel Hall used to call it, and he had cried in terror then. Never since, until now. Not long after that religious agony, he was able to defy his father and quit the Gospel Hall, though he could still grow troubled occasionally even now by what they had preached. *Be sure your sins will find you out* and *Boast not thyself of tomorrow*, and certainly not of the day after.

All the same, it was not guilt that told him to drop Denise. Good God, she was virtually a child, and he might be leading her into who knew what hazards – here and now hazards, not the Day of Judgement kind, not theological, but bone, blood and flesh? Her bones were small, her whole frame slight. Her hand felt lost inside his. She always seemed – the word that came to him and which he tried to shove away was 'breakable'. It returned.

He could plead she wanted him and would be devastated by a split-up, but recognised this as feeble, even evil. Just his way of disguising selfishness. Just his way of postponing a finish that would flatten him as well. Harpur was seeing her this afternoon. He would tell her then: keep it brief, with no blurring or wavering, and still no mention of Link Street, of course. These days fewer and fewer rules meant much to him, beyond the one that said you had to win, but some decencies there had to be and he felt he must not darken a young life.

Later this morning a sort of conference developed in Harpur's room. The Chief preferred impromptu get-togethers to more formal meetings. Lane, due at some official luncheon later, was in uniform, looking exceptionally unkempt even for him, and very down in the mouth. Harpur said: 'This is information, Chief, that came to Chief Inspector Garland from a, well, call-girl who gives him a whisper now and then. Maybe sound, maybe not.'

'Which lady is that, Francis?' Iles required, gazing fascinated at Garland. The ACC would be accompanying Lane to the lunch and was also in uniform. As ever, he looked consummately glossy, eyes bright with exhaustive unfriendliness, grey hair glinting in the *en brosse* style he switched to three weeks ago, following a Jean Gabin retrospective season at the Carlton. Boredom with the world and disregard for Lane fought constantly with each other to be the ACC's ruling passion. As was his habit, he stood near a window where he could now and then catch some kind of uplifting reflection of himself, like a woman in a Bond Street arcade.

'She's calling herself Elvira at present, sir,' Garland replied.

Iles considered. 'I know no Elvira. What age? Elvira? Sounds a maturer girl. Pony-skin jacket sort, platform soles. Up in the late twenties, even thirties or forties. Some want them like that, I know – older sister, teacher or nanny image – and I'm sure it's a perfectly fruitful taste. But I'm afraid I don't really understand it, sir – not *here*.' He pointed heartily at his crutch and then turned to Lane as if hoping that he could explain.

'And Elvira says what, Francis?' Lane asked. The Chief was sitting in the easy chair where Harpur had cried, Lane fiercely unrelaxed, gazing down most of the time, half his brain obviously somewhere else: rumour insistently said a London newspaper was growing interested in police matters on the patch and might send a big-name reporter. Nothing hag-rode Lane more than the investigative Press. The Chief had no shoes on. He went out of his way to avoid smartness. Little useless humanising touches were a preoccupation. 'He makes himself lowly for us, Col, because of rampaging pride,' Iles had said one day. 'Thinks he must dilute his grandeur.'

'Elvira operates out of Ralphy Ember's place, the Monty,' Garland told the Chief. 'It's about a taxi trip she saw him make, sir.'

'To where?' Lane said.

'We're not altogether sure,' Francis Garland replied.

Switching his eyes to the Chief, Iles pumped lavish deference into his tone: 'Forgive my throwing this one at Garland, sir, but I'd like him to say whether he's into a closeness with this lady, I mean on a nice, long-term, Darby and Joan basis.'

Lane winced and said: 'Oh, Desmond, do we—?'

'It's simply that these girls can be really honest and truthful with a man they go to habitually, and who pleases them,' Iles replied. 'Gifts and so on, Francis? Little Ratner ornaments for her dressing-table? It can be a most genuine, touching sort of relationship, as a matter of fact.' His eyes softened for a moment and the narrow, shining face grew wistful. Then he resumed briskly: 'But I mustn't embarrass you with sentimental autobiography, sir. Or is this girl simply someone who puts a word and so on your way once in a while, Garland? I'm talking purely about the status of the information. When you say she calls herself Elvira at present, what was her name previously?'

'Does that matter, Desmond?' the Chief replied. Lane, too, had a habit of gazing towards windows, but as though he wanted to escape through them.

'You might be right, sir,' Iles responded at once. 'But they're individuals, very much so. It can help to know whom one is dealing with. My only point.'

Garland said: 'Elvira's on good terms with the taxi driver involved – uses him for taking clients to her place. A day or two later she's chatting to him and happens to ask about Ralph Ember's outing. The taxi man said he dropped Ralph up near the Ernest Bevin. He walked off down Attlee Boulevard.'

'This is a lad with a new Rover in the Monty yard,' Harpur said. 'That's what puzzled the girl, sir.'

'So, he's going to drink in someone's house,' Lane replied. 'Doesn't want to be caught driving with a skinful. Everyone knows Ralph's becoming an eminence in the community. Responsible.'

'It's possible, sir,' Harpur said.

'Elvira's aware I'm always interested in Ralph,' Garland said. 'One day we'll have him.'

Iles grew thrilled: 'This sounds very much like a really first-class friend you've found, Francis. I'll never understand what the hell women see in you, but when these girls give loyalty they give loyalty.'

Mark Lane said: 'This is all very flimsy. A taxi ride.' He looked lost. Once, the Chief had been an untiring, inspired, ruthless detective on a neighbouring Force but, when he moved up, the big job seemed to turn out *too* big. More than once, Iles had told Harpur they were viewing a classic leadership predicament: talented people promoted a single disastrous stage beyond their range, and ruined. Ruined with Iles's help in this case, though the Assistant Chief always neglected to mention that. Iles did maintain that the opposite to Lane's experience had affected himself. Hadn't he been held at fifty rungs below his capacities through senior people scared sick by his talents, the unfairness driving him desperate?

'Flimsy, sir? Exactly,' Iles replied and then, as routine, ignored the Chief. 'Col, you think it's Ralphy taking pains, going clandestine, because he's into a planning mode? Some new job?'

'It's possible, sir. Ember's not a great one for planning, as a matter of fact – thinks it should all happen through inspiration, luck and guts. But, obviously, some basic preparations have to be done for any job.'

'Ralphy, guts?' Iles said.

'We don't know where he went, you say, Francis?' Lane asked.

'Only that it was near or on the Ernest Bevin,' Garland replied. 'Obviously, it's significant he didn't take the taxi right to the destination. No give-away.'

'Could be to see one of a dozen old lags with creative flair up there, still nursing the unconquerable hope,' Iles said. 'None of the Webbs, though, I think.'

The Chief hunched a little further forward and was crouched now, almost as Harpur had been. 'I'm reluctant to set anything moving on the word of a tart tipster, not when I've got this London Press prospect. Newspapers are staffed by talented, hard-driven people who revel in anti-police crusades.'

'They can't do anything on Link Street, sir,' Harpur said. 'Tinker and Hal Vernon have been charged. It's *sub judice*.'

'As I understand it they're interested not so much in Link Street simply as an incident, though God knows that's bad enough, but are suggesting all sorts about our use of grasses, Colin, and about possible heavy, illegal favours granted. This is root and branch stuff.'

Harpur said: 'Absurd, but an irritation, yes, sir.'

'Perhaps we should wait and see whether anything else shows,' Lane suggested. He glanced appealingly at the ACC.

'So, I'd propose a call on Ember at the Monty,' Iles replied. 'Reasonably soon. Colin and I. A few deep queries. It flatters Ralphy to have a Detective Chief Super and an ACC pay a visit, even a DCS like Harpur. Garland should stay out of it. Francis, if you're giving this girl a fine, lasting relationship it could be known – well, almost certainly is, and should you arrive with us, leaning on Ember, it might bring her very serious peril later. Some old thing game enough to rechristen herself Elvira I feel deserves consideration, don't you, Chief?'

Lane gave a short moan. 'Ember's developing civic clout. Letters in the paper. A lovely house, Low Pastures. The Rover. Doing a degree, for heaven's sake. I hear English, Religious Knowledge, Politics. I will not have him pressured, Desmond, Colin.'

'This goes without saying, I hope, sir,' Iles replied. 'I think well of Ralphy.'

Lane glanced around the room, taking in each of the other three in turn. 'Particularly when—'

'Oh, the reporter still bothers you, sir,' Iles remarked, a vast, consoling grin to Harpur. 'It's the *Searchlight* page of *This Morning*, I believe. Possibly a woman writer. Aren't all these papers at it now? A few big convictions overturned and suddenly the law and judiciary are fair game for every pipsqueak careerist editor and MP. Everyone in jail was framed! These media talents think they're Christ rolling away the stone. But we keep them all duly in the dark. Remember that television outfit who came to make similar agitation? *Where Is Truth?* was it, the brassy name of their slot? Well, where is *Where is* sodding *Truth* now?' He swivelled slightly to get a better look at himself in the window.

Lane said: 'God, I hate the ways our information has to be trawled for. Grasses, whores, pandering taxi men, the bloody foul and seedy Monty. Why is it still open? Desmond, policing could be deemed besmirched by these methods.' Little lines of pink in the Chief's sallow cheeks signalled his pain. Increasingly these days Harpur found himself wanting to plead with Lane to take a month off in the Seychelles, even if it meant Iles running the shop. Lane was a good man.

'Besmirched is certainly something none of us would wish to be deemed, sir,' the ACC replied.

Lane left soon afterwards to polish his speech for the lunch, shuffling swiftly in his socks, reminding Harpur of Chinese waiters in ancient movies about the East.

'I love that man,' Iles whispered simply when the door closed.

'He's hit a bad patch,' Harpur said.

'I say I love him,' Iles replied. 'The Chief is what the new policing is about – winning the public's support by open-dealing and scrupulousness. Let not those words distress you, Harpur. Lane is pre-Fall. I am sent to look after him – to come between the Chief and the spite and degradation of things as they are. He has a sweet and gorgeous soul and it's up to me to keep it holy, at the cost of my own.' He nodded a couple of times gently, slowly. 'Do you think I like being the way you people see me? What was it Sartre said?'

'That the one about not needing to be a chicken to know a bad egg, sir?' Harpur asked.

' "Hell is the inability to escape from others who prove and prove again to you that you are as they see you," ' Iles continued. 'Myself, I want to reach out to virtue, embrace the perfect. There's elements of those in all men – yes, all, even those we hunt, even Ralphy. Even those we kill. Harpur, we must talk when I get back from this piss-pious lunch with church-and-charity people about how we trap Ember.'

'I'm not around this afternoon, sir.'

Iles gave another lovely full smile, this time gross with congratulations: 'Ah, the student?' He greasily crooned a fragment of an old ballad: ' "*For youth cannot mate with age.*" No? Who said?' Iles frowned. 'Good Christ, have you been crying? Harpur, you poor, desperate old heavy. Are you telling me you've got a real emotional life going? Have I been clumsy?'

When Harpur met Denise, as usual in a side street off Cyprus Road after lunch, he found she had booked a hotel room for the afternoon. Before today it had always been Harpur who made the arrangements. For a few moments they sat in the old vehicle he was using these days. He had intended making the goodbyes in his car and leaving immediately. 'Also, *derrum-derrum*,' she declared, manufacturing a noise like a fanfare, and producing a half-bottle of Sainsbury's champagne from a carrier bag. She was jubilant. 'We're celebrating, Colin.'

'Yes?'

'I've not only got through my Part Ones, I'm in line for the Bell prize – for the best first-year student. Well, not just in line. I'm going to get it, no question. The information comes off the record, even secretly, from my adviser of studies. You *have* heard of off the record, secret kind of information, have you?'

'Wonderful, Denise. Are you sure it's me you'd like to celebrate with?'

She looked puzzled. 'Aren't you the only one I want? Some wine, some love, some more wine, some more love. I mean, who else?'

'Why's this adviser so forthcoming? What's in it for him?'

'Vile police mind. It's a woman.'

'Well? Which hotel?'

'All right, it's scruffier and cheaper than the ones you get.'

'Which, Denise?'

'I've seen the room. It's adequate, Col.'

'Which hotel? Now and then, or oftener, I arrest people in scruffy hotels.'

'They might recognise you? No, I'm sure it's respectable,' she said. 'Well, not hopelessly respectable. Oh, come on, Col, look pleased and excited for me.'

'Denise, love, I—'

'You're being seduced. Isn't that brilliant? Aren't *I* brilliant?'

56

'You're a star, Denise. A privilege to park in the same street.'

'Pig iron I've heard of, but pig irony?'

Jesus, the madness, the deadlock. He had wanted to break from her because she was a hurtable child with a lovely frame and lovely flesh, to be shunted away at once, while there was time, out of danger. Yet now he could not do it – because she was a hurtable child, so happily excited, and sure of his approval, and bearing gifts.

'Why do blue-stocking women go for you, then, Col? Your wife, me? Others?'

'Occasionally they, you, want a slab of the simple but wholesome – after so much word-play and litotes.'

'What the hell do you know about such things, Colin?' she said.

'I've seen life.'

'And your wife runs literary soirées. *Tristram Shandy*.'

'Oh, at least.'

They drove in two cars to the hotel and left the vehicles at a little distance. Then, for added discretion, they walked to it separately along a pavement where the dog shit went back to D-Day, she a short way ahead, proprietorially because she held the key this afternoon, and, possibly, also because she liked flashing her behind. He could hear a chinking sound from her brown and yellow Sainsbury's carrier bag. She must have brought glasses, as well. This girl could think things through. One day she would probably be distinguished, as long as she got the time: a big administrator in the Civil Service, perhaps, or ICI. People would head-hunt her.

And then, suddenly, that phrase became filthily graphic in his brain and for a second he glimpsed blood, straggling tissue from her neck: a ham-fisted severance. He quickly amended: organisations would compete for her. Where the hell did such foul pictures start from? 'Come on Harpur,' he muttered, 'you know where. They come from Link Street. You're putting her in peril. Can't you see anything but the telegraphing movements of an arse, selfish, libidinous, unyoung jerk?'

He tried to imagine what she would look like at her career peak. When? Thirty-two? His own age? One of the reasons he wanted her and could not let her go was that she was not his own age, was only just more than half it until her next birthday, when she would start closing the uncloseable gap. Why think of her older? When he was a child and his mother heard him long for time to hurry itself to the moment of some treat she'd say, 'Don't wish your life away.' Mostly she talked rubbish, his mother, but occasionally by the law of averages had a point. Was he wishing Denise's life away, then? The opposite, surely to God. Please God, surely. He wanted to think she

57

would get there safely: to thirty-two, or fifty-eight or eighty-eight, when he would be really well on. And, of course, he wanted her to look as she did now for as long as could be: the open, sharp-eyed, calm, querying, small-featured face under dark hair, and her non-smoker's skin, although she did smoke, and a lot, he thought, but never commented. So she smelled bad sometimes. Who didn't? Maybe by thirty-two she would look kippered and sooty-toothed, if she didn't chuck it. Perhaps he would settle for that. He'd be nothing like twice as old then, but probably with plenty of his own major blemishes. Christ, his hair was turning tail already and if he grew a beard it would be three-quarters grey, so he wouldn't.

Today, Denise was wearing cream light-weight trousers and a vermilion T-shirt with four carousing ochre hedgehogs in blue fedoras on it, front and back, and, following her on foot now towards this definitely off-off-Broadway hotel, he thought what a smooth-moving, lively, cheery body she had, and this very friendly bottom. How could he have imagined himself strong enough to ditch her? He wished they were walking together and that men in the road would look and suspect – no, know – that in twenty minutes he would be having her slowly, with her tongue in his ear: 'reciprocal invasion', as she called it. He hung back, though, doing the due drill.

As soon as she welcomed him into the room, Denise could tell he found it worse than he'd expected: the smile in favour was too big and airy. Once in a while he did stoop to diplomacy, and he wouldn't want to spoil her day. 'Any room would do,' she told him. 'What I love is closing the door and knowing we're sealed-off, safe.' Although struggling with the champagne cork, she was appalled to see his smile drop suddenly to nowhere. He grew very alert. So often with him she had the sense of a world she knew nothing of. God, she wanted to be older, wiser.

'What do you mean, safe?' he snarled.

She was shocked by his change of tone, stammered an answer: 'Well, no peepers, Col. It can happen, could happen – I mean, when we're in the back of the car, or one of those wrecked houses. I think of bypassers, voyeurs. Not here.' The cork flew and rapped on the once-cream wall, quite likely its first acquaintance with champagne. She poured. That pushy noise the bubbles made colonising a glass delighted her as always, and delighted her more when one of the glasses was for Colin. For a second, she almost recovered.

'You've seen someone watching us, Denise? You never said.'

'No. God, I'd die if I did. Just afraid it will happen one day when my toes are on the car ceiling.'

'What – you've sensed someone near? Exactly when?'

She was amazed at the fret. What obsessed him? He had grown so edgy, so intermittently remote lately, remote even for Colin. She would have liked to ask him again about the Link Street thing, but thought she had better leave it. Now and again that interrogation tone could take over his voice – the hardness, an automatic refusal to let go, a cop determination to spot between the lines what he started out looking for. You could see he might terrify people. Well, now and then, his job must be to terrify people and probably some of them took plenty of terrifying. 'I said no, didn't I, Colin? Only the possibility, love.'

She watched him walk across the room and examine the wood-work. 'Some door.'

'It's shut, it's locked. Nobody wants to batter it down. This is a hotel, not Mafeking, Col.' About doors she was touchy, because of that mock-solid, emblematic thing in Stafford. 'Here's to me,' she said, 'genius rampant.'

He came back, put his arm and hand holding the glass around her and drank the champagne with his face against hers. 'Yes, here's to you, lovely one,' he said. He seemed to have relaxed again. Today, he smelled nice: soap or shaving cream. Now and then when he arrived straight from work she felt sure she got a whiff of the cells from him, a mix of disinfectant and whatever it hopelessly fought there. She could put up with reminders he had a trade and that it wasn't perfumer. To keep him, she would put up with anything.

'Colin, I'm in charge here. Your veritable host – I mean, wine, glasses, cork removal, room.'

'Certainly. What difference will it make?'

'I'm thinking about that, savouring that.' And it was true she loved the notion of having him in her possession, enveloped in a room she personally had bought rights to, and split from his wife and his children and his job and his friends and his enemies, and those who were sometimes one and sometimes the other and you were never sure which: she had the idea those might add up to a stack, several in top police uniforms. It must be a glow for him to realise he was adored in the undivided way she adored him. She could give those twenty-five reasons why, even had them listed for herself on disc.

'I see a lifetime of you and me,' she said.

'I think so.' They lay on the bed, drinking.

'Oh, I might live with someone else or possibly marry. Reflex action. And you've got all that business at home, daughters and unquestionably a kind of kind wife. It's hardly going to make any difference to us, though, is it?'

'It would be a waste if it did.'

'Exactly,' she replied. 'We think in tandem. I'm not wearing knickers. They make a line through these trousers.'

'I'd noticed you're not.'

'I thought you would. Does it bother you? You said once you liked taking my knickers off me.'

'I've said it more than once. I'm entitled to fetishes.'

'I decided that since it was my party I could do things as I wanted today.'

'She who pays the piper leaves her knickers off. Can't fight folk wisdom.'

'But if you're disappointed, I could put a pair on now. I've got them in my handbag. What I mean is, in here there's nobody to see the ridges they make, except you, and you don't mind.'

'Logic's a boon. Yes, put them on.'

She got off the bed, removed her trousers, climbed into white knickers, replaced the trousers and then lay alongside him again with her glass.

'Now you seem more like the girl I know,' he said.

'Is that good?' She heard anxiety in her voice.

'Always.'

Of course, having him in her hold was only a game. It made her desperate to recognise that. At the end of three or four hours he would be away – to home and family or Parent-Teachers' or the nick or the scene of the crime or some slippery talking, bargaining spy. But because the afternoon was only an interlude, it had to be worked at harder while it lasted, and prized more: had to be milked. The ropy room, with its off-straight yellowish wardrobe, and a bedside table shakier than the plague, was for this moment where her life meant most. You had to learn to recognise these summits. She had an idea that the older you got the fewer there would be.

Summits. Yes, it was an attic, and the way the gables came steeply down, shaping the room, delighted Denise, as if about to close like a pair of compasses and squeeze her and Colin into each other. That must be a filched idea – those compasses in the Donne love poem? Colin was filched, too – from his wife and the rest – and Denise considered it wily to have freighted him here today, another victory for love over the standard, swarming institutional snags.

'Are there any other regulations – it being your outing?' he asked.

'Violence.'

'What?'

'I'd like more during sex.'

'How do you know? Has someone been giving you more?'

Interrogation room again. 'Keep calm, Col. Stop thinking like the sixties. I believe I'd like more because when we've had some I wanted it to go on.'

He was still staring off-and-on at the door. Denise decided to cut out the word 'safe' with him in future because to Colin it evidently raised the harsh reverse, and in extreme shape. Perhaps it did for all police. They lived with the knowledge that safety might any day splinter and drop you into chaos. They *did* feel under siege like Mafeking, or like *Fort Apache The Bronx*. She ought to think more carefully, learn more quickly.

'What sort of violence?' he asked.

'Oh, you know, scratching, slapping around.'

'Well, yes, scratching's OK – a kind of intimacy, another way of getting under your skin. Yes, any kind of closeness is lovely. I don't think I'd want to hit you, though.'

Denise watched him, wondering what her mother would make of it if she could see the two of them here, and resisting a scared giggle at the idea. Harpur was big and fair haired, though losing a little of it, and a bit misshapen around the nose and cheeks. Denise thought he looked like a not too useful boxer, one who finished a lot of bouts during a lot of years earning a good round of applause as the gallant loser, though not able to hear it above concussion timpani. She knew, really, that he would never be a gallant loser, and if necessary would turn dirty to make sure he wasn't – wasn't mistaken for gallant, that is: he might not always win, but he would hate to look sporting in defeat. This was one of the itemised things she loved and wanted to learn from him; the will and skill to stay yourself, not kow-tow to currents, to keep on deftly satanising if nothing else would work. Denise reckoned she had been born into a tough world, which would get tougher, and you needed to take measures against it: maybe why she had finished up with a cop, an older cop, one probably as capable as anybody at taking measures against it.

Except, of course, she had not finished up with him. He was someone else's, many people's, stolen for special afternoons and evenings, and once – big deal – overnight. Half the time his mind could be anywhere, keeping ahead. She suspected it was three points brighter than hers, and five points brighter than anyone's who taught her, although he played philistine, even was, and could talk and look punch-drunk whenever it suited, in fact often. Three different admirable aspects of his brain power came high in the listed pluses on her computer. So what worried him today? It would not be chickenfeed.

'Hitting would be a busman's holiday?' she asked. 'So maybe burn me. With a cigarette?'

'I don't smoke,' he said.

'I could lend you a ciggy. I'd like marks. Show I belong. I know kids who do it. Well, I can't wear a ring, can I?'

'No, no burning.' He rolled away and lay on his back. She saw his mind had completely left her.

'All right,' she told him. 'No burning. Sorry. Look, don't limbo plunge.'

'No burning.' He was almost shouting, and she found herself glancing at the flimsy door, as he had. It would not stop much sound.

'I said OK,' she told him.

In his head he had sight of a girlfriend of Iles – really a serious and even touching affair – brought out dead from a torched building not long ago and looking, as the ACC had mentioned at the time, like charred turf. Celia Mars was the only person Harpur knew who had ever got really close to Iles, and that included the ACC's wife, Sarah. Celia had been accidentally caught up in a gang war, just on the very outermost edge, but the very outermost edge where the arson was. What might Denise be on the outermost edge of? Everyone touched the fringes of so many ways of life, and it could bring bad problems. There ought to have been an eleventh commandment: *Thou shalt not overlap.*

He put his glass on the floor. 'You've got to think long-term,' he said. 'Husband, live-in lover – they'd get ratty about alien initials in scars.'

'So stuff them. C.H. for Colin Harpur? It could mean Carmelite House, a convent. But we won't make a thing of it, Col.'

'I'm a tenderness person.'

'Well, that's nice, too.'

He saw she had picked up how troubled he was and, keen to keep the day happy, turned back towards her, pushing the memories and parallels and fears hard away. Iles had got over it not too badly, eventually, as far as anyone could tell with him. He and Sarah had a child now, and that seemed to delight, even almost stabilise him. Gently Harpur tugged the hedgehogs off Denise and then the rest of her clothes, making quite a performance with the knickers because of the discussion they'd had. Then he lay with his head on her middle, listening to her stomach gurglings, drawing his nails down her arm, under and over, pretty softly at this stage, leaving only a delicate line that disappeared almost at once. She pushed and pulled a bit at his clothes – his shirt and the belt of his trousers – a sort of impatience, but nothing too committed, as if she were concentrating on whatever she was getting herself out of lying there flat with his ear on her navel and having her arm given this steady, sharp massage. It was all sleepy, half-pace, lovely. Early on, he liked this kind of silence and some hang-fire leisureliness. Leisureliness you could get in a room, even a room like this, less so in a car or rubble.

Harpur decided you'd never identify anyone from the noise of their gut juices, so it was not all that personal and close, really, this position, but it always comforted him to eavesdrop on her innards' mild hullabaloo, the one-to-oneness of it, her teenage body talking to him, proclaiming everything still working fine. It would have talked like that to anyone, of course. It would have talked to a stethoscope, and talked more intelligibly. But he was the one who was there now: what he had meant about making men in the street imaginative and envious if the two of them had walked together to the hotel. She was his. He could look after her. He was gazing down the half length of her, from her bush to her knees to her shins and feet. It was all noted, what he had to take care of, head to toe: brow, chin, shoulders, armpits, breasts, ribs, and then so on below. If you'd been in police work a long while it could make you think of a body as components.

Her hand on his clothes began to grow more forceful. He raised his head from her stomach. She turned away for a moment to put her glass down alongside the bed and then turned back and with both hands started to pull at his shirt and tie, not that nice, considerate kind of treatment he had given the hedgehogs, but button busting. Often she had a directness about her, even when she was not running the show. Harpur sometimes saw it as youth doing a let's-cut-the-crap thing, a sort of reproach for his easy, older pace. He did not mind too much. Adjust. He learned, or was reminded, of what things were like at nineteen. Some urgencies were more urgent then. His own urgencies would turn up all right pretty soon, and then they would hit it together, nearly always together whatever the embittered, feminist guide books said about the myth of it, her tongue out of his ear by that stage because their heads were too full of movement, but his invasion of her giving a lovely surge of all the usual unique pleasures.

He left the bed and hurriedly got out of his clothes, then went close again. They were lying on top of the covers in the grand early summer warmth of the attic. The sun made a really serious go at battling through the window grime.

'I see you looking and looking at my skin – a sort of reverence,' she grunted. Now and then her voice seemed all wrong for her frame.

'Why not?'

'It's distancing.'

'Well, I'll stop it then,' he said. She was right, without really knowing why she was right. The distance was into the future, where his worries about her skin and her scalp and her blood lay.

'Why I wanted the marking and knocking about and so on. It brings things down to earth.'

'What's great about being brought down to earth? Ask a boxer.'

She gave it a thought. 'Too much talk.' She put an arm around him and her hand fluttered over his back and shoulders and neck. He must have scared her off the violence, even scratching. 'Anyway, I love your skin, too, Col.'

'Reverence it?'

'Love it. It's been around, seen trouble.'

She meant his own scarring and he felt himself starting to grow proud of his few wounds. Quickly he put a stop to such oafishness.

She bent up one leg and rested it on his hip, so he could find her with his fingers and give the sort of messages that preceded the final rough and jubilant message, when she would usually be under but often above, who cared? Her face was against his, her eyes dark and loving and doing what they always did – trying to read him, with every bit of brain she had gleaming in those victorious irises. Sometimes he half wished she could manage it. But who could read anyone? You made do with scratching the skin for nearness, and with sinking in for as far as you could go for as long as you could keep it there: after all, in politer times newspapers used to term that being intimate.

'We make love like farewells,' she muttered, staring up at him.

'No, like for ever.' It had to be possible, and it was what she wanted to hear. And what he wanted to say, come to that, at the moment.

Chapter Eight

'She buys champagne,' Doug Webb said. 'I'm watching her, in Sainsbury's. Plus two glasses. She holds them up to the light, grinning, like they're something so beautiful and with good tidings just for her, the Wise Men and the star. You see what I'm getting at, Courtney, Ralphy? Not the wide old common things they used to do for champagne, the Babycham buckets, but proper delicate flute glasses, that type I tell you Lamb's sure to have at his bloody summer do. How come a student's buying champagne, supposed to be hard up? Well, because it's a celebration, a big day – turning these couple of glasses around in window sunbeams, really lapping up the sight. Maybe a saint with some holy vision. What big day? Her boyfriend's killed someone, that's what, and she's doing the catering. Saint Mouth. They go off toasting themselves, and what follows in the hotel. Harpur's pulled a coup with her aid, and so a party for blowing a backward kid's chest out and two others taken. The kind of world we live in today.' Webb found his voice sinking. After a while he muttered: 'Don't worry, I'm not breaking down, but it makes its mark.'

'You did well, Doug,' Sanquhar-Perry replied. 'Controlling yourself on our project's behalf. This is maturity, if you don't mind me saying.'

Webb minded him saying, the oozy bastard. Maturity was natural when you were fifty-one. Webb let it go, though. His voice picked up again. 'You could hear the glasses touch the bottle when she walked. Victory bells. Who do they think they're fooling, Courtney, Ralphy? He walks behind her to this flophouse, as if they never met, and you can see him smacking his lips. They're like that, gun cops: kill someone then bed someone – blood up, hooked on thrill. I was sobbing. I heard the glasses sounding off. A glory procession, like bringing home the Football League Cup. Next thing, she'll be down getting a giggle out of his funeral.'

'Which hotel?' Sanquhar-Perry asked.

'The Tenbury. Out they come eventually and it's the same – she

65

walking in front, him twenty metres behind, but strolling now. Well, they've said it all, done it all. She's got the Sainsbury's bag again but now only the glasses, no weight, yet still a happy little tinkling. She's thinking they'll be able to use them again. Maybe.'

'Tenbury?' Sanquhar-Perry said. 'That's a comedown. I heard usually the San Francisco or High Table.'

'You're saying I've got it wrong – that this wasn't those two?'

'Not at all, Doug. No, indeed,' Sanquhar-Perry replied in a hurry.

'I hope not. I'm close. Not too close, never observed, but I'm with that girl non-stop – student flats, supermarket, then meeting him. No knickers, I'd say. That's how some of them are these days. Who's going to get Harpur wrong, anyway – that face and the neck?'

Ember said: 'Look, Doug, how's she even going to know Harpur did Martin? It's not in the papers or anywhere.'

'He tells her. This is one-up for him and one-up for her, who helped. This is Harpur VC. On the phone he says, "You heard about that business in Link Street, Denise – some scum blasted following useful information? Take a guess who saw to him. I can't tell you, but there's nothing to stop you wondering." We've got an intelligent girl here who can read in the spaces, an undergrad. "Oh, Colin," she replies, "my gorgeous one. Festival time. My treat." '

'Harpur wouldn't talk like that,' Ember said. 'As they go, he's almost civilised, and he'll never make the top. Nobody talks like that. You torture yourself, Doug – jabbing a wound.'

'I haven't got wounds. That was Martin. Remember?'

'This girl's no part of it, and we're not even sure ourselves Harpur did the killing,' Ember said.

'We're sure,' Sanquhar-Perry replied. 'The word's out.'

'Civilised? Blasting off at a slow-wit? I had to identify him. You ever seen anyone hit from so close? Perhaps you have. You've been in sorties. You seen a son hit from so close, though? Why do you have to take care of Harpur, anyway, Ralphy, or his messenger-girl?'

'No, not like that at all,' Ember said. 'I feel for you, Doug. I just don't want you giving yourself pain if there's doubt. Extra pain, I mean.'

'No extra pain. Just pain. And it's sending me a plea. It's sending all sorts of his loved ones a plea.'

'Which we'll listen to, Doug, no question, when we're ready,' Sanquhar-Perry replied. 'It's great you're still ready to work, even before the funeral.'

'Like I said, I have to be occupied. Anyway, this was timetabled. I don't back out.'

66

'Great,' Sanquhar-Perry said. 'Isn't it, Ralph?'

'Responsible,' Ember replied. He was driving them in the Rover, Sanquhar-Perry alongside him, Webb behind. Webb wanted to be reasonable, despite it all. They were going to inspect the target Sanquhar-Perry's inside contact said would be fruitful any time now. Courtney still reckoned to feed the police a wrong tip through Lamb and clean up. Webb, gazing at the back of their heads in the Rover, knew they could not understand what he was talking about, would not even understand why his voice had failed. Oh, they heard the words and were sorry about Martin, but had no feel of how it was to lose a lovely hard dumbo boy, and then see the ones who did it or gave a hand skipping off to their seaminess, thinking they fooled the universe, thinking sex and love made them special and would keep them forever safe. These two, Ember and Courtney, did not know about family suffering. They had things cut and dried. Ember smug in his club and Low Pastures – almost as big as Lamb's Darien, they said – paddocks, and with his daughters riding in gymkhanas, getting a smart education and on no Records computer, yet. True, Courtney lived measly, though without kids to worry over and no commitment to anybody much except himself. The women came and went, gave their bit of tempest now and then, but minor consequence. Did he have to cope with a wife and mother grieving the way Kay was? Grieving? All Sanquhar-Perry thought of was his cheeky curls. He'd been training them into a nice fat cluster on the back of his neck.

'I heard Harpur was pretty sick. Might take counselling,' Ember said.

'Did he look sick to me?' Webb answered. 'He looked like home is the hunter and due something juicy.'

'Right here, Ralph, and the bank's a couple of hundred yards down on the left,' Sanquhar-Perry said. 'Barclays. Borough Walk. Ralph and I would have worn black ties, Doug, but they could be noticeable on a reconnoitre, all three of us.'

'Martin would understand,' Webb replied.

They drove slowly but not so slowly it told a story. Ralph would be thinking this was a traceable car and might find a home in someone's memory.

Go into something with Ember and even with Courtney and you could never be sure of the ins and outs. They might have professional interlocks all over. Here's Ember falling over himself to say the best about Harpur every chance, like he was his uncle. Here's Courtney playing for delays on the girl. There could be a real business structure behind it all, and they would not let it come apart because some nothing Webb kid got shot on a nothing raid. These were operators, even Courtney in that rubbish house with the glued furniture and murdered carpet. They might have their arrangements. They would think hitting back for Martin not on at all, not necessary and what they would call a spasm. That was obvious about Ralphy, but probably the same for Courtney, too, no matter how committed the bugger talked. When it came to settling up you were on your own. Perhaps that was fair enough: produce a liability kid and it's your liability. But he had in mind that girl's behind when she was walking ahead of Harpur, so proud of itself and cheery, busy with come-on, while Martin's body would be flat on an individual freeze slab and she put it there.

'Inside, the bank's too tough,' Sanquhar-Perry went on. 'Bars and reinforced glass to the ceiling and steel sheets behind veneer for doors. Plus alarms, of course. But a cash pick up by Larch Security twice a week, the van parked here, three men including the driver.'

They passed the Barclays, not too much staring, though adequate for a first visit. 'We can go around again,' Ember said. 'Or stop and have a walk. Not together, obviously. Well, obviously.'

'Yes, walk. That's what I mean – the ties, Doug,' Sanquhar-Perry said.

'A link to Link Street,' Webb said.

'I love the way you can still be witty and wry, Doug,' Sanquhar-Perry replied.

'So you're menuing what sort of money, Courtney?' Ember asked.

'I hear upwards of a hundred grand. Some days it could be twice that.'

'Do we get to know which?' Ember replied.

'Which what?' Sanquhar-Perry said.

'Which days it's two hundred?' Ember replied.

'I'm given very sound information.'

'Numerate?' Ember said. He turned left at the end of Borough Walk and looked for a side street where they could leave the Rover.

'How do you mean, numerate?' Webb asked.

'Can the information tell us which are the one hundred days and which the two hundred?' Ember said slowly, like spelling it out for an idiot.

Sanquhar-Perry chuckled. 'I love the way you stick at it, Ralph. I love the way you think maximisation, my own gospel. Some would regard a hundred grand elegant and anything above was luck. You've seen bumper times, Ralph, I know it. You're from a fine past.'

'Just an equation: risk, reward. That's my point – numerate.' Ember pulled in. Webb saw it was a street of big houses mostly converted to offices. There were plenty of cars on the firms, Rovers included. Ember's would not stand out.

'Yes, of course,' Sanquhar-Perry said. 'We're told when it's a bonus day.'

Webb could guess what they were thinking, though they would never say it while he could hear. They were thinking this job meant healthy money, not the kind of rock-bottom, veg-smelling little sortie where Martin died. Class. All right, he'd let that go for now, too.

They left the car at intervals and strolled back separately towards the bank, not even glancing at one another. This was the kind of work Webb knew he could do better than anybody. When he looked at a street, really looked, the picture stayed in his head for as long as it had to, a picture where he could see detail, like shop doorways that might give cover, lane entrances that might be a crisis exit. Using this picture, he could recall distances to within a couple of feet. It featured steps and kerbs and broken flagstones that might bring you down as hard as a bullet could, if you were running like a fool and carrying a sackful. Locales kept their shape in his memory the way girls' bodies did in other men's as wanking kit. Himself, he preferred streets. He had a Polaroid in his head. So how did Martin get Shredded Wheat in his? Kay's fault? She had a daft aunty somewhere.

There was no security van loading now. His street picture would be missing important items, such as the size and type of vehicle, the size and type of guard, the kind of safe, in case it came to busting the van and not just the crew – time-lock, keys, combination? Courtney's contact might provide. Webb would have liked to have on file in his mind the colour of the van, the shape of the door hinges, the registration number, the kind of lettering that did the company's name, the brand of window grilles, even the radiator grille. Things like that that would seem nothing to most made a target live and become familiar and manageable. The only van in sight was a hamburger mobile for sale in a second hand car yard with a notice on the windscreen, 'One gourmet owner.'

In this sort of career there were always blind spots. If you asked for perfection you'd never move. Ahead of him, Ember turned and walked back. He was gazing about, maybe counting people on the pavement, numerating, numerating. That could be important on the day – obstructions or even bloody nuisance heroes – but who knew how many there would be then? To Webb, Ember looked pretty sick. It took some believing he had piled up gains, yet the fact was he had. Glance at Low Pastures – not that he'd invite you there. The bugger thought he looked like Charlton Heston. He didn't, thank God, or someone might notice and remember him walking past, full of fright, El Cid gone wobbly.

Webb and Ember passed each other, as if neither existed. Webb had an idea Ember wished it was true, about him. Ember seemed to be assessing the traffic flow now, working out how it might affect their flit. More uselessness. You never knew how traffic would be. Sanquhar-Perry stood opposite the bank, gazing, which was not too clever either, really. Banks did not like being stared at. 'Saunter, you curly sod,' Webb muttered. Now and then and oftener he wondered what kind of people he was tying himself to – intelligent but dim? He liked the way he summed them up for himself before – they thought they were strategists was what they thought.

In the car on their way back Sanquhar-Perry said: 'Looks workable?'

'It's a bank and a street,' Webb replied. 'Then a van.'

Sanquhar-Perry had another chuckle. 'I like it. The fundamentals, Doug.'

'Afterwards?' Webb replied. 'We disperse with the shares? What about my main business?'

'Repaying for Martin? We reassemble, obviously,' Sanquhar-Perry said. 'In due course, or sooner.'

'Well, I hope so, Courtney.'

'It's all in hand,' Sanquhar-Perry replied.

Now and again, Webb did see what they meant about vengeance. It could be stupid. Vengeance slammed a duty on and took away your thinking. It said, Do it, and you could not ask why, but if you did the answer was, Do it because it's got to be done and the task is sacred. It nagged and gave you orders, even if you'd spent your life making sure nobody gave you orders, except when you were inside, of course. And yet, when he thought again of Harpur and the girl getting their merriment and their steam up out of Martin torn open among no-account shoppers he knew it had to be balanced. Revenge was straight and clean, not like niggling grab questions about how much would be on offer this day or that. Revenge was holy – more holy than those sun-bright champagne glasses and what they stood for. Revenge was about someone else, not just selfish. He had looked at the girl's jaunty rear through one layer of material and seen a statement that life went on and was rich fun and full, for some. That arse laughed at agony – Kay's, Martin's and his own.

'Look, you say all these nice matters about Denise, Ralph, but a couple of days before Link Street she's right up there at Lamb's place. In the house, for God's sake, taking info,' Webb said. 'I happen to know this.'

'Yes, I saw you waiting around near Darien, Doug,' Sanquhar-Perry replied. He turned in the front seat, nodding the yellow mat in very friendly style.

'You fucking what?' Webb yelled. These sods wanted to make themselves sound so fly. 'You telling me you saw me and I didn't see you, Courtney? That'll be the day. There's nobody could watch me and me not spot him.'

'I just thought I'd have a look at her,' Sanquhar-Perry said. 'I kept out of your way, not wanting to throw you.'

Webb shouted again: 'No, this is—'

'Tony Towler was at Darien, too. Yes? The grass's grass,' Sanquhar-Perry replied. 'Three-way conference?'

Webb's voice had another collapse. After a few seconds he managed in a whisper: 'Christ, Courtney, you *were* there.'

Sanquhar-Perry turned back to look ahead and spoke over his shoulder. 'Towler's going to be so useful, the slime. I've got him nibbling.'

Webb said: 'Towler's another we ought to—'

'We will, Doug,' Sanquhar-Perry replied. 'Eventually. A word you don't like, but there's wisdom in it, believe me. Let him help us for now. He's a recruit, you could say.'

This coolness, this long-distance planning: Webb felt like a moron or a child again, stuck on one idea, not able to step around it, even for a moment. So he said: 'What I don't understand – anyone can get in and out of Lamb's place, no problem. Open house. Why not just go there and do him?'

'Me, I wouldn't like to go after him on his own ground, Doug,' Sanquhar-Perry said.

'You really want to finish him, you two?' Webb replied.

Sanquhar-Perry turned around again, smiling kindly, and gazing blue-eyed at Webb, as he had gazed at the bank: 'I hate it when you slip into that disbelieving mode, Doug. You did it before.'

'Towler's going to be at the funeral,' Webb replied.

Sanquhar-Perry said: 'Towler's everywhere, buttering, sucking up, sucking in. His trade. Don't let it provoke you, Doug.'

'And you boys?' Webb asked. 'Can we expect you?'

'I don't think that would be clever, Doug,' Ember replied. 'Regrettably. Best we don't proclaim a connection – what you'd bravely call a link – not at this moment, in view of the bank. Harpur will have eyes there.'

'Ralph's right, Doug, I'm afraid. Pointers would be no good to any of us. We'll send flowers, naturally. The names had better be codes. Yes, police and the Press look at these things, the hard, prying sods. I thought "From Agnes and Neville" – that's my parents' names, so there's authenticity, giving a family dimension. How about you, Ralph?'

'I discussed it with Margaret, of course,' Ember replied. 'We thought, "From Hugh and Gordon, two staunch old mates of Martin, a great guy." Cut flowers, not a wreath. Margaret and I both think wreaths are fine – but maybe a bit formal for "staunch old mates". We'll get them out of town and a cash payment, so no possibility of any line back to us. I've got to think of our team.'

'The papers gave real display to the death and mentioned the time of the funeral,' Sanquhar-Perry said. 'You'll have a huge crowd. We won't be missed.'

'Well you will be,' Webb replied.

'That's kind of you,' Ember said.

'I'll look after weapons for the job,' Sanquhar-Perry said. 'We can't go without. This is three to three, so we've got to give ourselves extra weight.'

'No question,' Webb replied.

Sanquhar-Perry said: 'That's really—'

'Courtney, you think I'm going to back off firearms because of Martin? You don't know Doug Webb. Get me something man-stopping, Courtney.'

'You're grand, Doug,' Ember told him.

'You're this team's backbone,' Sanquhar-Perry said. 'No less.'

72

Chapter Nine

'A veritable hood funeral, Denise. Here, read the paper. We must go. Sure to be atmospheric heavies from all over and heart-shaped wreaths, plus his faithful red setter on a lead, like Chicago or the East End. Real downtown local colour. I adore it.' Mandy prodded her shoulder. 'Oh, wake up, Denise, it's ten o'clock.'

'What you talking about?' Denise muttered from the bed, opening an eye. Bliss, these tail-end summer-term days – no work, no pressure, sex, more sex. How could you fix it so the next sixty years were like this?

'If we're in the big city we ought to see how the big city lives – and dies. An education. This is for that kid, knocked over in the Post Office raid? Last post. Look, it's been a really subfusc term and I need something spectacular to talk about when I go home to the heart of rural England, so help me. This will wow them. Anyway, all sunny day funerals are impressive – brass handles aglow, bees flirting with the wreaths. In the Valencia. You should be interested, you with your top-cop boyfriend. That *is* still on?'

'What?'

'You and the dick supremo, as it were,' Mandy said.

'Just about,' Denise replied. She sat up slowly in bed. There was a fatty smell of cooking. The door stood open and she could see across the corridor to Mandy's flat. Her door was open too and her flat horribly tidy. Mandy was dressed and eating a bacon sandwich. 'Colin worries,' Denise told her.

'What – guilt re wifey and so on? I've come across that in men myself, penny-and-bunning bastards.'

'That. Other things.' Denise slumped back.

'Like? Don't doze off again. Experience beckons, slut. What other things?'

Denise spoke from the pillow, eyes closed: 'Oh, I had this dread he meant to end it. You know the way it can come to you – not certain, but almost – a shadow, a horrible vague premonition of something, these last couple of weeks. Colin frets over my safety, as if I were a damn child. I'm supposed to be in danger, can you believe? I see him looking at my body, not the usual way, although he does that as well I'm pleased to say, but as if imagining it – imagining it in a mess. Cut about, et cetera. So, turn me loose, that's what he'd decided, I think – supposed to be for my own good. I gave him a yarn about winning the Bell prize and wanting to celebrate. I knew he couldn't ditch me then. He's too kind.'

'And what's the Bell prize?'

'I made it up.'

'Isn't he going to find out? He *is* a detective.'

'I'll deal with that, if and when. I just needed something to get me over a crisis, didn't I?'

'There you are then. It's still on, so you owe it to him.'

'What?'

'To see this funeral. It's a feather in their cap. Your duty to share the triumph and witness the pay-off. You can tell him about it.'

'I don't think so. You don't know him.'

'He could even have been part of it. Someone pulled the trigger. Or is he too big wheel?'

'Probably. He didn't say anything. He wouldn't, though. The sod's made of secrets.'

'So, we'll go?'

'Where?'

'The funeral. Spectate. Bit of practical social anthropology. Underclass on parade. We shall not look upon their like again – at least, I won't, where I live in deepest Somerset. And I go home soon, sooner than you if you're staying for that summer ball thing. Jonson Court's going to be nearly empty. You'll be all right?'

'Of course.'

'If you say so. Well, come on then.'

'What?'

'Let's join the obsequies.'

Part of Denise loathed the notion: gawping, crowing over people's distress. Yet what Mandy said had reached her: perhaps she ought to see something of the world where Colin spent his working life. It was wrong, diminishing, to think of him as just a lover.

But outside the nice, sprawling, ugly church, Denise knew immediately that sightseeing was a callous mistake. Some of these people arriving looked hammered by real misery. Well, of course. A boy was dead. Did it matter he had been crooked? He was still their boy. Now, Mandy probably regretted coming, too, but would never admit it. She was not hard or stupid, just impulsive and could get stuck with the results. They stood among a cluster of locals at the

74

churchyard gates, and Denise would have liked there to be more, a crowd to hide her.

'The faces,' Mandy whispered. 'Auditioning for *Godfather IV*?'

'That's from bloody Woody Allen. Let's go,' Denise replied. Her face did not fit, she knew it, nor Mandy's. Their faces were rich, rural Somerset and middle-rank, new executive estate, Stafford. This was the Valencia, run down, dirty, sure of its bleak self: hard, old, used to spitting out what it didn't want. They were slumming, and it must show. This was not the same as coming to the Valencia with Colin. Now, they were looking for a giggle in people's loss: flippant, privileged sows.

Mandy said: 'Five more minutes, since we're here. This has to be his mother.'

The woman entering the churchyard gate was not weeping and walked unaided, but Denise thought Mandy might be right. This woman looked at nobody in the crowd, her eyes on the church door, as though needing to put all her concentration on getting there. She was tall and fair skinned, mid-forties, long, slim legs, hair assisted-blonde, though not madly assisted, strong features, her eyes seeming empty now and bright blue. The paper had described the dead boy as handsome, and looking at her you'd believe it. She wore a navy suit, gleaming white blouse, no hat. To Denise, she seemed like someone who had seen a lot of pain even before today and made the best of it by guts and toughness. You'd pick her out anywhere as a mother of robbers or priests.

A man walked a little way behind. He would be a bit older, his face long and craggy and bitter, not handsome at all. He wore a grey suit from newsreel shots of the first Labour Government. For a moment, his eyes seemed to take in Denise and fixed angrily on hers. Very troubled, she looked away. The recognition she had feared was in his glance: he must see they came to peep at a low-life pageant. When she turned back, both had disappeared inside the brownstone church. More mourners entered and not long afterwards she could just hear the vicar intoning, 'I am the resurrection and the life,' and then a hymn started, 'The day thou gaveth, Lord, hath ended', the voices an assault. She found herself crying and saw that Mandy had lowered her head and might be sobbing, too.

A Daimler hearse waited near them for the crematorium run, its tailgate already raised to receive the body. The driver in navy peaked cap gazed about like the officer of the watch. Wreaths and cut flowers were crammed against the windows and driver's partition, around the coffin space. Mandy had it right again, and through the glass Denise saw a large heart-shaped wreath of pink carnations, its card apparently in a child's handwriting: Goodbye, Uncle Martin. God bless you for ever and ever, Bobby, Sue and Mike. A couple of men who had been watching from the other side of the road came quickly over now and one of them walked down the offside of the Daimler, apparently reading the inscriptions, while the other stood near Denise and did the same on the pavement side. They were young, both in shirt sleeves, jeans and trainers, both fit looking, both intent. She wondered if they were Colin's people, and wondered if she liked it if they were. She almost asked the man at her side, but feared questions in return. Colin would get ratty if he heard she had come here, and in his sombre style see it as another step into peril. The men made no notes. That would be too obvious. They worked systematically along, reading the messages that were visible, memorising.

Pushed up to near the roof, was a simple wreath of white roses bearing a card on which Denise could see, From Agnes and Neville, ever friends of dear Martin, and ever proud of him. She heard bright defiance in that – a wish to let the world know, and the prying men know, that at least these two, Agnes and Neville, stood by their friend, regardless. It was touching and she began to cry again. This was a community they had come to peek at and patronise – perhaps a rough community, but one with its own bonds, grief and genuineness, that above all. You would not find such loyalties on a chi-chi estate in Stafford. Names like Agnes and Neville – traditional, unfancy, even noble – brought the day a richer dignity. She had never seen so many flowers at a funeral.

A spray of dahlias seemed in danger of falling from the open back of the hearse. The card with them said its piece more clearly still: From Hugh and Gordon, two staunch 'old mates' of Martin, a great guy. Denise took a couple of steps and carefully placed the bunch more securely inside the hearse. The concentrated scent from the mass of blooms enveloped her suddenly and invaded the street, doing their standard, hopeless bit to sweeten tragedy. One of the two men had watched Denise with the flowers and she gazed back at him, her eyes still wet with tears, giving the same sort of honest defiance as she saw on the cards. Now, she felt glad they had come, after all. She had learned something. Into her head from somewhere swam that shagged-out Tennyson line, *Tears, idle tears, I know not what they mean*. She knew what hers meant.

Tony Towler followed Webb and Kay into the church and watched them walk slowly up the central aisle to a pew at the front to take places alongside their two other sons, Rodney and Bernard, and some more relatives from this section of Webb's life. Towler did not feel too great, had almost chickened out of coming, but knew he could not. This was a ceremony he had to attend and be seen to attend, and his flowers, with their message of heavy bereavement, yet also happy memories of Martin, had to be noticed by Doug and his people. To stay away, to fail to send a tribute, would proclaim fear or shame, or both, and get people wondering – or wondering more – if he had anything to do with Link Street.

Towler took a spot in the body of the church and stared at the back of Webb's neck above the collar of that bloody suit, as if he could read there whether Doug knew he had come, and whether he had any special ideas. Towler was happy to see other mourners enter the pew with him. He had dreaded being left seated alone like a disease. Strange to realise he had never felt more in danger than now, yet this was the House of God. Today, the House of God would be a no-go area for police and maybe for God himself. Webb and Kay sat next to each other, but to Towler it looked as though there was no contact between them – their bodies stiff and apart, Kay concerned only with the coffin in front of them. Everyone knew Doug still worshipped her, and that she no longer had any time for him. She stayed, though. Kay was very strong on family, strong on contracts.

The coffin lay so close to them on its shiny rubber-wheeled trolley that Webb realised he could have reached out and touched it. He didn't, but Kay did, once, letting her hand pause for two or three seconds on the lid, then withdrawing it slowly, her eyes still dry. After she had done that he knew he couldn't. It would have looked forced on him. He knew he should not touch Kay, either, or speak to her, but must leave her alone with the pain. She made it plain he could give no comfort, and would not let him try. It was as though she blamed him, and the exclusion hurt Webb nearly as much as Martin's death. Sitting there, half listening to the vicar's address about the grand strengths of meekness and long-suffering, he let his mind find hatred once again. That was easy enough.

As he and Kay walked to the church he had spotted Tony Towler arriving in his funeral gear, and the sight of the girl outside had also driven him almost sick with rage. They never gave up, that syndicate – Harpur, Iles, Lamb – and their filthy in-betweens. They killed, made sure you went all the way to the oven, and listed those who showed sympathy. He had noticed two plain-clothes police standing opposite the church and another on a flat roof filming. Normal, and he could not object to their professional interest. This would be true even of Towler. The girl was not the same, looking so sympathetic and bloody refined, but undoubtedly there to snoop on labels and see what she could see, then report back. A mockery. How could a pretty kid like that sink into such rottenness? Sanquhar-Perry and Ralphy Ember should have been here to observe it, the sods. They might understand a bit better then. Might see why he had to struggle to keep cool, act cool – or not act, only bide his time for business reasons. Far down, though, he thought those two were probably wise. Very far down.

Of course, they considerately stayed away and sent their tasteful floral tributes with the loud, nobody messages, which the girl outside would be reading now. Webb would have binned the flowers and cards as soon as they arrived, and Towler's. Kay said no. Kay said if your whole life was a fraud why would funerals be different? Kay had a brain, and she could use it like a knife. How did she produce a half-head like Martin. She did not seem to realise, though, or maybe did not care, that the flower cards from that lot yelled loyalty while the senders kept in hiding, heads down, a cold insult to Martin, who was cold enough.

And, sitting there then, Webb felt as if the coldness came at him all at once out of the casket, folding around his face and shoulders like a sudden fog. He was part of Martin. Yes. He could imagine those bullets had reached him, too, and his chest grew tight. Always there had been that extra closeness between him and this boy. Gasping, Webb slumped forward about forty degrees, like going into urgent prayer. He sensed the vicar glance across anxiously and as a result tangle some helpful things he was saying – possibly about grace, or one of those similar church fitments, such as the other cheek. Kay kept staring in front, above the coffin, head up, face fixed, and took no notice. Christ, he could have been having a coronary here, but did she care? Didn't she believe he could suffer, too?

Webb straightened in his pew. *Kay, look at me, I count for something. Didn't I love him?* Rodney leant forward and stared around her at Webb, obviously troubled. Rodney was not Kay, though. Rodney had always been a bit bloody soft. Among the sons of this one of Webb's households, Rodney possessed most of the intelligence, yet somehow went in for a lot of consideration. Strange: Rodney looked harder than Martin, who people used to say was like some tremendous poet. Martin had had the real core, though, and not just because he was too stupid to see risk.

It was Rodney who had picked the final hymn, 'The Lord's My Shepherd'. Webb didn't mind it too much, although it was not the Lord who made Martin lie down, and what they had here was not

78

the 'shadow of death' but the item in full. 'The shadow of death' was what was around that girl and Towler and some others, if they only knew. But best they did not.

It pleased him that they took the coffin off the trolley and carried it out on shoulders to the hearse – some of the undertaker's people plus Rodney and Bernard. That gave the human touch, not those foul, stout, quiet wheels on greased axles, rushing Martin to the check-out. He and Kay walked slowly behind, she still fine, still nowhere near him, not really. Outside, the girl and the two detectives seemed to have gone, though the lad with the camera was still at it. People came up and said what a first-class boy Martin had been despite – some of them people Webb hardly knew. He found it warming. Briefly, he felt built up again by pride.

Towler made himself go forward and shake Doug's hand. Lamb had suggested that. It was all right for him – he could stay home in Darien. Lamb had worked out with him, too, some words to speak, but to speak with breaks and throaty humility: 'What can I say, Doug, except that all my memories of him are grand memories, and they will stay with me and help me? That doesn't take away your sadness, I know, but for me he lives.'

'Thanks, Tony. It was really fine of you to come.'

Towler, trying to read Doug's face through the curtain of mourning, thought, This smart old bastard knows. 'What else could I do but come, Doug? This funeral is a statement. I wanted to be part of it. Had to be. I would have felt small if not.'

'Yes, I think we've made a little mark today, Tony.'

'This will stand out, Doug. It's already written in to the history of our area, our people.' Some of these words he had put together with Lamb, too.

'Thank you, Tony. Can you come back to the house afterwards? A few of our closest.'

'Privileged.'

Towler wondered if that might indicate something good, after all. Surely to God Doug would not ask him home if he thought anything? They had a saying this way: If they break your bread you don't break their head.

Webb nodded and turned away. You went through the game because games were for going through, but a little of Towler was enough. Although for work Towler liked check jackets, today he wore what Webb saw was a really perfect dark suit, made for him, no question, and costing as much as the coffin. Towler might go to a lot of funerals. He had smooth dark hair and very neat features, though these would not necessarily last.

Webb moved to the front of the hearse on his own while they put Martin in. He knew this driver from way back in other work and had specially asked for him, a famous all-rounder. 'See a girl doing a survey of the flowers at all, Charlie?' he asked.

'Handling.'

'Handling?'

'Handling, Doug.'

'You mean the bitch entered our vehicle?'

'Right.'

'To read a label better?'

'What else? One of theirs?' He nodded up towards the photographer.

'A helper.'

'Worse. They'd sink us all. They sank Martin. You've got to consider, where was that hand last night, the night before?'

Charlie had hit it. This was a girl who would be fondling Harpur, if what Courtney and Ember said was true – then down here among Martin's remembrance flowers. Webb almost retched. He watched the box's prow slide up on steel runners towards the partition. The Carlisle, they called this coffin – one of the most truly wooden and priced at over a grand. You stood the loss, didn't cut corners when it was a lovely kid shot at work. The story went, they never burned the superior caskets but did a switch and used them over and over. He must not think about that, pass-the-parcel with Martin. Crookedness had no limits.

From the other end, Kay was watching the coffin take its place, too. Webb saw the clergyman come out in his black robes and official little hat and speak to her, a message of consolation, obviously. Training supplied the right thoughts for all kinds of moments. She would take it from him, and gave a good, small, weary smile and shook his hand. He held on to hers for a while, two handed, but surely to God that would not mean anything, a vicar, with Martin stretched so damaged right alongside. Was that a sex response halfway down the bugger's robe?

Webb felt satisfied with the turnout in the church. That big place had been almost full, and then more here along the pavements. The family had respect and affection. With reverence they shut the tailgate and the vicar climbed into the passenger seat. That pleased Webb, too. It was good to think of Martin going the last distance with someone very likely decent and holy, despite the incident just now. That gummy villain, Charlie Burnett, had a lot of suitable points, but was not one for the spiritual side.

In the crematorium chapel, just after the curtain came across in

80

front of Martin by electricity, Rodney stood suddenly. He was weeping. 'I'm going to turn to God,' he cried, staring about. 'I hear the call of God.'

Jesus, this noisy jerk was a Webb? Kay kept gazing at the red curtain and did not look up at their son, though he was next to her. You'd think she was used to it.

'All right, Rodney,' Webb called. 'Sit down now, lad.' *God calling him.* For Christ's sake, there could be Press here. This would shoot holes in the total occasion.

'Yes, God wants us different,' Rodney declared. 'I know it now. Today.' Webb loathed the way Rodney said that word, 'God' – his voice full of boom and affection, as though God was a charmer with thousands of good ideas ready to share. Rodney had half turned and was addressing the congregation. Webb looked at the faces and saw among them Towler staring, eyes on fire, lapping it up. Even if there were no reporters here, the world would soon hear of this. The vicar left his reading platform and went quickly towards Rodney. Webb stood and moved around to the kid, also.

'This is perfectly natural,' the vicar said, taking Rodney's arm. 'Even to your credit.'

'Of course it is,' Webb told him. 'He loved Martin. We all did.'

'A moment of great emotion, a moment of great revelation, also,' the vicar added. 'I think of Saul of Tarsus.'

'Right,' Webb said. He felt this family was getting ripped to pieces – first Martin, now the cleverest son of them all. That could happen. A decay would start and take hold if you let it. He had seen this with others, the horrible slide of a good family into ordinariness. Gradually he drew Rodney away from the vicar and took him out to an undertaker's limo and put him in the back. Webb sat at his side. Rodney still cried. That was all right. People did at funerals, even men. But not the rubbish talk.

'I meant it,' Rodney said.

'Nobody holds it against you,' Webb replied.

'I'm going to do some real thinking.'

'We all have to, son. In a quiet way.'

'We can't win the sort of battles we fight. Don't you see, we're being told that?' He shouted this, and turned and gripped Doug Webb's lapels hard.

But you could not take offence with someone deep in stress. He waited a minute and then got Rodney's hands off the coat. 'Rest now,' he said. 'We're all down.' Bernard joined them in the car, looking very confused. He was only a kid. 'It's all fine,' Webb told him.

The vicar turned up at the house for drinks and cold meat. This was all right. He had done a fair job at the two services, getting Martin's names right, and went on giving Kay comfort now. It did not seem to bother him, the kind of company he was in. That would be his training, also – leading him to accept publicans and sinners, plus, for today, pushers, and rough-house and wage-grab and menaces folk, as well as their women. Webb stayed near Rodney, waiting for him to pull through, watching that he did not drink too much and set off all the awful purple distress again. Yes, he looked big and promising, but there had always been this creepy sensitiveness lurking.

The last part of the day had been an agony – Towler so caring behind that suit, the girl with her soiled hands in the hearse, then Rodney splintering, and now this chirpy fucking vicar taking over, sitting with Kay, gazing around, giving the whisky a turn, long legs under his skirts stretched out as if he lived here and had ideas for redecorating. It was the girl who had started the whole lot, and who was there near the end, too. He had had enough of her.

But even in his lonely fury Doug Webb did still recognise that Sanquhar-Perry and Ember were probably right when they said she must not be touched – not touched yet. Handling the flowers was something else to be remembered against her. She would be with Harpur or Lamb now, anyway, giving the picture. Oh, yes, the shadows were gathering to her. It might take a little while.

Towler could be another thing, though. He was talking to Kay and the vicar on the other side of the room, and seemed ready to leave. Who would worry much about Towler, except his mother, if he had one? There was a lot to be said for starting the clean up with Tony. For one thing, it would stop the bugger having a chortle among friends and contacts over Rodney. Courtney might not like it, of course. He made out he was going to use Towler to place the false trail. Well, Courtney could find someone else. Webb felt he had to do something today, now. 'Will you be all right?' he asked Rodney. 'Remember, you're among friends. I might go out for a while shortly. Well, would you say I'm needed here?'

Towler, chatting to Kay and the vicar, watched Webb and saw that things were not right. Webby had him marked, no question. That face was not what you would call an open book, but you could read any hellishness that got into it, and it was into it now. Of course, in Towler's kind of trade you never felt safe. There were times, though, when you felt worse than others, and this was one. He thought it might be time for some subtle police protection. Jack

82

Lamb should be able to fix that. They listened to Jack. You bet they listened. Towler would go to Darien again.

Denise drove Mandy back to the Jonson Court student flats and then made for an area of trees and bushes on the stretch of foreshore known locally as Carnality Strand, to meet Colin Harpur in his lunch time. During the trip to the flats, Mandy stayed unusually quiet, still as if in shock, and Denise was grateful. The funeral had left her confused. She really felt for the family and their solid community, and regarded the snooping, heartless police as – as snooping, heartless police: how her mother and father and that generation believed they all were.

But thinking about those mourners now, and most about the man glaring hate from the church path, she also began to wonder about the perils of Colin's job. How did you fight a community like that, if they were crooked and had to be contained? They would join to repel you. They outnumbered you and yours and might know dirtier tactics. Dirtier than Colin's?

Even now, away from the church, in the city's crowded centre, and near the familiar, grandiose buildings of the university, Denise remained scared by the loathing that had reached her from that man – Martin Webb's father? The memory of his desperate face dogged her, and had such ferocious clarity that she wondered if it was the only time she had seen him. Had there long been an impression of those features in her mind, waiting to be focused by head-on encounter? This must be crazy, a sort of paranoia. Where would she have seen or met him, for God's sake? She forced herself to think about that systematically, and found no answer. Or only an absurd, feverish answer: somehow Denise associated him with the afternoon she and Colin had gone to the hotel, she bearing champagne and glasses, to celebrate that fictitious prize. Pummelling her memory, she tried to see again faces of people in the street that day. Men had certainly lech-looked, and as ever she had ignored them. Half ignored them. Now, she wished she hadn't, for once. In any case, she had been too preoccupied with the dread of losing Colin to notice much – or at least to know she had noticed it.

'What's wrong?' Mandy said, as she left the car.
'What?'
'You're very white.'
'Funerals.'
'You should have said.'
'You don't look great yourself.'
'I couldn't stop seeing chest holes under the shroud.'

It was Colin's turn to bring supplies and he had promised sand-wiches and beer. Just the same, on her way to the foreshore she bought a couple of custard slices, because he never seemed to think of the sweet, an age-gap thing, though she could not tell him that. Parking among the trees, she waited, then realised she was gazing around at the few other lunch-break love cars already in place, searching for that face again. She stopped it. People here disliked being looked at. And her fears were fatuous, anyway.

They had used this rendezvous frequently before. When she first suggested the place, Colin objected, saying it was notorious and unsuitable for a police officer, pompous git: maybe age, maybe status-mania – tripey, whichever. Eventually, he gave in, though, and there had never been any trouble. Her own suspicion was that he used to make love to another woman here previously. For a cop, he could be remarkably sensitive. Now and then she thought of asking him, aware it would be entirely pointless. Anyway, in the hope of being unrecognised, he always used old anonymous cars, even for genuine duty trips. Nobody down here was about to shout, 'I spy police,' but Colin had this bleak obsession with secrecy. If that's what the job did to you you could keep it. You could keep it, full stop. Who wanted to case hearses as a career? And who wanted to fight big tribes of hard enemies day in, day out?

When they were eating and drinking in the front of his Ital she said: 'You seem strained, Colin.'

'My daughters are both doing exams.'

'That gets to you?'

'They worry, so I do. Perhaps academic stuff comes easily to you. Bell prize winner and so on.'

'I thought it might be something in the job.'

'The job goes its usual sweet and gentle way. And you? Resting on your laurels? Dozing in bed all morning?'

'Too true.'

'You look a bit peaky. Not enough fresh air? When will you go home?'

'To Stafford? I've got to have my results officially and pick my courses for next year. Then Jack Lamb's do. Why? You want me to go home?'

'Not at all.'

Or perhaps. Harpur had given up the idea of dropping her as too agonising, but, yes, he would like her safely away from here for a while, a good long while – at least the length of a university vacation. The funeral of Martin Webb had sharpened all his anxieties and regrets. Although he did not go near it himself, and thought the family should be left to their pain unharassed, Iles insisted on a brute presence there and filming. 'You're a bit unhinged, Col, through blowing young Webby into his box,' the ACC had said. 'But worry not, I'll do your thinking for you. Well, don't I always? One of our war's first principles is, Get the enemy down and keep him there. They'll see our men around the funeral, naturally. This is not covert. These folk have to feel we've only just started.'

'They could be allowed their privacy, sir.'

'Young Marty, yes. The grave's a fine and private place.'

'He's to be burned.'

'It's called cremated. Have you thought more about getting counselled, Harpur? You're into extremes – language, soft-heartedness.'

'I'm still considering it.'

'You feel bad?'

He felt bad, lingering bad, but not disabled. 'I've killed someone, sir.'

'Who would have killed one of ours, and one of our best. But death's an item, no denying, creep or not. The Chief continues his anguish over you. Two of a grossly caring kind, you and Lane. I'll adore the obsequies film, and the flower list with its stalwart, bogus names, won't you? Isn't the officiator that hale divine who was shagging our finger-print girl in the vestry post matins Wednesdays and Thursdays? Webby might not like the police connection for his lad if he knew.'

'Webb's not too bad.'

'Kindly. Get this, Harpur, will you: he's not too bad because we don't let the sod get too bad,' Iles had said. 'It's termed policing? We want people like Webb inside or eternally pissing themselves for fear they're going to be. This is termed law and order.'

Harpur left then. Now, in the Ital, he looked when he could at the other vehicles around Carnality Strand. It was one of the reasons he had always hated this spot: cars could park here, half hidden by trees and billowing bushes, the occupants careful about being seen, because that was the way couples behaved. Who said it was lovers in every car, though?

And Denise sensed his worries. She felt they had talked themselves into glumness, as they did now and then these days, and wanted something bright and warming to get them out. They finished the custard slices. Perhaps it was one of those rare moments when she could offer him as much consolation and comfort as he generally gave her. 'You'll have to return to the nick soon, Col.'

'We should get in the back.'

'That's an idea,' she replied.

The little scrambled change of geography, from front seats to rear, transformed things, as she had known it would. Back-seat love might strike many as crude, and Denise herself sometimes preferred bed, but she also had a full thesis in her head on a car's compensations. Youthfulness was one, and possibly the most important – that US student jalopy tradition: important for someone getting on, like Colin, and she could watch and feel him shed years and anxieties as he shed his clothes. 'You're mine,' she said.

'Do I argue?'

'Your life argues for you.'

'Did you say wife?'

'Her as well.'

When Denise returned to the flat she found her mother there with Mandy. 'Surprise,' Sybil Prior cried, amid giggles. 'I was saying to your friend, I intended doing this secretly but find I can't handle it.'

'Do what?' Denise replied. 'Lovely to see you, obviously, but please Mummy, do what?'

'Check up. I've been out to this man Lamb's place.'

'Darien? Check up on Jack Lamb?'

'I told your mother I know nothing about him myself.'

'Don't get cross, Denise. I didn't go in, or see anyone. That's what I mean, I couldn't handle it. What on earth would I say? But I want you to take me to meet him and his girl. Look, I must know if he's – well, if he's like Gatsby.' She drew back from saying 'if he's shady'. Instead, Sybil Prior thought a reference to this smart book should lighten things.

'It's mad, Mummy.'

'Denise, I will see these people. Peace of mind.' She let her voice roughen. 'I swear I'll return there alone if you won't take me, and this time I *will* go in. I'm entitled to know the kind of friends my lovely daughter has. Where on earth have you been today, by the way?'

Denise almost laughed. Her mother had on what she probably felt was the mature version of her sixties denim – brown leather bomber jacket, man's check shirt and narrow-cut beige slacks. These far-off echoes of far-off youth failed to fit at all with the blaring, pindown, mid-life views. The idea of taking her to Jack's appalled Denise. The idea of her scratching around there alone appalled Denise more. Christ, who knew what she might find? Who knew what might happen to her? 'They're probably not even at home,' she said.

'Let's try.' This time, Sybil spoke heavily, as though on a mission and without choice.

Denise went down to the booths at the other end of the building and telephoned Darien. Jack himself answered. 'I'm sorry about this, but my mother insists on meeting you,' she said.

'Wonderful. She can meet *my* mother, too.'

Mandy was waiting in the corridor. 'She seemed so jumpy, Denise. Obviously, I didn't tell her about the funeral. Our story is we spent the morning at college – seeing advisers, and so on. Been with Colin? What's her big fret, anyway?'

'Oh, like all *croulants*: she's afraid I'm reliving her student days. Main part envy, small part fright.'

'Will it be all right out there?'

'Why ever not? What could happen at Darien? I mean, what do you expect, Mandy? Lamb's a gem and a gent.'

Mandy mumbled: 'But you had doubts – didn't you say?'

'Never.'

At Jack's house, Sybil Prior declared: 'Oh, Mr Lamb, this is such a super place. Do I recognise the Latin on the gates? Horace? And "Darien" – a resonant name, even without picking up the Keats and Chapman's Homer reference.'

'Chapman crapman,' Mrs Lamb replied. 'What interests you, I expect, Mrs Prior, is not the property but how the hell someone like Jack got it and what's liable to happen to your daughter here. I mean, does Jack Lamb look manor house?'

'And I adore the pictures,' Mrs Prior replied.

'You're wondering how he got those, too? You don't give up.'

'I really love it here,' Mrs Prior said. They were in Lamb's office-library-den upstairs.

'I understand a mother's worries,' Mrs Lamb went on. 'Clearly. Don't I worry about Jack?'

Denise saw her mother stop a smile. 'Even now?' Mrs Prior replied. She waved a hand, half pointing at Jack, as if saying he seemed well beyond a mother's anxieties. Today, more formal than usual, he wore a fine grey silk light-weight suit and looked huge, established, secure – as always, whatever he had on.

'Jack's not so old,' Mrs Lamb said. 'I'd like to think he'll get, say, three or four years older – nice and lined and living. Motherhood's a long-term assignment, Mrs Prior, with certain aims. You come out here wanting to know about Jack! Some chance. I'd like to know about him myself. We bring them into the world, and they shut us out of theirs.'

Her yellowish dress seemed to be muslin, one Denise had not seen before. It hung on to her as though without strength or hope left, and Denise could not imagine anyone actually packing it to bring. In the bright sunshine of late afternoon, she could look from the half-open window across Darien's wide grounds down to a small lake and the beginning of woodland. On lawns between the woodland and the house the marquees for the summer ball would stand. Visualising the charming, civilised, happy scene was a thrill. Her mother's worries about Jack and Helen appeared ludicrous, and her own worries about letting her mother meet them.

For a moment it all seemed brilliantly peaceful and then, far off, near what must be the edge of Chase Woods, Denise saw a man running. He had come out of one clump of trees and seemed to be trying to reach another – bigger, denser. What struck her as strange was that he seemed so well-dressed, so urban-well-dressed, for this setting. He wore a dark suit, what might be black patent-leather shoes, a white shirt and a tie which also seemed dark, though she could not be sure at the distance. Perhaps because such things were high in her mind, the clothes looked like a funeral outfit. They somehow made the running man appear frantic, desperate: he was hugely out of his element and ran as if he knew it and wanted to get back to his own kind of territory, or at least get to that thicker wedge of trees and lose himself until it grew safe to leave.

Behind her in the den, Helen said: 'Denise has really settled in superbly, Mrs Prior. I have friends who went away to university and spent all the first year trying to get used to a new place. Not Denise. She's really built herself a life.'

'You've helped me, you and Jack,' Denise replied over her shoulder, still staring towards the woods. The running man turned his head, perhaps expecting pursuit and, at the same moment, lost one of his black shoes. Denise saw it roll away behind him, down steep-sloped ground, like a shot cat. For a second he paused, obviously contemplated going back for it, but then decided to write the shoe off and kept going, running now as though he had a limp, so his action looked even more frightened. She said nothing – it occurred to her suddenly that she was getting used to saying nothing about what could be crucial situations – but was aware that Lamb also had joined her at the window and seen what was happening.

Then Helen called him back. She had laid out plans of the grounds on a desk to show Mrs Prior how the ball would be run and Denise heard them discussing the guest list. She stayed at the window and, behind the running man, she now saw another, not as young, but moving with good speed and power all the same. At once she had the idea that this was the figure who had dogged her or dogged her fancy for days – the man who radiated disgust from the church path this morning. He also had on a suit, perhaps his funeral suit, too, and she could almost make out that long, anguished, worn face. Or she thought she could. That had to be idiotic, and she tried to drop the notion. It persisted, and grew stronger as she looked.

The man ahead had now reached the patch of trees, despite his lop-sided running. *Go, go, go.* She was bound to sympathise, because he might be on the end of the same disgust as herself. Behind Denise, Mrs Lamb remarked: 'Asking the Lord Lieutenant is not the same as getting the little bastard to show.'

Denise watched the first man reach the trees and disappear. His body seemed to lose some of its tension and she could almost share his relief. A minute or so later, the pursuer followed him in. Finding someone in there would be difficult. Thank God.

Lamb returned to the window: 'Myself, I like the grounds best in winter. All this cheerful greenery – tedious. Nature's getting above itself.'

'You have to be boss, haven't you, Jack?' Mrs Lamb said.

She came after him to the window and then Mrs Prior and Helen moved over, also. They gazed out at the shimmering woodland. From somewhere within the patch of trees came a protracted, raw, showy scream, and then another, quieter, compliant. They all remained silent, awaiting a repetition.

In a while, Sybil Prior said: 'What was that, for heaven's sake.'

'What I mean,' Lamb replied. 'Nature red in tooth and claw, I'm afraid.'

Denise knew he would not have spoken about it if no one else had.

'Some animal?' Sybil Prior asked.

'Caught by another. Stoats, weasels hunt in the early evening.'

'You're telling us that was Brer Fucking Rabbit, Jack?' Mrs Lamb remarked. 'So, how big do they come around here, and trained by Pavarotti?'

Mrs Prior said: 'There's a moving Georgian poem about someone hearing a rabbit caught in a snare and trying urgently to find it.'

'No snares, Mrs Prior, just predators,' Jack told her.

'Predators everywhere,' Mrs Lamb said. 'What I meant about Jack's chance of getting older. Or those connected with him. But I can't worry about *them*. I'm not their mother.'

Driving her mother back to the station, Denise asked: 'So, what did you think?'

'Mrs Lamb's clothes!'

'She rôle-plays.'

Sybil Prior found she had no wish to seem like that eccentric, elderly, negative, interfering woman. This was the kind of nuisance figure she and her generation had strugged to neutralise or escape from in the 1960s. Perhaps the battle still had to be fought. 'A sumptuous house, Denise. And Jack and Helen seem so – so suited, regardless.'

'Yes.'

'In fact, I really liked them both.'

'I knew you would.'

'Not what I expected.'

'What did you?'

'Well something – how would I say? – something quite sinister.'

'Oh, yes – Gatsby. Not quite.'

'I know. The mother, though, was something different. That luridness over the rabbit.'

'As Jack says. She sees urban America everywhere, even in the English countryside. A sort of colonising violence.'

'Silly old bag. Pray God I never get like that.'

'Impossible, Mummy.'

When Denise Prior and her mother had gone, Mrs Lamb said to Jack: 'You'll want to take a look at whatever happened in the woods. Alone, you country lad. We understand, don't we, Helen? So, the wall and the educated gates can't keep it out. We understand that, too, don't we, kid?'

'Keep what out, mother?'

'Carry something when you go,' she replied. 'You might get mugged by a stoat.'

'Who's going?' Lamb said. 'I'm not part of whatever the lady called it – a Georgian poem?'

'Oh, Mrs Prior has read a book or two, various lingos, but she's not stupid, all the same. That girl's a liability to her. Hey, you're not screwing Denise as well as Helen, are you? Is he, Helen?'

'Mrs Prior knew art, too,' Jack replied. 'She picked out a Stuart Davis downstairs.'

'Carry something.'

He had to leave it until evening, when his mother and Helen went out in the Mercedes to a Gospel rally under canvas in one of the city parks. Mrs Lamb loved all that – vivid singing, hell hints, bellowed renunciations of sin.

When making for Chase Woods, he did carry something – a flashlight. He had recognised Tony Towler running, apparently scared frantic, poor, negligible sod, and beautifully dressed, as though he had come straight from that boy Webb's funeral, which he would have had to turn up at: low, to use mourning as a blind, but a blind was a blind and blinds were scarce, so you did what you could. What you could was not always enough.

Denise Prior had certainly seen Towler, too, and had perhaps seen more than that, though she said nothing. This troubled Lamb: maybe she had learned editing from Harpur. But then, it all troubled Lamb. He had not needed his mother to tell him dirt spread and that the rough elements of his life might reach Darien. Sometimes, in fact, he invited the rough elements in. For Towler, though, he felt responsibility. Lamb felt responsible for anyone who fed him, however small-time. In the normal way, Tony disliked coming out here, so he must have been seeking help, maybe a sort of sanctuary, and it looked as if he had not found them. This hurt.

He located Tony quickly, and, despite poor light among the trees, had no need of his torch to see why Towler had screamed, or why he had stopped. A knife had been used, first deep into his stomach, a single straight wound there, so that a thick but small circle of blood marked the quality white shirt just above his trouser band. Lamb was sure of the sequence because Towler could have screamed during that blow and a little later, but not after what had then happened to his throat, which was hacked right across, jagged, a tear more than a cut, from ear to ear, or as near as made no difference, and especially no difference to him. The mourning tie sat in place but drenched, like the shirt collar and the jacket lapels. His head slumped at a bad angle to the side, like a door on one hinge. There had always been an impression of sad tone to Towler's lean face and flat-brushed dark hair, and, looking down at him now, Lamb thought of pictures he had seen of young, dead, body-broken officers in the 1914–18 war.

The lapels had been given their own knife treatment and so had the rest of the suit, almost as if it and not Tony Towler were the enemy. His trousers were slit up the length of both legs and the jacket shredded, not only the lapels but all the front of it, twenty or twenty-five slashes. It was just the suit material: the knife had not gone through to his body or legs at those points, as far as Lamb could tell. He switched on the flashlight to check now, and could make out no marks on the skin, except the stomach and throat wounds. Perhaps the back of the jacket had been destroyed, too. Towler was face up, eyes open, mouth frozen open, too, and Lamb did not feel like turning him over to find out, particularly with the head so wonky. The man with the knife looked like a thorough worker, though, and probably would not want any part of Towler's mock-grief finery left whole. It had to be daddy Webb, possibly with one or both his other sons, more likely solo: Doug had famous reserves of impatience.

This was killing-ground Webb would love. He must have loved the screams, too. They meant Lamb was almost sure to come looking, find the body in this little grass-floored clearing on the edge of his land, and would want nobody else to know. Quick and efficient disposal became vital. Webb could guess that Tony discovered dead here would create all kinds of unwanted questions about his connection with Lamb, and, from there, about Lamb's connection with Harpur, and Harpur's happy influence on Lamb's career.

Switching off the flashlight he had a think about how to get rid of Tony. Graves were hopelessly fallible. Graves on your own ground were more or less a confession, even though you hadn't done the killing. If he brought a vehicle down to move him, tyre marks would stay obvious for a time, and detectable for a long time after. Of course, his mother would spot the tracks instantly, and let her dark brain loose on them. Even in his fury, Webb would never have hacked the commiserations suit if he did not know Towler was sure to be found, found by Lamb. Otherwise, that damage would immediately point police to someone dealing with a funeral insult. Lamb chose what to do and eventually left.

Late in the evening, after Helen and his mother had returned, the telephone rang and a man's voice, high and disguised, said: 'Look in the woods. Grass on grass.' Webby must have decided he could not rely on the screams alone to make Lamb search.

'Anything among the trees?' Mrs Lamb asked.

'That still bothering you? I don't know, mother. Perhaps we'll all have a walk down there tomorrow.'

'Take a picnic,' Helen said.

'That's an idea,' Lamb replied.

'Done what's necessary, have you?' his mother asked. 'You're a class player, Jack.'

Iles wanted to view the funeral film as soon as possible, and Harpur had to stay on with him in the evening. The two boys who had been sent to inventory the wreaths were also present to help with a commentary, and Erogynous Jones, because he knew the community inside out and coud do identifications.

'Don't think I exult in their pain, Harpur,' Iles remarked. 'Don't any of you think it. I challenge any bastard to say I'm short on qualms. This is Doug Webb now, yes, Erogynous?' he said, bending forward in his chair to stare at the screen. 'Stop it there a minute, will you?' he called to the operator. The frame held Webb on the

92

church path. 'Dual-purpose suit? He lags the pipes with it in winter,' Iles said. 'And Kay behind him, as if she'd rather not know? Still a noble fuck, I'd say.' He bent further forward. 'Warm legs, yet not boxy. These would be up your street, Harpur.'

'Kay's timeless,' Harpur replied.

'So, what the hell is Doug staring at?' Iles asked. 'Do I read contempt in that fine old rag-and-bone face? Hatred? Blame?'

'Someone obscured by the hearse, sir?' Erogynous replied.

'Who was there, boys?' Iles asked the flower-inventory pair. 'You didn't attend, did you, Col? It's that sort of look he's giving someone – occasion-related.'

'Just a little crowd of locals, sir,' Seabourne told him.

'Plus a couple of girls around nineteen, twenty, who didn't look the part,' Carl Diamond said.

'How?' Iles asked.

'Outsiders, sir. Bit dreamy? Educated, even,' Diamond replied.

'Martin had been having something up-town – two up-town – and Doug objected?' Iles suggested. 'They're fussy about class, people like Doug. Run it on,' he told the operator.

Erogynous named other mourners who followed Doug and Kay into the church. Some, Harpur knew already, a few not – piffle villains. All levels would have to turn out for a Webb funeral. It was like Ascot, and it was like a soccer match.

'One loves to think of Mencken,' Iles said. ' "There is no death!" "No, madam, but there are funerals." '

'Tony Towler,' Erogynous told them.

'Now, that *is* a suit,' Iles replied. 'This man's a bit of an eminence?'

'Might be a newsboy to a grass,' Erogynous said. 'We don't know.'

'We're getting a really nice type of person into informing these days,' Iles remarked. 'Who's this? It has to be Marty's bird – one of them.'

The film showed a girl come out from around the back of the hearse and fondle the flowers through the raised tailgate. 'Miss Heartbreak,' Iles said.

Harpur at once recognised Denise. Christ, what was she doing there? He had been sharing a girl with Martin Webb? He had killed one of her other boyfriends?'

'Known to us?' Iles asked.

'She looked at me like I was leprosy,' Piers Seabourne replied.

'Stupendous arse,' Iles said.

'This is one of the girls I mentioned,' Diamond confirmed.

'Martin was brain-damaged but lovely with it, I believe,' Iles said. 'Didn't I hear like an undersized god with not a curl crooked?'

'That another of your fucking quotes, sir?' Harpur replied.

'What's up with you, then?' Iles said.

'She might be just sightseeing,' Harpur replied.

'And touching up the carnations?' Iles said. 'Not likely.'

No, not likely. Denise went out of sight. The film blacked out for a while and then resumed as the coffin emerged. They saw Webb talk with the hearse driver while Kay took consolation from the clergyman.

'Yes, that's the vicar who was banging our finger-print lady, isn't it?' Iles asked. 'The one they called Holy Hardon?'

After the viewing, when Harpur and Iles went out to the car, a woman of about thirty in a fine denim skirt and silk ochre blouse approached them, smiling an exceedingly genial welcome. 'This has to be the sodding Press, Col,' Iles muttered. 'I love reporters – their tenacity, acumen, intuition, plus the grandeur of the principle they represent: the public's right to know. I'd wipe out the lot.'

'Mr Iles, Mr Harpur?' she said, full Oxbridge languor. 'I wonder if I might have a word.'

'I certainly don't see why not,' Iles replied.

She had a good, open, cheerful face and slim body on heavyish legs. The denim seams coped with stress. Harpur would not have said journalist straight away, but Iles was always swift and impeccable on a scent. She had a slightly bustling, confident way of walking, as if certain that nothing important could happen anywhere, or not properly happen, without her presence. So Iles probably did have it right. They thought Livingstone would not have existed without Stanley, or Hitler without Gerd Heidemann. When she came a little closer Harpur could make out in her eyes a bright, hearty friendliness, industriously fabricated, so there could be no doubt that she was from a big, responsible London paper and investigative right through.

Before she came into earshot Iles said: 'Bloody fine shoes, not Gucci – or not both of them, anyway – but close. I could do business with this one, except for that happy-hour smile. I'm not averse to legs that can take a grip. Doesn't it make you weep, Harpur, to think of them spending years at Somerville or wherever, burnishing fine points, and then coming out to stir shit in carparks?' She stopped near. 'Here's a treat,' Iles continued. 'You're Audience Research, madam? Harpur's snobbish in his viewing – watches only Remembrance Day at the Cenotaph – the Queen and so on – so no good talking to him in summer. Try me, though. The darts, or anything ethnic.'

'I'm from the *Searchlight* section of *This Morning*. Name's Wendy Sellick.'

'More than a treat – a privilege,' Iles replied. 'Naturally, we've heard of your work.'

'Well, we don't get by-lines on Searchlight.'

'A disgrace,' Iles said. 'Harpur's often spoken of it when we've been studying Searchlight together, thirsty for revelations.'

'I'm here for the funeral.'

'Marty? I hear it was a very nice affair,' Iles replied.

'Not really to cover the thing as such.'

'Well, no, not as such,' Iles said.

'Our news people will do that.'

Martin would have delighted to know he was news in London. A near-idiot, yet right for the world's Press.

'We're looking behind this death – a wider inquiry,' the girl went on. 'That's Searchlight's brief.'

'This is intriguing, Wendy,' Iles remarked. 'An eye-opener. A Searchlight roams the whole scene, obviously. We've had people with that kind of more fundamental task here before, the cosmic. "In depth" I believe it's termed. We're fond of them, flattered by their attention.' They stood around Iles's Scorpio.

'I didn't want to come into HQ,' she said. 'I felt you could talk more easily outside.'

'Tact,' Iles replied.

'Particularly I'm interested in how the information reached you – you, Mr Harpur.' She widened her grin. 'Not just about the Post Office raid, in fact, but—'

'The vaster tableau,' Iles said.

'You should approach our Press Officer,' Harpur told her. 'Chief Inspector Tarr. He'd be happy to help.'

She said: 'That's not really how Searchlight—'

'Operates,' Iles said, laughing. 'Harpur's a bit of an old bureaucrat, I'm afraid, Wendy. Press Officer, indeed! This is Searchlight, man. You're a fountainhead person, Wendy. Anyone could see that. Anyone but Harpur. Not somebody to have truck with functionaries.'

'I'm a functionary,' Harpur replied.

'Look, I know how information is received can be a very sensitive matter, Mr Harpur,' she said, 'but—'

'Sensitive matters are your food and drink,' Iles commented. 'And you know how to digest without eructations.'

She said: 'We understand—'

'How to protect those who help you,' Iles remarked. 'Discretion is your middle name.'

She said: 'To be frank—'

'I love it,' Iles said.

'To be frank we hear there's an informant here, on your patch, who gets unparalleled police favour. What I mean, has been allowed to build a thriving illicit business because he's so useful. Clearly, we do a lot of pre-digging before we come to you head-on.'

'Clearly,' Iles replied. 'Plus the local corr can earn a peseta or two giving you the standard scuttlebutt. This will be *quid pro quo*? I'm not going to say I've never heard of such juicy confederacies. That supergrass business in the Met?'

Harpur said: 'You don't really expect us to comment on ridiculous rumour?'

'Plus a network of minor figures – all decently provided for – who feed this central grass. It hasn't been easy stuff to unearth. It's dangerous.'

'But you stuck at it,' Iles gloried. 'Wasn't there someone at the *Sunday Times* they called the Badger? I'm damn glad you've raised this. As a matter of fact, I've often worried myself over how detectives get their inside knowledge. Yes, often.'

'When I was at the funeral, in fact, I spotted two people I understand are what police call "newsboys" – feeds to a principal informant.'

' "Newsboys"?' Iles replied. 'Not something from that wonderful spy-speak le Carré used in his Smiley confections?'

She said: 'This is a man called Towler and a girl we haven't identified yet. We will. The pieces come together if you persist.'

Mellowly, Iles replied: 'Pieces coming together. That's such a comforting image, I always think. Childlike, as in jigsaws, and yet wondrous – Genesis, the Creation: those six divinely complementary days. Order, a scheme, optimism. I really think this is thorough, don't you, Harpur? Wendy, you people have your methods, methods proved by long practice. I find it admirable. Towler? Not a name I've come across. How about you, Col?'

'Any first name?' Harpur asked.

'Anthony. Really rather an aristocratic-looking guy. Smooth hair. Patent shoes. Magnificent tailoring today.'

'This is something to go on,' Iles replied. 'Tony Towler.'

'No, never heard of him,' Harpur said.

'Have you thought you could be putting these people in real peril?' the girl asked.

'This Fowler?' Iles replied.

'Towler.'

'This Towler and the girl?' Iles said.

'Exactly.'

'It's certainly a point, Col. And will you be putting them in peril if you talk to them, Wendy – if you publish?'

'They're not our targets. They're only incidental.'

'I hope the stonemason can spell that for the memorial. So, poor old Col's your target, is he? Myself?' Iles replied.

'It's what journalism at my level is all about,' she said. 'This is abuse of office. Could be.'

'Like Nixon. Col, boy, you're on the end of another Watergate. That's what all you people dream of, isn't it, Wendy? Wholly fine. We'll be in touch. Count on it. Have to get home to Scrabble and the wife. Some people spend their lives in suburbs, and not for any urgent reason.' He drove away.

She said: 'Off his head? So he can quote E. M. Forster, but doesn't he see the turmoil here?'

'The ACC has his own ways. Often they work.'

'Look, Mr Harpur, your arrangement with Lamb? How does *that* work?'

'As Mr Iles said, we're going to be in touch?'

'And you – you pulled the trigger?'

'Is Wendy much of a name for someone intrepid?'

Harpur also went home and Megan said: 'You're looking pretty bad, Colin. Us?' It was the kind of question she asked now and then to show she kept up an interest.

'A job problem or two.'

'Work?' She sounded relieved. 'This funeral? Trouble over the boy killed? But why? From what you tell me, your man had to shoot to save another officer. I'd have thought that entirely justifiable. Not one of your wild blast-off people, was he? I mean, a tragedy, obviously, but reasonable.'

Megan was good on fine points.

'It's to do with Jack Lamb,' he replied.

'Oh, Lamb.' Her tone altered. Jack, face to face or on the telephone, gave her offence, and she let him know.

'Your best fink, Dad?' Hazel said.

'You should be in bed,' Harpur replied.

As Harpur went higher in rank, Megan had come to accept most of the standard hostilities to police, and the children had picked these up from her, and from friends at school, naturally. If you married someone whose parents were Highgate doctors, and an uncle and aunt Hampstead Fabians, you had to expect the reach-me-down decent squeamishnesses about law enforcement. He had never blamed her too much for that. In any case, occasionally, Megan could be more or less understanding. He had a policy of telling her a few items about his work: those he thought wouldn't annoy and make matters between them darker still. She found out a few things for herself, though: that could not be helped when you lived with someone as sharp as Megan, no matter how much space you gave each other.

'Lamb's been rumbled?' Hazel continued. 'How the dickens will you survive? He goes or gets wasted, you'll never make ACC.'

Megan came to his help. She must have seen he was weary. 'You can't be responsible for everyone, Col. Not for marksmen, not for the way all information is gathered.'

'Lamb's a friend.'

'A mouth,' Jill remarked.

'Go to bed,' he replied. 'Hazel as well.'

'Yes, go to bed, both of you,' Megan said.

They left then.

'Perhaps it would be for the best if Lamb did disappear from your life, Col. I hate that contact – the horrible dependency, the sliminess, and above all the reciprocity.'

These terms, or similar, he had frequently heard from Megan. With repetition they did grow easier to take, though each time they came out he knew they shoved the two of them further apart, closer to others. Harpur remained willing to take her points seriously and argue. That was marriage and so far they stayed married, for the children. 'Policing – my sort – needs clairvoyance, love. Jack's clairvoyant.'

'I don't know about telling fortunes. He's made one, though. And that girl he's with.'

'Nineteen, possibly twenty.'

'Exactly.'

'She knows her mind.'

The television was running – some *Late Show* interview with an author whose book went backwards. Megan leaned over and switched it off. 'I'll video it,' she said. 'Fascinating. Oh, Col, take your chance, if it is a chance. Get shot of Jack Lamb.'

He was not happy hearing the word 'shot', even used like that. 'You'd really be happier?' he asked. Of course, she was saying more than break from a grass.

'Don't you see, it would prove policing can be clean. Cleanish, Col. Yes, it might make things better.'

Now and then she spoke of Jack as if he were a sexual rival. That role had gone to someone else – several someone elses over the years. He had his needs. 'Better for you and me?' he asked.

'It's possible.'

He stretched out in his chair, savouring the video recorder's tiny sound, because it reminded him the literary smarm still dripped and that he would never have to see or listen: like having a tooth deep drilled under anaesthetic. 'Newspaper people are looking for ways of getting at Jack, via his sources – some well-known leaker and a girl nobody's heard of. It's dangerous for them, all of them, Lamb included.'

'Col, Col, cut loose. It's so unnecessary, so degrading.'

He realised suddenly that she really thought he might. She had bed in her voice, reconciliation. Of course it was heartening. For a moment, he heard the way things used to be for them. She understood so little, was so clever, and so thick. Did she genuinely imagine he could ditch Lamb, leave him to the enemy? Or even ditch Towler? Above all, he could not ditch Denise, who had been sucked into all this in ways that baffled him. Naturally, Denise did not reach her reckoning at all, but was powerful and immoveable in his.

They went to bed then and she was loving and ferocious. Women could be like that these days, and nights. Think of Denise wanting violence, burning. God. You did what you could. He knew how to switch on, and Megan knew how to, also. It made for a minor affirmation and was therefore a plus. Nothing was resolved, but love-making was not designed to resolve. Such nearness as was offered you took and enjoyed and treated for a few moments as if it spoke of the future, even of the long-distance future.

Chapter Ten

When Denise arrived at Darien next day to see Helen she found them all – Helen, Jack and his mother – preparing for a walk to the edge of Chase Woods, which bordered the grounds. 'Scream hunting,' Mrs Lamb told her. 'You remember, kid? That sound with a tale to tell, but nobody listening.' She had on a kind of trouser suit in navy.

'Mother gets her teeth into something,' Jack said.

Helen seemed uneasy but had made a picnic. 'Come with us, Denise. There's plenty. The woods are lovely now. Bluebells are over, but other stuff. I'll show you the actual spots where the marquees will go, and all that.'

'I love almost anything rural,' Mrs Lamb remarked. 'Often you can feel a kind of virtue there. What's that phrase you hear – I'm "into it".'

'Fifteen years ago people said that,' Jack told her.

'Well, I'm into the countryside,' she said. 'It goes its own way. Cow bells.'

'I'm not sure,' Denise replied. 'There's still things to do at college.' She knew Mrs Lamb's feelings about the wood and its tale to tell might be right. Denise had seen the two men go in. Perhaps she was the only one who had. It was knowledge she did not wish to extend, and she wanted no further contact with that hate-filled, grief-pitted face of the second man. He had been the pursuer when she saw the two of them. Who could say things stayed like that? Who could be sure the screams had not come from him? He might still be there. Even if not, the wood would give her a kind of contact with him, and above all she wanted to avoid that.

'You saw more than you've said, Denise?' Mrs Lamb asked. 'Afraid you're going to stumble over something?'

'Like what?' Helen asked.

'This place, Darien, doesn't stand alone, girl. It's in a context. That context could have sharp edges. Every time I come from the States, I ask myself, This going to be the time it happens?'

100

'What? We find bits of a rabbit?' Jack said.

'Of a pigeon.'

Lamb remarked: 'I love the woods at almost any time. I'm all in favour. I hope you'll come with us, Denise.'

'Please,' Helen said.

And so she caved in. Lamb seemed nervous, as if in need of reassurance. Denise did not see how she might help him, but she went.

'Don't think of me as an oracle, Denise,' Mrs Lamb declared, when they were drinking tea and eating a pie and sandwiches among the trees. 'I don't know any more than you about how Jack puts it in the bank, puts pictures on the walls. I see nothing here but greenery, which is what the sod knew I'd see. Helen was scared, though.'

'Some other area you want to inspect, mother?' Lamb asked.

'Crow away.'

Lamb knew she had been right about Helen's fears. Helen had a bright sense of things – not intuition, but a continuous, brilliant feel for what might be going on. Now, though, she seemed happier. It would be fine for a while down here.

Last night, unable to forget all the tales he had heard of discovered graves, marauding foxes and the like, and worried about moving Towler at this moment by vehicle, Lamb had suddenly come to feel that if you owned a wood and good trees, thick with summer, the place to hide a body temporarily might be up, not down or away. It would be difficult, but the very strangeness was a plus: should it come to a search, who would look in high foliage?

After dark, with the help of a ladder and a couple of pulleys he had pulled Tony up into a healthy oak and lashed him to a branch. This took some unseemliness with the ropes, but whichever way you got rid of him would mean rough handling. That sickened Lamb. Tony had been a reasonable lad, repeatedly taking trouble to spell out the gospel of grassing, facing up honestly to the furtive side of it and finding a justification. He had been excellent on subtleties – the morality and local culture aspects. He was minor, yes, but to hear him explain like that had often brought Lamb strength, and he must treat him properly now.

It was a comfort that Lamb had been able to manage things with the rope around Towler's chest and under his arms, not the ankles and upside down. Lamb dreaded to picture Towler's head hanging like that after the wounds, and all the sliced bits of suit folded back and fluttering like gala ribbons. God knew, his head looked bad enough when he was hauled up the right way. Bringing him from

101

the end of the rope on to a branch had meant Lamb's face was pressed to his for a while, a sort of intimacy in death which had not really been too bad, despite the coldness.

Tony would get emaciated and therefore insecure after a while, but Lamb's mother might be less watchful by then, and he could bring a vehicle down for a night removal. Ultimately, Towler would have to go weighted into the sea, up the coast a long way. As a matter of fact, during the picnic his mother said she would like to see a couple of the small ports to the north. 'Ships in dry dock, propped by beams. A cautionary sight, don't you think, Denise?' she asked.

'Well, yes.'

Lamb could keep an eye open for a convenient piece of foreshore during those outings, perhaps, then get a small boat somehow, preferably not hired, no traces. He had made sure the picnic was nowhere near Tony's tree and while the three women chatted about the Yugoslav political situation, which his mother had lately become an expert on, Lamb took a small stroll and had a good gaze up and around, to check nothing was obvious. Of course, his mother would notice and have her thoughts, but could not possibly make any precise guesses.

It had taken Lamb four and a half hours altogether getting Towler into position. Helen knew he had been out of bed, and he realised this could account for her worries today. A girl like that deserved a decent life, and for most of the time Lamb thought he provided it. As his mother said, though, it was a life which did touch the outside now and then, like any life was bound to. When he had his little tour during the picnic, he was particularly on the watch for fragments of Tony's suit. He felt very nervous about missing items or particles because when he had Tony hanging on the rope last night he suddenly noticed one of his shoes was gone, and it had taken him an age to find it in the dark. Putting the shoe back on him had not been a treat, either. Lamb had to consider that one or more of those suit strips could easily have been torn loose during the hauling, as the body banged against the trunk and lower branches. Serge in the undergrowth would really say something to his mother. As he tied Tony to the branch in the night he made a methodical inspection of him, to ensure all the suit was present, though slashed, and he had also scrutinised the soil, but by then his torch was starting to fail. He might have missed something. This search in daylight was important.

'Find what you're looking for, Jack?' his mother shouted.

'What am I looking for?'

'Innocence?'

'Never lost it.'

Fixing Tony to a branch had seemed easy enough as a notion, but the practicalities turned out tough. The branch had to be high, for concealment, and reasonably straight and broad to give support. The higher Lamb took him, though, the slimmer the branches grew, and the sharper the angle of growth. He did it in two stages, climbing to a first platform to secure the pulley, descending, then heaving Towler up to there. Temporarily, Lamb lashed him anyhow to a branch then climbed higher, refixed the pulley, went down, unroped Towler and drew him up the next ten or twelve feet. A couple of times while Lamb tried to get him stretched out along a branch up there, Towler almost fell, and by then Lamb was so tired he knew he would not be able to bring him back to that height if he did go.

Eventually he secured him, not so much along a branch as roped to the actual trunk, legs on each side of a branch, his feet dangling, but pretty well hidden by foliage. Lamb would have liked to have him sitting on the branch but the body was too rigid. In the dark, it had been impossible to know for certain whether the feet were discernible from the ground, say when a breeze moved the leaves. He had played the flashlight on what seemed to be the key areas for a long time and everything appeared fine. In the day, now, he looked again and was satisfied. He had been tempted to get out of bed once more at first light and do this survey. That would have unsettled Helen even more, though, and he had decided to risk it.

He did not know much about the speed at which the flesh went from a body and supposed that at some point the shoes might drop off. That would surely be weeks, even months, and he would have moved Tony by then. Perhaps he would do it straight after the ball: besides the security, it would not seem right to leave Towler up there longer than was needed – going to pieces, crudely roped, a branch in his crutch and his head askew. It might not seem much more right to sink him at sea, yet people did finish that way, over the side from under a flag. Some old sailors even insisted.

Towler had no relatives locally that Lamb knew about, and no steady woman at present, though he did all right casually, what with the tasty clothes and his nicely smoothed dark hair. Eventually, it would be necessary to look for family. Not yet: it could undo everything if there was a fuss. Somehow they would have to be informed that he was dead. You could not let a nice lad like Tony just disappear, even if he hardly rated.

When Lamb returned to the picnic scene, Helen was saying: 'Oh, can you imagine! I forgot to mention, Denise. The Lord Lieutenant has accepted.'

'Yes,' Lamb added, 'we're all very gratified – really rather brown-nose gratified, I suppose.'

Denise saw real shame in the big, heavy face, and big, heavy body. 'Recognition, that's all, Jack,' she said. 'Deserved. It's a kind of distinction, yes, but why not? You've made your mark in this society as much as anyone else. So, why shouldn't he want to enjoy himself here? He sees he's on to a good thing.'

'What I say, too,' Helen remarked.

'Next, the CBE, or something, Jack,' Denise told him. 'You've helped put this city on the art map.'

'The art did that. I'm a dealer.'

Mrs Lamb said: 'If there are screams from the woods on the big night, at least the bands will drown it.'

'No ghosts here,' Helen replied, handing Mrs Lamb a meringue. She ate it in a picky, very reluctant way, and then took two more.

Looking about, she remarked: 'My husband always maintained that if you went among trees think like a squirrel.'

'What's that mean?' Helen asked.

'Squirrels don't have Lord Lieutenants,' Mrs Lamb said. 'But my husband was full of would-be maxims that didn't add up. Jack's got his way to make just like any—'

'Businessman,' Denise commented. Now, she felt a lot easier. She realised she had been looking for blood on ferns and maybe even a finger poking from a hasty grave. For a while, she had wondered why she did not do what Colin suggested and go home to Stafford.

'Businessman,' Mrs Lamb remarked. 'Something like that. There's a lot about Jack that's almost forgivable.'

Chapter Eleven

It brought Doug Webb a lot of golden therapy, the way things turned out in the woods with Tony Towler, but he knew he would have to see to that girl soon as well – the one who mouthed like Towler to Lamb and Harpur, the one who had soiled Martin's floral tributes, getting her talking hands into the hearse for a memory job on the cards. A girl stuck on a man, even on a thug cop like Harpur, would do anything for him, no matter how dirty. The idea of her messing with those flowers tore at his stomach and he was glad not to have seen it because the memory would sicken him for ever. It fouled the human race. One of the lads – Dean Knighton, the boy they called Amuck – had done such a nice video of a lot of the funeral, but, of course, he was inside the church when that girl invaded the sprays and wreaths.

Amuck had his camera going even during the service, though the vicar said it was banned. So, stuff the vicar. Think of the way he went for Kay. Some of that was on Amuck's video. Yet this was supposed to be moments of wholesome, general grief rather than freshing with a dead boy's mother. She said he had been a real comfort and could talk about so many topics that interested her, not just Katharine Hepburn, but travel, foreign mountains, planets and even books. It was well known that women did go for clergymen because of all the factual conversation, plus confidential smiles and delicate fingers. They were trained for it.

Kay had started attending services since the funeral, for binding up the wounds, she said. Could be. She was not someone you asked too many questions. So, religion was doing filthy damage to one of his families – probably the one he thought most of – which was not what religion should be about at all, clearly. Who wanted a vicar sniffing at Kay, and Rodney turning holy crazed like that, frothing publicly in the crem chapel? Webb blamed Towler and the girl for starting all this trouble in some of those he loved, and the girl was going to pay, like dear old Tone had had to. What they had done was a sin.

Sanquhar-Perry and Panicking Ralph wanted another meeting about the raid, and this time it was going to be in a railway-station buffet because Sanquhar-Perry worried over using his house again, and Panicking never allowed work in the club or at his home. Doug wouldn't have them in his place, either.

This meeting would probably be to do with Tony Towler dropping out of sight, just a sudden, total absence, no tracks. That was sure to enrage Sanquhar-Perry, because he would have to find someone else to carry the dud stuff to Lamb. A pity, but Webb could still not regret settling Towler. Anyway, he had never really believed Lamb and Harpur would be fooled. Towler himself might not have been. Any bright grass's grass like Tony came to feel the difference between truth and rubbish. A grass dead made things safer, not otherwise. Naturally, Webb would act sorry and puzzled, even with these two at the buffet – *where the hell* had *dear old Tone gone after the funeral*, et cetera – but the delight at what he had managed warmed him and he felt the world was cleaner, more like God would want it. On the seventh day He might have seen off all the grasses, if they had been about at that juncture.

What also pleased Webb was that, although Towler scampered hard towards the woods, at the end he was so brave. There was nothing more sickening than going for someone who just fell to pieces – not if it was a man, at any rate. It might be different when the girl's turn came shortly.

Sanquhar-Perry and Panicking would not want her done, either, and some of that might come out fierce at this station meeting. They were afraid it would fire up Harpur, and Ember considered killing women off-colour, anyway. Ignore them. There were different sorts of killings, and some had to be. You did not need to feel evil, only sure and intelligent.

With Towler in the woods, it had been a hunt, yes, but for five or six minutes nobody could have known who was hunting and who was hunted. Webb went in among the trees, taking his time, walking, never running, and at first he heard nothing that said Towler and saw nothing that said Towler. This was not Webb's sort of ground, nor Tone's either, as far as he knew.

Eventually, the thing that did Tony no good at all was he was not carrying anything, simple as that. Webb had picked up the knife during sandwiches and lager back at the house after the funeral. Tone probably never carried anything. Not his style. Not any grass's style. They listened, they spoke – that was their style. Armament was heavy, and their work fitted another category.

Just inside the patch of trees, Webb had stood very still, getting

106

himself used to the different light and the ordinary sounds of a wood. For quite a while, he kept the knife hidden. If they had been seen from the house, Lamb and possibly others might come down, and provocation of Lamb was stupid.

At the time, Webb did not know for sure whether Towler had anything with him, of course. So, he put his back to a tree for those first minutes and crouched a bit, thinking what a fool he would look if he was done by someone like Tony Towler among leaves. Webb never considered giving up, whatever Towler was supposed to do for the project, laying the wrong leads. It was too late. Would a brain such as Tone Towler think after this chase to Chase Woods that he might get truthful whispers from a team with Webb in it? Now, he'd know absolutely they were plants. Towler had to go. It was the right day for it, spot on.

The certainty made him feel grand – that day in the woods, and now, as he drove to the buffet conference. Sanquhar-Perry liked plenty of conferences. They excited Courtney and made him think the teamwork was hot. It did no harm. Webb knew how people like Courtney saw him. He was Webby, getting old, thick hairs growing from his nose, no intellectual zing, always low with money through carrying two families, pussy-whipped by a couple of wives, kids gobbling all the pay and croaking for more. He would not quarrel with that as a picture of himself.

To end Tony, though, would mark him out, did mark him out, as a constructive one, a tidy one, one with the beautiful, unlearnable gift of timing. Nobody would know, of course, except himself. That was the tidiness. Towler would disappear, had disappeared. Everyone else would be mystified, was. If, now, he could deal with the girl too, it would be an utmost achievement. He would be notable. Again, only notable to himself, but that would do fine. Between the three of them they could manage Lamb, one day, maybe. Very maybe. Doing those two pieces of linkage would give him a new rating, though, whatever happened – or didn't – later, and even as he stood among the Nature that day, huddled, scared, worried he might come out of this a dead idiot, he felt grander than he had for years. For a little while then he could even forget it was the funeral day of a sweet, film-star-face, half-daft son.

After a few minutes, Webb had moved ahead in the wood and come to a small clearing, unshaded by trees. Grass grew there and a mix of wild flowers, pink, white and blue. He hung back on the edge of this space, realising that anyone crossing it would be on show from all round the compass. What he did not want was conversation with Tone – talk where the old times were mentioned, or friendship, or what Tony would refer to as friendship, anyway, and the street solidarities. Towler could persuade.

When Tony stood up suddenly from where he had hidden behind bushes on the far side of the clearing, Webb acted at once. Towler seemed to think he was safe now, as if Webb had given up or gone on further into Chase Woods. Tony brushed his suit down and gave a little flick to the hair over both ears, making sure it was lying flat, like going to a management job interview. It was then Webb decided to slice the tailoring afterwards, Towler's funeral clothes were so precious to the bastard, and such a brilliant insult.

What Webb meant by brave was that when he stepped out on to the grass of the clearing holding the knife and Towler saw him and it he did that again, brushed down his suit, had a glance to check it was hanging right. Best look presentable to have your throat cut in a picnic area. Then he bent down fast and picked up a fat branch that had dropped, but anyone could tell it only dropped because it was dead, a tubby piece of decay, and if he had hit Webb with it it would have been like getting hammered with a roll of bin liners. Towler must have realised straight away it was useless. He had stood there, gazing at Webb, the stick hanging from his right hand, no smile, but no twitch, either. Tone was lop-sided through losing a shoe, but he still had presence. And he did not talk. Well, he would know his grass gospel was not going to work, not funeral day, not after fixing the ambush of a dear three-parts-barmy kid.

He gave Tony the knife in the stomach first, just beneath the waistcoat, because he wanted to get even with that solemn suit as well as him himself straight away. Towler did not fall for a while, but staggered around and even tried to run again, just a few steps, a giddy child, spinning, his legs tangling themselves. It could have been funny if you were hard, but Webb felt a bit sad for that moment. A man's legs in a suit like that ought to give strength and dignity.

Towler had a hand over the hole and Webb watched his fingers get red one at a time from the top, like jam trickling down the layers of a sponge cake. He was still quiet, and was still quiet when at last he did tumble and Webb finished him with what he had hoped would be a quite easy swing of the knife across, but which took a hell of a lot of digging and leverage. He knew nothing about what necks were made of inside, that was the trouble. The dragged-out labour of it distressed Webb so much that he screamed and, after a moment, screamed again, though more quietly this second time. For a second or two he stood near Tony as he twitched and gurgled and maybe at last did struggle to get out a word or two – 'Doug'? 'My father'?

'Martin'? – then Webb wiped the knife on the funeral jacket before starting to shred the whole suit. He took care, though, not to damage Tony himself any further. That would be nuttiness, bloody nuttiness.

Webb's nausea over the killing had not lasted too long, and he could soon enjoy the thought of Tony's courage, and the thought that a start had been made in putting Martin's death right, plus the trouble that came for the two boys in the Post Office with him.

Now, at the rail buffet, Sanquhar-Perry said: 'Vanished. Totally. I never heard of anything like it.' That boyish, innocent face had real worry built in today, as he sat down at their table not too near the window and carefully dealt with old bun crumbs on the Formica.

Webb replied: 'Tone was always one on his own.' The buffet was not a bad idea, busy, people edgy, waiting for their connections, no time to notice others. As cover, Sanquhar-Perry had brought a big case with him today. It was empty but when he arrived Courtney acted bent over, like clothes for six months in Lapland.

'Clever, the luggage,' Ralph Ember said. 'Courtney, you should go far. Change at Crewe.'

'I take it Tony was at the funeral, Douglas?' Sanquhar-Perry asked.

'Looking rare,' Webb said. He got it into his voice that if these two wanted funeral knowledge they should have been there, not lurking at home behind flowers.

'And afterwards at the house for commemorative snacks, I heard,' Sanquhar-Perry said.

'My way of showing I had nothing against him, Courtney. Part of the project. So he'd believe what we gave him?'

'Right. You did remarkably there, Doug,' Panicking said. 'This was a talented suppression of all your natural resentment and contempt.'

'The kind of game we're in, Ralphy. No sensational ability required. What's the profit in anger?'

'All the same,' Ember replied.

'What interests me is the time that comes after this trip to your house – no trace,' Sanquhar-Perry said. 'Any idea where he went, Doug?'

Well, of course it was the time after the house. 'As far as I know, home. I couldn't give him attention. That caring vicar's trying to get a hand up Kay's mauve mourning skirt.'

'Just this total gap when he leaves your place,' Sanquhar-Perry remarked, from behind tea.

'Christ, shall I tell you what this is like, it's like a Harpur quiz,'

Webb replied. 'Can I have a solicitor? So what you saying, Courtney?'

'I'm saying if he fails to show soon we find another way to send Lamb wrong stuff.'

'Oh, he'll show,' Webb answered. 'Is there a girl? I heard he travelled for a bird in the old days. Swansea way? Bury St Edmunds? There's quite a slab of romance in Tone. Did you ever hear him sing "Always"?'

When Webb left, Ember said: 'The fucker's done Towler?'

'Obviously. I heard he was wild at the funeral, looking like epidemics.'

'So, what's he done with him?' Ember asked.

'Got rid.'

'Doug? He couldn't manage it. He could finish him, yes. Doug's a really fine lad. Terrific stuff behind that sprout face – not a brain, obviously, but stamina, grand savagery. He's not up to losing a body, though. And not a word in the papers, nothing.'

'Yes, a gem, but it makes me wish to Christ we'd never brought him in. Something low there, something sick-dim? To be harsh, Ralph, tell me this – how does he produce a zombie kid like Martin, otherwise? Genes. That's not Kay's side. She's bright as dawn on a looking-glass. Kay can talk to vicars. We'll have to take decisions about Doug. He'll want to finish the girl next.'

'Oh, no,' Ember replied.

'He's got bigger. It's visible. He thinks he can do anything.'

'The girl—'

'Which means Harpur berserk and into no-stone-unturning.'

'That girl—'

'Webby's found himself a mission, Ralph. He's after a personality extension. I've read about this in articles. If you were Doug, wouldn't you want to be something more?'

'So money wouldn't do that? The job?'

'Money's only wherewithal. Doug's looking for nobility, for ways to get through to Kay. He has to pay the score for a dead boy. It's manhood, it's fatherhood.'

'*Hamlet* but backwards.' Ember had begun to wonder whether he would give this raid a miss, even if Towler was still alive and came back in time to send the police wrong. They seemed a fragile crew, Sanquhar-Perry and Webb, and hellishly liable to push Ember into one of his panics at any time.

And changeable. Sanquhar-Perry said: 'I'm talking about forgetting Doug, yet I know it's not on really, is it? Look, we're stuck

110

with him, Ralphy. And he's unbeatable at memorising a site. We must take account of his agony. It affects behaviour.'

'Probably.'

'I love the way he lies – no flicker. This is someone who's come through interrogation. Formidable. The job's crucial to me. This girl I'm with now – Zena. I feel a certain debt, Ralph. She's not used to my sort of place, council breeze-block. I've learned as fact her mother had a big kitchen with God knows how many hobs and drainers. People think, names like mine – Courtney, Sanquhar-Perry, the Scottish aspect and the last bit difficult to pronounce with the q and the u and so on – they think I ought to be in something a lot glossier. I can accept this. So, funds required. Briefly, this job is the one, Ralph.'

'Your place – nothing wrong with it at all, Courtney.'

'Not Low Pastures, is it? You come into my house looking for bats hanging on the light flex.' Sanquhar-Perry's voice grew hard and loud. Ember glanced around. Christ, did he want his address yelled here? Were they as crazy as each other, these two he had linked with? 'Ralph, you're beautifully fixed up – property, the club, unit trusts I should think, kids in some fine school, and the cat-and-dog man's wife on the side, plus her own dormobile, a girl and a half, I hear, and dotty for you. Then there's Webby, blinded by hate, envy, money worries, and used to living on bacon rind. He doesn't really care if this job happens or not because he can always find something small-time – all he's used to. Instead, he's after dignity. I've got to hold this confederation together. You hear me?'

Ember did. Others might.

Sanquhar-Perry grew quieter. He knew there was no point in bellowing at someone like Ember. Ralph had worked with very big people and came out of it on top, even if he did look faded now. 'You see the detail, I know that, Ralph. Foresight is natural to you. You're thinking, if Towler turns up dead and they find out we're working with Doug we'll catch for that, too. Harpur and Iles would love to bring us in on a killing, and they could. They've got marvellous framing flair. From what I hear, they're always ready to say, If he didn't do this one he did another, so all's square.'

'Tony will show.' Jesus, to be done for helping murder something like Towler, especially when you hadn't.

'It might be enough for him,' Sanquhar-Perry said.

'Who?'

'Doug.'

'How do you mean?'

'He might forget about seeing off the girl – or forget until after the job. All I ask.'

'No, no, he won't go for the girl, Courtney.'

'He's got a mission, I tell you, Ralph.'

'Don't forget to stagger with the case,' Ember replied, standing.

Ember was skilfully replenishing the pickled eggs jar in the Monty that night, spilling no vinegar on the mahogany, when he suddenly sensed tension at the bar and looking up saw Iles and Harpur approaching, Iles wearing a three-hundred-quid double-breasted silver-buttoned navy blazer, and smiling in that joyful, all-round, crucifying way of his, as always glorying in the fright he caused, his eyes merry with recognition of club members he had sent down or expected to. This was probably supposed to be a routine visit about licensing and fire precautions, but you never knew. Yes you did. It wasn't. Normally, the nobodies, not chiefs, handled that kind of small-hours chore. This pair just liked coming to make pain, especially Iles. He lived for terror. You could watch him wondering all the time whether career-wise he should have picked villainy not the police, perhaps seeing a difference. Harpur, though, definitely hung on to microscopic fragments of civilisation, despite rank and his appearance.

'Ralphy,' Iles cried, 'what an eminent turn-out here tonight. Some really resonant crumpet. You know Harpur, do you? Very up-and-coming. For years. Ember's into higher education, Col. Gilding the lily, I'd say. How's Margaret and so on, Ralph?'

'The usual?' Ember replied.

'We remain booze snobs, I'm afraid, Ralphy,' Iles remarked. He accepted a port and lemon and Harpur took cider and a quadruple gin mixed in a pint glass. 'So, not at the Webb funeral? I heard you missed a quite bracing do.'

'Hardly part of my world, Mr Iles,' Ember replied.

'Oh, I thought maybe through the club. Not flowers even? I'm sure you're not on our nosegay list. But I suppose you're less than close to Doug, Ralph?'

There was that list, and the list they would get into their heads of everybody they knew here tonight, admittedly plenty. That's how they worked, these two, trying to pick up signs, seeing signs when there were none, making things fit what they required. This was detection. They must have had a whisper on something: one reason Ember never allowed shop talk in the Monty if it involved himself. Suppose he had been conferring with Sanquhar-Perry and Webby when they walked in, for God's sake. That mention of the funeral made him nervous, the suggestion he might be in the Webbs' circle. Iles and Harpur never asked him anything straight out, because they knew he would not talk to police. They did their deducing, though.

So, what tip brought them tonight? He had been careful when making for Sanquhar-Perry's dump on the Ernest Bevin, keeping his car right out of it, and today he made very sure there was nobody behind him going to the station buffet. These two, Iles and Harpur, said things without saying them, Iles especially – always it was Iles especially. Look for what they called at the university a 'subtext', meaning diabolical hints. Ember wondered again whether he would back out of the raid. That was supposing he could now. After all, Sanquhar-Perry saw his future in it, had invested his soul and Scotch family pride, and would probably turn vicious if Ember quit. Pressures were massing. He started to sweat.

'You still knocking off that sweet piece in the multi-storey, Ralph? Two-hour ticket, is it, Tuesdays?' Iles said.

'Harpur's moved on from your wife, Sarah, I hear,' Ember replied.

'How did the university first year go?' Harpur inquired. 'Politics your main subject, I gather.'

'All I'd hoped it would be,' Ember replied. 'Half hogwash, but I was expecting two-thirds.'

'Thatcher's tightened them up,' Iles said. 'Even screwed the Oxford troupe.'

'So you're through all right?' Harpur asked.

'I hope so. First-year results aren't out yet.'

'You might win the Bell prize.'

'What's that?'

'Best first-year student.'

'Never heard of it.'

'The Chief and I, not to mention Harpur, are pleased to see you've really settled down, Ralphy,' Iles remarked. 'Become a civic plus. I expect you're meeting an altogether nicer class of person.'

'Nicer than whom?'

' "Whom." That's great. This is education, Harpur. Nicer than the camel droppings you used to run with, Ralphy.'

They were asking who – or fucking whom – he was running with now, of course. They bounced these insults at you and waited for you to return something giveaway: asked questions without asking questions and heard the answers they wanted – interrogation as chit-chat. You wondered whether they knew about Sanquhar-Perry and Webb, and had speculations. Christ, he must get out of this raid.

'And look who else has come to do you homage now,' Iles remarked. A woman Ralph had never seen before entered the club and walked towards the bar, smiling at him as if they were old friends. She wore red cord trousers, a white shirt and gold and red striped cravat. Her shoes were black, elegant, fragile-looking and dear. 'This is Wendy Sellick, distinguished *Searchlight* journalist,' Iles cooed. 'Wendy's inexhaustibly investigative.'

'Madam, I'm afraid this is a private club.'

'Oh, Harpur will vouch for her, Ralph,' Iles said. 'And I'll vouch for Harpur, up to a point.'

'I knew it must be you.' The girl leaned across the bar and extended her smile.

'Ah, because people told you he looks like Charlton Heston,' Iles said. 'Astonishing resemblance, yes? That scene where he plays stone dead on the nag in *El Cid*? So Ralphy.'

'Well, I've been unsuccessfully looking for someone,' she replied. 'I was told, try the Monty.'

'Fine advice,' Iles said. 'Anyone worth a light wants to be seen here. Mention the Monty to your social scene editor. Make a change from Chelsea Arts and the Groucho.' He waved a hand. 'Look around. Mark the members. Sullen gnomes at rest from dark satanic labours.'

'Ah, an adaptation of a pastiche line by Roy Fuller,' she replied. 'It's a man called Towler I'm urgently looking for.'

'Towler?' Ralph replied.

'Anthony Towler – Tony or Tone,' she said.

'I think you spoke of him previously,' Iles remarked.

'You bet I bloody spoke of him.'

'But we had no knowledge, Ralph,' Iles said.

'He's not at home and the neighbours haven't seen him for days. It's worrying,' the reporter said.

'Can't help,' Ember replied.

'But you know him?'

'We get so many people in here. As you can see. All sorts. Gingerish? Stoutish?' Ember was glad to note the club seemed to be relaxing again. People talked and argued around the pool tables. Paul Simon was on the juke box: Ember was still able to keep rap out, so far.

'Is Towler an official missing person, Col?' Iles asked. 'Do you have any other first names for him, Wendy – Anthony Something Something Towler, possibly?'

'Not that I've heard,' Harpur said. It frightened him, if Towler really had gone. Towler was linked to Lamb. Denise could also be thought to link to Lamb, and in the funeral video Doug Webb gazed with clear hate at the spot where she'd been standing. 'What have you done to find him, Wendy?'

'All the usual. Called time and again and all hours at the house, rung time and again and all hours. Asked around in the street.' She straightened up from the bar and faced Iles. 'Look, I mention his name to you two one day and the next he's very absent. What the hell's happening?'

Harpur considered it not a bad question. Iles said: 'So, tell me, is Towler important in some way? And what are you going to drink? And the same again for us, Ralphy. Why I love the Monty. All at once it turns into party time.'

In the car on the way home, Iles remarked: 'Someone congenitally tawdry like Ember can't be expected to understand that previous situation – you, me, Sarah.'

'I wouldn't have thought so, sir.'

'Sarah looked around, considerably unhinged at the time. Obviously. You were there, that's all. You've a kindly disposition, Harpur, and aren't intellectually threatening.'

'Thank you, sir.'

'It's totally over now.'

'Totally.'

'She's a lovely wife and a great mother to our child. As far as I can tell I haven't picked up anything dire, though I never actually had the tests. It would seem an unpleasant reflection on you.'

'You're among the whitest men I know, sir.'

Iles pulled up at Harpur's house. 'That episode will certainly not hold back your career, as far as I'm concerned.'

'Thank you, again. I knew that.'

'Could I be petty? Is that Desmond Iles?'

The ACC did not go in for rhetorical questions and Harpur answered: 'Never, sir.'

Iles barked on. 'You had Sarah for months, so does that make you unfitted for the highest ranks?'

'A *non sequitur*, sir.'

Startled, he stared at Harpur. 'Where did you learn phrasing like that? No, it's your general lack of venom that does for you, Col. Intransigently fair-minded. But policing's a dark science. Don't imagine that because an old eclair like Mark Lane can get to the top others similar can follow. He's a one-off. All right, you can kill a man like young Webby – very nice and necessary shooting – but then you fret, sweat, contemplate counselling, hiccough guilt. I can feel it all the time. That wholesomeness – part of what Sarah saw in you, I suppose. In our vocation, a desperate flaw.'

'Ralphy seemed jumpy. I mean, more jumpy than Ralphy's famous for.'

'Oh, he's into something. Fancy the reporter at all? The legs are not utterly unacceptable. She spends all that on shoes but is mean about dentistry. Some like jagged teeth. They bring a medieval touch to the face and make a woman whistle in climax, like an old-time kettle. I thought she gave me heavy come-on.'

'Unquestionably, sir.'

'You don't?'

'I felt she loved the blazer, sir.'

'You have to catch women journalists young because one ear gets bigger than the other, through intensive phoning. Happy thoughts to Megan, Col.'

Chapter Twelve

Harpur broke into Anthony Towler's house in a *cul-de-sac* off Corporation Street. It was late at night and the house dark. Although he had a torch with him he did not use it yet. Behind the house was a building site and security lamps from there gave enough light to show him he was in the kitchen, lavish, very up-to-date, and exceptionally tidy. Work surfaces stretched and glinted like runways. What you would expect for Tony.

From outside, too, the house looked made for him. A Victorian villa, it was neat and carefully tended, the pointing first class. Harpur had stayed watchful when he arrived, in case the girl reporter, Sellick, had also come on one of her visits, waiting for Towler to return, keen to doorstep him. He did not see her, though, nor any likely looking parked vehicles.

This kind of work always enraptured Harpur. To invade other people's property alone, on the quiet, and deftly go through their personal things, made his heart dance. This was not crudely turning a place over – 'spinning a drum' in police lingo – when you ripped everything apart, looking for stolen goods or drugs or a weapon, and when some supplied what they hunted if it failed to show. On his visits, Harpur was searching for nothing special but longed only to get past the curtains and dwell on intimate normalities of a life. With luck, you could see an identity unfold then: an act of contemplation, of osmosis, needing a kind of reverence as much as intrusiveness.

Or he thought of it as like psychiatry, except psychiatry was a doddle. In both games you exposed the secrets of a personality by delicately picking away: the psychiatrist entering a mind's recesses, Harpur charting the bits and pieces of domesticity. Whenever he made an illicit break-in, he knew he had chosen the supreme career, and, standing in the dark in someone's modest living-room or kitchen, he saw horizons glow and widen gloriously, as though reaching the essence of this particular target might bring communion with

117

the souls of men, or women, everywhere. 'Oh, stuff the whimsy, Harpur,' he grunted. 'Get on with it.'

Harpur moved from the kitchen and came to the living-room. Here, the curtains were open and street light shone in, so he still did not use the torch. He shifted around very carefully, sometimes on all fours, to keep below window level. Towler had furnished in harmony with the house, and owned some good Victorian pieces, including a Pembroke table, a gleaming Wellington chest and what looked like a genuine old chesterfield, re-covered in black leather. No wonder they called Towler Tone. The television and music centre damaged period feel, but there had to be latitude. Towler's compact discs were not Victorian, either: Harpur liked the title of Fishbone's rock album which he could just make out, *The Reality of my Surroundings*: verbiage heavier than the beat these days. Towler's own surroundings seemed a bit dishevelled here, and this room looked much less tidy than the kitchen. CDs and cassettes lay strewn on the varnished hardwood floor and bits of the *Daily Telegraph* straggled, part on the chesterfield and part on a decent Indian rug alongside it. What seemed to be a dark blue tie had been flung anyhow on to a brocade armchair.

For a second, Harpur wondered whether someone had been through before him, searching clumsily. Improbable: books on alcove shelves looked undisturbed and the drawers in the Wellington properly closed. The books were what he would have expected – a set of volumes by one or other of the Lawrences in blue mock-leather, and additional respectable slabs with smart bindings such as Graham Greene, Tolstoy and Americans like Stephen King. Towler must be in a mail order club, to confer depth. Anyone giving the room a rough, quick look-through would not bother shutting drawers and would sweep books to the ground, in case there was something behind or between, or among the pages. More likely, Towler had gone out in a hurry, and meant to put things right when he returned. Perhaps he had been uncertain about attending the funeral and left the decision late. That would make total sense.

To look over the house had been a sudden, unplanned idea, which came earlier that night while Harpur loitered outside the student flats where Denise lived. Mounting an occasional watch there had become a habit. Very anxious about her lately, he would drive two or three times a day, and at night, near Jonson Court, occasionally stopping for a better look around. The early visions of her body smashed and lifeless had begun to return repeatedly, and return with foul, extra clarity. He could have counted wounds and done a full police run-down of her injuries then, had he wanted to. He didn't.

118

Jesus, the Webb shooting really had blasted his mind. Why hadn't he taken counselling? Playing Mr Impregnable? He felt powerless and appallingly alone. And he felt responsible for her, and knew this to be stupid: she was not his wife nor his child. She was nobody's child now, but a clever adult. He could think of hardly anyone to tell his dreads to: obviously not Megan, obviously not Iles or the Chief – in fact nobody at headquarters, except maybe Francis Garland if things grew completely intolerable. Nor could he tell Denise herself. Strangely, the impossibility of consulting Megan disturbed him most: nearly two decades of marriage built habits and dependence, even this marriage. *Megan, I'm in an affair with a delightful undergrad liable to get butchered in error, or maybe not in error. How would you handle it, dear?*

He and Denise had been out together a couple of times in the afternoons, once to the sea, once to the Tenbury, but he never asked why she had been flower-arranging at the Webb funeral, nor what that Bell prize might be, the one she was due to win and which Ralphy Ember said did not exist. If she wanted to tell him anything she would. You did not interrogate a lover. And this was not just a lover, but someone who a year ago had been a schoolgirl – what Iles would call a kid, still occasionally showing traces of her childhood, even if officially a grown-up brain box. Go gently. But, of course, although you did not grill this kid, you might not tell her everything, either. No lovers of any age did that, if they hoped to continue. Denise apparently had her own secrets. Now and then during those two outings he really studied her, but could see no sign of sorrow for Martin Webb. She baffled him. He remained convinced, though, that he could never let her go and amazed he had ever thought he might. The hours he spent with her were so joyful he would not sour them with inquisition. A sign of ageing: make the most of what came, regardless, because you'd known droughts.

He took Towler's discarded tie out into the hallway and under the stairs. There he risked the flashlight. The tie *was* very dark blue and seemed new. Towler might have bought it for the funeral and then thought he'd better go whole hog and wear black: if you engineered a death, make the mourning copious. Towler had been all-round nervy over this outing. He'd forced himself to attend, just the same. Yes, he had guts. Had? Harpur found himself growing more and more uneasy.

This was the end of a wearing, not very profitable day. First thing that morning, he had rung Jack Lamb to say he wanted an early meeting – what Lamb sometimes called a séance. This was unusual: generally Lamb made the move. Jack had agreed a rendezvous for

119

early that evening, all the same. It always struck Harpur as a bit mad, but most informants allowed only the barest talk by phone, Jack particularly. He and his sort had read about professional and amateur taps, about car phone chat unaccountably crashing into local radio broadcasts, and of operators eavesdropping for fun and/or backhanders. So, the detective and his grass had to tête-à-tête. And the dangers in that always looked greater to Harpur: two big men – Jack huge – in closed conversation at what they hoped was some clandestine venue, but might not be. You did what the informant wanted, though, without question. It was his future, his bones and balls.

They had a string of alternative venues, referred to by childish codes, and this time Harpur had stipulated the station buffet. Somehow, he felt most comfortable there, most anonymous, liking the constant movement of travellers, many from elsewhere, and most too concerned about connections and timetables to notice other people. He was soothed by the warmth, the grubby cosiness, the Whitsun Treat sound of mass tea-making. Arriving first, he had cleared food debris from a Formica-topped table at a far point from the window and bought Cokes. Lamb came not long afterwards. 'So what's the panic, Col?' he asked comfortingly. Once in a while Lamb could show stress. Generally, he acted rocklike.

'Two things. There's a woman journalist around, naming names – yours, mine, Iles's, Tone Towler's. This is a quality paper, no rag. Police information methods obsess them. They get their own stuff any way they like, but don't think we should. To look virtuous and penetrative they'll splash the lot, and sod *sub judice* and general peril. Be careful, Jack. Is the Summer Ball still on? Can't you drop it this year, for God's sake?'

'I've got the Lord Loot.'

'All the same, I—'

'You're thinking of Denise.'

'I'm thinking of a number of people.' Yes, he was thinking of Denise.

'We've had Press persecution before. These papers want crime beaten but can't comprehend the ways of doing it. Their reporters tire, get brick-walled, retreat to London.'

'You sound like Des Iles.'

'I knew I'd make it one day.'

'She'll come to see you.'

'I'll behave beautifully.'

'Second, Towler's missing.'

'Towler? Missing? What's that mean? Who's Towler, Col,

anyway? You mentioned him. Mature age? Someone entitled to go missing?'

'Anthony Towler. You use him.'

'I think I've heard of this lad,' Lamb replied. He drained his plastic cup.

'Don't fuck about. No time.'

'Youngish? Lives Corporation Street way, near the DIY?'

'When did you see him last?'

'Missing? What's it mean?' Lamb had repeated.

'The Press can't find him.'

'Away on business? Women? Gone to see one, or done a runner to dodge one?' Lamb had dressed for once, thank God, in fairly sober clothes, except for a large purple 'Free Mandela' badge on his lapel. Often causes safely won won him. Jack would fret about telephone leaks but occasionally made these meetings a display by sporting crazy gear, including once a vast, thick brown cloak with fur trim, and twice a navy sombrero. Today he had been in a greenish country suit and plaid tie and might have been making for a country landowners' shindig. He had the face for it, too – heavy, large-chinned, wide, wily, genial. People expected grasses to be small and ratty-looking. It was one of his innumerable plusses that he wasn't.

Harpur said: 'Tone Towler fed you the stuff on Marty?'

'I should think this Towler will turn up. Journalists – they red letter. It's their trade.'

'Has Towler been in touch since the funeral, Jack?'

'And Helen would be so upset if I called off the ball. With these young girls you tread delicately. But, as you know.'

'Towler gone. Who's next, Jack? It could lead to you, and to Denise. At a spree like that – unbulletproof marquees, woods for sly access and exit, people three-quarters pissed and off-guard, night, shadows – everyone's exposed. An invitation.'

'I'd love to send you one, so you'd give protection in your famed, Maginot style, Col,' Lamb answered, with one of his great laughs. People in the buffet glanced at them.

'Jack, is there a way of raising Towler?'

Lamb had seemed to look startled for a second. 'Raising him?'

'In a crisis. If he's off somewhere, I'd like to hear he's safe.'

'Oh, *raising* him. A lot of these people, they go where the jobs take them,' Lamb said. He stood.

'Bugger it, Jack, what's going on?'

'Luckily, these things have a way of sorting themselves out,' he explained. 'My mother argues theology, as you know, and I said to her only yesterday, we must believe goodness will win, or what's the world but hell? She's sceptical. Negative.'

Harpur sided with Mrs Lamb. Goodness might not win. It needed a lot of help, some of it shady, and even then was inclined to fall short. Harpur had driven down to Jonson Court and sat for a while, looking about. Because he and Denise wanted no gossip, he had never been inside the building, but he knew the rooms and could see her light behind the curtains. Things seemed all right. He spotted nobody waiting around, not Doug Webb, nor anyone else. All the same, he stayed until the room went dark at just after eleven o'clock.

Then the decision out of nowhere to look at Towler's place. He had the address in his mind, even before Lamb mentioned it, because he never sank all his hopes in one informant, not even Jack: impossible to know how long a grass would go on grassing – would stay alive to go on grassing, or would think it paid to go on grassing, or, as suspicions about him spread, could go on hearing stuff good enough to go on grassing with – so you discovered where to deal direct with his sources.

Harpur had driven a little way on in Corporation Street, parked, and, slipping a flashlight into his pocket, walked towards the rear of the house. It backed on to what was once an industrial area of foundries, small workshops and a couple of warehouses. For a decade the buildings had stood derelict. Now they were gone and crescents of cement brick, so-called town properties, were going up, town meaning cramped. Probably as part of the planning deal, the builders had provided Towler and his neighbours with a new rear wall each, about three feet high. Towler, in his prim way, had fixed trellis work to this, giving him an extra couple of feet of screen. His neighbour had not bothered, though, and Harpur climbed on to that wall and jumped down into Towler's garden. In the dark, at least, it looked well kept, and he could smell honeysuckle and mint. The original rear door from the house into the garden had been replaced with a modern one, which pleased him. Years ago a girlfriend working at city hall gave him a set of keys able to open almost everything on the Ernest Bevin council estate, and he had found that one or more of them would usually work on private sector simple locks, too. It had taken him a couple of minutes to make his entry into the kitchen.

Under Towler's stairs now, Harpur switched off the flashlight, went back into the room and replaced the dark blue tie on its chair. In a wickerwork wastepaper basket near the Pembroke table he saw what seemed to be torn pieces of white card. He lifted these out and took them under the stairs, too. Using the flashlight again, he was able after a while to fit together on the tiled floor three different handwritten messages, in very black, grieving ink, obviously meant to escort funeral flowers. Towler must have had trouble hitting the right style, and who'd blame him?

From Anthony, in affectionate memory of a . . . The first one tailed off there, as though Towler had panicked and jacked it in at the thought of defining his relationship with Marty Webb. That, again, was natural enough. *Martin – we long for you, old son, but happy memories linger on, Tone.* This one had been ripped across and lengthways. Perhaps Towler grew suddenly sickened by the ripeness of it, and feared others would, too. *Goodbye, Martin, God bless – with profound regret from Anthony Towler.* That did not seem too bad. The rip went right through 'regret', though. Sensitivity might be a real Towler weakness, and Iles often said it was with Harpur. He would have to check the inventory to see what Tony finally came up with. It would be tasteful, no question and not, *Goodbye Martin. We'll miss you. Harpur didn't.* Anyway, the bastard couldn't know, couldn't possibly.

He switched off again, returned to the room and scattered the pieces in the basket. He put each cushion back. Then he noticed another card propped up by a book on the Wellington, and obviously meant to be seen by visitors. It was an embossed invitation to the Summer Ball – *Helen Surtees and Jack Lamb request the pleasure of the company of Mr Anthony Towler at a Summer Occasion on June 26, from 9 p.m. Dress, Unspeakably Elegant. RSVP.* Good for Tony.

Quickly mounting the stairs, Harpur looked at the bathroom and two bedrooms and once more had the feeling that Towler went out in a hurry, expecting to return. In the bathroom his electric shaver remained connected, and a toothbrush lay in the washbasin, as if it had been used and dropped during the rush. A discarded violet-striped shirt had been thrown on the duvet in Towler's bedroom and a pair of brown suede shoes, still laced up, were in front of an immense mahogany Victorian wardrobe, whose curved and carved pediment almost touched the ceiling. Period, yes, but period for a mansion. The piece must come apart or Towler would never have got it up the stairs. He had probably kicked off the suedes to put on thoroughly condolencing black, as with the tie.

Harpur had noticed some mail under the letter box and he descended now and collected it. This time, he took a cushion from the chesterfield, and made himself reasonably comfortable under the stairs. People spent whole nights like this during the Blitz. He put the flashlight on once more and worked through the letters. Three looked like bills, from which he would probably learn nothing, and he set them aside. The other was a handwritten envelope with a Paignton, Devon, postmark. He hesitated for a moment or two over this, though obviously not because it was personal. Should he take this away, steam it open, then reseal and redeliver? After all, Towler might be back home tomorrow, or next week, or sometime. And, if he wasn't home tomorrow or next week or sometime, it must be because he had grave trouble, and tomorrow or next week or sometime the house would be full of police, himself included, and colleagues would not expect to find one of Towler's letters interfered with. Well, they wouldn't. He could take this with him. He tore it open.

The address at the top was Blagdon, Devon, which must be a village near Paignton. *My dear Anthony*, it began. From the envelope, Harpur had already decided the writing was a man's. He turned to the end and saw a neat signature: *Your loving father*. The letter instantly captivated Harpur. This was just the sort of deeply private material he thrilled to ransack.

My dear Anthony,
It was grand to see you last week, I don't think you should worry too much about the development at the end of your garden. This is the way of the world these days, I fear. Everywhere ugly modern housing and little regard for a locality's historical ambience. But you should be able to maintain your privacy, my boy, and who knows, by some wondrous chance your new neighbours over the rear wall might turn out to be passable folk. There are some still left in this country.

I must admit that I remain hazy about how you earn your living these days, although you did patiently try to explain the intricacies of entrepreneurial business. To a middle-aged school master these things have to remain a mystery, I fear. At any rate, you seem to be doing well at it, even in these days of recession.

It was also pleasant to meet your friend, Mr Sanquhar-Perry – so amiable. I really do intend to apply some of my (very) amateur genealogist skills to his interesting surname and particularly, of course, the Sanquhar, as promised. Perry should be an easier matter. There is, of course, a Scottish town, Sanquhar. Your friend will wish to know, though, his forebears' historical role and status there. This I shall look into. What seemed certain from your friend's general manner is that he has distinguished lineage behind him. I'm pleased you have such well-bred company.

Please keep in touch Anthony. Too much time passed since our last 'get-together'. I do feel the need now I am alone. There are just the two of us left. The occasional telephone call is good, but I like the 'luxury' of a meeting and of a nice long letter.

Your loving father.

Harpur glanced back at the date and saw it was the day before yesterday's. Somehow, he must check whether Towler had turned up there since the letter was written: little chance, unless he was deliberately lying low. No wonder Mr Towler found it hard to fathom his son's trade. Harpur would have enjoyed hearing Anthony spin that splendid tale. Touching that Towler senior should mistake Courtncy for class. Folding the letter and envelope, he put them in his pocket. Tony's link with Sanquhar-Perry, off-cut of the Scottish gentry, strongly interested him. Towler had been taking a professional sniff at Courtney's future plans? Did Courtney explain to Mr Towler how *he* earned a living, too? That would be even more tricky.

He decided on one more quick look around upstairs, and then home, via the student flats area. A man's bedroom ought to say a lot. He replaced the cushion on the chesterfield and the unopened bills beneath the letter box. If any of them had looked like an Income Tax demand or telephone account he would have opened those as well, but one was Gas, the other Electricity, the third hand-delivered with a newsagent's name printed on the envelope. Harpur could do without knowing how Towler kept warm and what paper he took on Sundays.

In the bedroom he opened the wardrobe and found half a dozen good suits, a lurid silk summer jacket, high-quality leather coats and four pairs of silk summer trousers. Towler really did spend. Would he have left this lot if he had planned to disappear? The bedsheets seemed to be silk, too. Perhaps he had tender skin. Christ, that could be a liability in his world. Tony's father was right, though – the lad seemed to be riding the recession. You could not keep a good grass down. He must work damned hard. Had he extended his listening to Sanquhar-Perry, and maybe others? Harpur would look at that.

Glancing down from the front window, he saw a sign of what he had feared when first arriving: a new Sierra parked right outside, lights off, empty. It had certainly not been there when he first examined the street. The number plates were local. Hired? This could be the reporter. He moved back fast and sat on the bed.

Despite what Jack said, these people did not flag. They wanted to know, and the urge pushed them hard. Sellick could be anywhere around outside. He must not be seen here, or God knew what she and her paper would make of it.

After a few minutes, he heard something from the back of the house which he could not immediately identify – a small, delicate noise, repeated three times. After that came silence for a few seconds, then a different, larger-scale sound, though still subdued. Suddenly he realised he had been listening to someone making a small hole in a window, then opening the catch. It was no novice: minimum disturbance. Christ, but this was unforgivable. Investigative reporting might be fair enough, but not breaking and entering.

Soon, he became aware of her moving about downstairs. It worried Harpur that, also like himself, she had fixed on Towler, or on Towler's disappearance, as key. The girl was bright. She would come upstairs shortly. Even if she found nothing of importance in the house – and she wouldn't – journalists loved to festoon their stuff with descriptions of relevant places, especially off-limits places.

Harpur took a straight-backed chair from beside the bed, set it near the wardrobe and climbed up. With painful effort he was able to get down behind the ornate pediment, between the top of the wardrobe and the ceiling. As long as she could not risk a light up here, either, he might be unobserved. Did the position remind him of some cartoon about a seal on a bedroom wardrobe?

He waited and watched the door. A career might be involved, his, not hers. And then he realised all at once that she was not alone. At least two people had entered. He could make out whispering – not the words yet, but definitely voices. These people operated in teams. Jesus, a photographer. He had already visualised the kind of headline his position might produce. But pictures? His face behind this fancy mahogany, his arse jammed against the ceiling. Not even the Chief, the ever kindly, constructive Lane, could save him then.

Stairs squeaked. The whispering had ended, but he thought he could distinguish two sets of footsteps, moving quietly, cautiously. Of course, it might not be the reporter at all. From the whispering he had been unable to tell gender. All sorts might come looking for Towler. Nobody qualified better as a target, except possibly Lamb, and himself. And if they came they could come in strength. Two might not be the whole story. What hope of defending himself confined like this?

When the whispering resumed, though, he knew the voice was Sellick's. They must have gone into the bathroom first. All doors upstairs were open, so it was possible now to pick up sense. In fact, the reporter had begun speaking at almost normal pitch. They must feel confident the house was empty.

'The whole place makes me certain something unexpected and terrible has happened to him,' she said. 'Gut feeling.'

For a while there was silence, except that Harpur heard someone moving about in the bathroom, possibly noticing the razor and toothbrush. 'Gut feelings should be avoided, Wendy,' Desmond Iles replied. 'No clout in a court of law.'

'I don't have to cater for a court of law.'

'You can't rely on anything you see in this house. Someone has been in before us,' Iles said.

'What? How in God's name can you tell?'

'The wild scattering of the bits of card in the wastepaper basket. Too wild. Likewise the letters. They wouldn't fall like that. And only useless bills. Something more apropros taken? The cushion, nicely plumped up and immaculate on the chesterfield. It's probably been replaced.'

In a moment she said: 'You know, you amaze me, Iles.'

'Desmond. Amazing is what I'm celebrated for. And a general perceived snottiness.'

'Why you're here at all, for instance,' she replied.

'I thought I'd like to see you. You're interested in Towler. It made sense to bump into you at his house.'

'And letting me in.'

'I didn't let you in. We broke in. If you want to see the house, why not? It will put your fine investigative mind at rest and show we've nothing to hide.'

'We?'

'The police, obviously.'

Astonished for a few seconds at hearing the ACC, Harpur recovered now. The shock must be another sign of ageing?

The two of them came into the bedroom and examined it at first from the doorway. Harpur watched through the hand-crafted twirls of wood. They did not put the light on.

'What colour are those sheets?' Sellick asked. 'Blue?'

'More turquoise. I know you people love accuracy, when it suits.' Harpur kept his breathing subdued.

'I'd like to look in the wardrobe,' she said. 'Get his style.'

'Of course.'

They crossed the room and, standing right beneath Harpur, opened the wide doors.

'Nice gear and lots,' Iles said. 'I don't know why this lad didn't come to my notice before.'

'You mean if he's such a successful grass?'

'Oh, we don't deal with grasses, Wendy. The Chief's utterly opposed.'

'But Harpur? It's Harpur we get the persistent rumours about. The reciprocal arrangements.'

'Col? He wouldn't have the subtlety. Don't get me wrong, for God's sake. A good man. Even a kind of high flier, at a middling level. Definitely a goodish man. But intellectually unadventurous.' They closed the wardrobe doors.

'I want to have another look at those card fragments in the waste basket,' she said.

'Someone's fitted the bits together then chucked them back, I'd say. Though what would one learn? Mourning's so formula.'

They went out of the room and Harpur heard them descend the stairs. As much as he could without noise, he rearranged himself for comfort. Possibly they would go soon. Three minutes later they were back in the bedroom ferociously plucking at each other's clothes. Iles was in civvies, so the buttons were not resistant.

'Look, Iles, never have I had a cop. I'm not suggesting a lot of experience, anyway, but I admit I could be said to have eschewed police.'

Iles did not reply. He was kissing her, low.

'That's very nice,' she told him, 'but bloody answer, will you?'

'What?' he mumbled.

'Say you've never had a reporter, of course.'

'Never.'

'Don't stop that yet,' she replied. After some minutes she said: 'But did you eschew us?'

'Eschew is not a word in my active vocabulary. Chew is.'

'Oh, yes. Yes.' In a while she went on: 'I don't know if I can believe a thing you say.'

'That's what comes of being high in the police. I blame the judges.'

'Can we hit the turquoise sheets now?' she asked later.

The Assistant Chief threw Towler's shirt off the duvet, then lifted her on to the bed. Out of her clothes, she looked younger – narrow shouldered, narrow hipped, the legs somehow not so bulky, supple, soft.

'We don't have to hurry, do we?' she asked.

'Why should we?'

'Is he going to come back?'

'Wendy, are you still working?'

'Working? Does it feel like it? But will he turn up?'

'I don't know. I'd find an explanation. Bound to be a way of explaining two visitors in his bed.'

'So, anyway, we needn't rush.'

'I don't know how to.'

'Oh, God,' Harpur muttered.

In a while she said: 'You're so gentle, so giving.'

'I know it, you know it. Thousands don't.'

'Shall we keep it like that?'

'Keep it like this?'

'Keep it like that for a while. How about your wife?'

'What?'

'Does she know you're gentle and giving?'

'Sarah? I don't think she'd care one way or the other.'

'I don't understand. Honestly. You're altogether a lovely man, you know.'

'That far I wouldn't go. Sarah's now and then seemed to need somebody else. One accepts. One has no ownership.'

'I love your body, your gameness, your eyes, and greyness, and put-on arrogance.'

'I love your looks, the taste of you, your walk, your underarms, your clothes, your absence of clothes, your charming and sizable tits on such a narrow frame, your consummate nosiness. We might have been picked for each other by Computerdate.'

They became still and silent. Harpur feared they had gone to sleep. Then she said: 'Now, don't keep it like that.'

'Exactly what I thought.'

'On the other hand—'

'I'm not going to rush. Am I likely to, on account of some jerk grass with silk trousers?'

'He *is* a grass then?'

'You say so. What we know is the silk trousers.'

'He gets invited to Jack Lamb's.'

'If you were a big grass would you advertise it by asking little grasses into your social life?'

'So he is a little grass?'

They left just before dawn. Iles had been right: the girl's teeth did make her whistle during the high points. She said: 'Des, I hope I haven't got to drop you in it. I mean, notwithstanding.'

'Others have tried.'

When he was sure they had gone, Harpur came down and went to the bedroom door, wanting to see whether the chair looked natural against the wardrobe. Had Iles known he was there? The first assumption if you suspected someone had searched a house

129

before you arrived was always that he might be still there. Also, Iles could have spotted his car, although it was at a distance, old and reasonably anonymous. Iles did spot things. He was not in his job by luck and definitely not by ingratiation. On the other hand, the insults the ACC had spoken about him had been mild, which might suggest he did not realise Harpur was listening.

All the same, Harpur decided that if he himself came into a room and saw a chair in that position it would strike him as unusual. So, did Iles like to be watched screwing, or at least screwing the Press? Did he think that Harpur liked to view? Did Harpur? He decided yes, but not enough to pay. This was human nature at its very best – and especially Iles's at its – so why not witness and take heart?

Harpur was uncertain whether to replace the chair alongside the bed. That would look right should Towler return. But if Iles brought the girl back he would put two and two together, even if he hadn't tonight. Harpur decided to leave the chair as it was. Towler probably would not be back. Iles and Sellick might.

Chapter Thirteen

Jack Lamb took another call – a lad he knew, though not too well. A voice. A very apprentice voice. Lamb had dealt with him once or twice before, receiving useless snippets, but accurate snippets, as it turned out. You encouraged such people, played them along in case they developed, and, now Tone Towler had gone, even more so.

'Business material,' this lad, Gary, said on the phone. 'Might be your sort of thing. In fact, almost definitely, Mr Lamb. I'm beginning to learn your taste. Quite large scale.'

'Nice of you to think of me, Gary.' To him, large scale might mean anything more than a bike without lights.

'Shall we say the usual?' Gary replied.

The contractors were arriving today to set up the marquees, but Helen could supervise that. 'Fine, Gary.'

It was a holiday caravan park, a little way up the coast, with lettings by the week or fortnight and a constant change-over of cars and people, so they were almost all strangers to one another. You could park and stand and talk somewhere and they thought you were discussing your van's telly reception, or did not think about you at all. It had been Gary's idea, and a good one. He could turn into something valuable.

'This is full and exact in some aspects, Mr Lamb, but in others not at all.'

'Normal, Gary. Our caper's not like a Royal Commission.'

'Full and exact in terms of weaponry. This is undoubtedly sawn-offs. I know your gospel, you see.'

'Thanks, Gary.'

'You're not interested unless it's life in danger – innocent life: the public, shoppers, kiddies, bank clerks.'

'It's a bank, Gary?' Lamb fought to keep incredulity out of his voice. For Gary to be tipping about a bank would be a move up faster than Speedy Gonzalez.

They were standing near a thick hedge alongside what seemed to be an empty green and gold caravan with a type name big on it,

Status. Gary had left his jacket in the car and stood with sleeves rolled up, acting a holiday maker. He was a tubby, red faced lad with a very heavy, untidy black moustache that went down to both sides of his mouth. A lot of novice villains cultivated this sort of thing, or beards, certain that in emergency they could shave and become someone else. As an overnight measure, though, Gary would have trouble shaving his gut. He spoke with a nice, sing-song accent – maybe Welsh, maybe Liverpool-Irish – made for spilling.

'What's your source, Gary?'

He closed up and looked confused, hurt. 'Mr Lamb, I—'

'No, not the name, obviously. Who asks names? Type of source. Status.'

'Solid.'

'Gary—'

'Excuse me, Mr Lamb. Your drift is I never came up with banks, sawn-offs before – that league.'

He had nous. 'I'm thinking of the questions I'll face – if I take things further. These are disbelieving people.'

'Well, I understand that, Mr Lamb.'

'The nature of the source.'

'Of course.' He came a bit closer. That was all right. 'Someone who's been asked to do a reconnoitre of the bank and hinterland. The people actually handling the work are from outside – London, naturally – and needing a local eye. Someone with the flavour and the geography.'

'That's normal, too. So, he's telling you this, Gary – this local eye? Why? That could be hazardous for a lot of people. Look, I'm being blunt because I know you can take it.'

'Right. Simply big-heading, I'd say. He's proud to be so famous that they ask for him. Mind, he didn't tell me direct.'

'Oh? This is via in-betweens?'

'I was present. In the room. Would I trouble you with secondhand? He was talking to someone else, someone closer. But he knew I was listening. He wanted me to pick it up, sort of accidentally? His way of big-heading without big-heading, you know?'

'It could be.'

'In a way, it's no big deal, is it? They get him to describe some main street architecture and do traffic and road-works updates. He's a periscope. But they asked for him by name, which means he's big – how he sees it. To be relied on.'

'And when you say bank? This is hit a bank in a raid, do a cash delivery to a bank, or wriggle in at a weekend and fillet deposit boxes?'

'Sawn-offs, Mr Lamb. No wriggling. Head-on. Getting behind the counter and into the safes, filling sacks and away.'

'Heavy man-power.'

'I hear five, plus driver.'

'Big sum, then, to divide six ways, and crumbs for your source.'

'I'm vague here, Mr Lamb, I admit. Haven't got a figure. But my source says six don't come from London and employ a local spotter without a return.' He paused. 'Sorry, that's your point.'

'And we know the bank and date? Names?'

'We know the bank and date. Names? Again, we go approximately, Mr Lamb. But does it matter, that's the thing? All I've got is the boy running it is called David.'

'First name or surname?'

'First. My source says David this, David the other. Familiarity.'

'You're guessing it's a first name?'

'How's that?'

'Your source uses it to show they're mates. How you read it?'

'It's said like a first name. That feel?'

'Fair enough, Gary. It might mean something to people in the know – people in the London know, and I'm not.'

'Even you have limits, Mr Lamb. And a sawn-off is a sawn-off, whoever.'

'That's an argument. But—'

'You're still bothered about the people you tell?'

'They're going to ask. Nothing surer. I'll give them your answer: what's it matter who's behind sawn-offs?'

Gary grinned. 'Thanks, Mr Lamb. It makes sense, yes? I mean, even when reporting to the highest level.'

'Tell me how it happened, Gary, will you?' Lamb asked.

'What?'

'The way you picked this up.'

'Well, I did tell you, Mr Lamb. Like an accident.'

'But I don't understand how you were in the room in the first place with these people. How you were where you could hear something like this. You obviously know these people well?'

'I work with one of them now and then. It's normal for us to have meetings – make a decision or two, consider a project.'

'And the other one, the one he was talking to?'

'Well, I've heard of him, seen him around, but I don't really know him,' Gary said. 'That doesn't matter, though, does it Mr Lamb?'

'When you say "a room". Someone's house?'

'Mr Lamb, I really don't like all this. I came here in good faith.

133

I know you've got to be careful, but this is out of order, this is hurtful.'

'Gary, it's basic. I've got my own long-term cred to think of.'

'When I say "a room", not anyone's house. Not really a room. This is one of those old concrete defence bunkers on the foreshore.'

Lamb smiled and said: 'Thanks, Gary. I know them.' They had better come off the list of spots he and Harpur used.

'You can talk there, no interruptions, except kids now and then. I'd have told you straight off, but—'

'Oh, I know there are rules, Gary. It's impressive you're so careful.'

'Thanks, Mr Lamb. So, OK now?'

'Fine.'

You could look three ways at what this lad said. First, he was lying and knew it. Second, he had been fed rot and did not know it. Last, he had heard what he said he heard and what he heard was right. With Towler you could always eliminate the first and probably the second, Tony being straightish and so experienced. Tony put material through the sieve before he thought of bringing it. Gary? Lamb didn't really know him. No profit in yearning for Towler, though. He had been hoist on a tree for trying to better the world. Echoes there. 'Well, I'll have time, place and date, Gary. If this comes off you're going to be very handsomely placed, indeed. I see a future.'

'This sort of situation – well, I believe like you, Mr Lamb. A duty.'

Chapter Fourteen

It really thrilled Denise to be part of it – watching with Helen and Mrs Lamb the arrival of the marquees, dance flooring, bars and lights in the glorious grounds of Darien. There were shadows, of course there were, but she tried to snuff out in her memory that picture of the two running men at the edge of the woods, and the screams. She found it hardest to forget the man in front, the one she did not recognise. About him she had seemed to see terrible, scuttling despair, a kind of awful acceptance, as if he knew he deserved whatever was about to happen. But, after all, nothing had been found, no more had been said, not even by Mrs Lamb. Denise's bright brain disliked the unexplainable and her training said not much, if anything, was. Experience had begun to tell her that some things might be better unexplained, though: so just voyeur and keep quiet.

As a child, Denise had once seen a circus assembling in a local park. It was that kind of bustling excitement now – the sparkling promise of gaiety and high spirits. The park today, though, was not a general, public place, but somewhere she had privileged access, somewhere she had come to feel was another home, thanks to Jack's kindness.

She arrived at nine thirty in the morning, wanting to miss nothing. On this brilliant June day, the sun was already hot, the grass and trees richly green: stillness everywhere, except where the men worked. The party itself was still a couple of days off but Helen said Jack wanted it all set up early so there'd be time to right anything wrong. There wouldn't – mustn't, couldn't – be anything wrong! She felt certain as they looked at the canvas rise in this sweet setting that it would all go superbly. The weather was going to hold. The forecast said so, and, in any case, it just had to!

Helen had brought out a couple of brightly painted mountain bikes – hers and Jack's – and she and Denise rode around the grounds in their shorts keeping an eye, pretending to supervise, in Helen's words. Near the woods, Denise was conscious of those shadows again – the face of the man she had seen before, the terror of the one she hadn't – yet she still found herself hoping the marquee team thought she belonged to this household. Whatever had happened, she loved the association with Darien. It gave her such a feel of style and space and of – well, of mattering a bit. Imagine getting on a mountain bike to look around the garden in Stafford! Marquees? It might just take a frame tent.

Snobbery. As always, shame closed in on her for these ideas. Her delight in the preparations and the place stayed, though. Not even a May Ball at the smartest Oxbridge college could match this. She wanted to thank Jack again for making it all happen, for opening up her life, but he was out on business somewhere this morning.

His mother, in one of her dresses and a US admiral-style cap, lay on a lounger up near the kitchen garden. They cycled back to her. 'Isn't it beautiful, Mrs Lamb?' Denise said. 'Like, oh, I don't know, a royal palace garden party.'

Mrs Lamb's eyes were shut and she did not open them. 'I'd like it to go well, of course. People do break through into legitimacy. We had friends. Their daughter came close to marrying a Senator.' Now, she did open her eyes and glanced down at the thin legs in loose, pale stockings poking out from under her seven-quid frock. 'My age – you see beyond the immediate, you know. I watched the workforce while you cycled around. What they see, and gaze at, kids, is some bronzed flashes of thigh, buttocks on saddles, pussy on wide wheels. These things merge – the two of you merge in the minds of men. Flesh.'

Helen giggled. 'Oh, Alice—'

The old face gleamed fiercely. You could imagine her holding her own in Detroit. 'I'm not just talking smart and coarse. You understand what I'm getting at, Denise? It's like before. Now, though, I see the how. You, you're a visitor up here, and very, very welcome. Jack, Helen, even myself, we're staff and know we're into risk. Then think of someone wanting to get Jack, and there must be plenty. So, they decide Jack's too difficult, too big, too wide awake, too connected-protected. Get his girl instead then. That'll hurt him as much. They farm these jobs out. My husband used to say, one thing about top hoods, they know how to delegate better than McArthur. So, people are sent down and they need to identify this lady of Jack. They observe a while. Well, there's a nice-looking girl in and out of Darien all the time, like she belongs – pretty, legs, full of fun, happy, not too much behind – just the sort of thing Jack goes for. Get it, Denise?'

'I could be mistaken for her?' Denise replied.

Helen said: 'Oh, Alice, you're not telling us that people putting up these tents—'

'Not at all. They're only suckers for flesh on a hot day. No, it was just watching them, I had this insight, this feeling the two of you kind of intermingle? The sort of people they'd hire for that job, it's what's known as a hit job – they're not always strong on fine distinctions. They shoot or whatever, and then get the name later? Am I clear?'

'This is crazy,' Helen said.

'Well, I hope so,' Mrs Lamb replied. She touched Helen's arm again. 'Look, my dear, I worry about you, too, but—'

'If I can't take a joke I shouldn't have joined, and Denise hasn't joined?'

Gazing at the gnarled, all-knowing face, Denise said suddenly, 'Alice, what was it among the trees? I mean, everything's so normal now. I don't need to have the detail – one is young, but understands confidentiality. Just was it something serious?'

'Whatever happens, you're a sweet, brave kid, Helen,' Mrs Lamb replied. 'Jack's lucky.'

'I love him, Alice.'

'What I said – he's lucky. With a chin like that? Lots don't love him. Every day I read that in his face. Sometimes when I look in his face all I see is target practice.'

'I read it, too,' Helen replied slowly. 'Not every day. Now and then. When I see it, I must show all the more I love him. He needs that.'

'What I said – he's lucky.' Mrs Lamb lay back and turned on her side. She spoke over her bony shoulder. 'Maybe forget it, Denise – all I tell you. Maybe I fret, look too wide, too deep. My husband always said narrowness was fortitude, the glib superponce. So, here's Jack now, trying to look unnefarious, with average success.'

Lamb, driving Helen's Maestro, parked in front of the house and for a while watched the men working on the marquees. Why couldn't he feel more pleasure in it?

Lamb walked over to the women. He still saw the friendship between Helen and Denise as mostly a happy thing, but he had started to worry about it, too. Harpur obviously thought Denise might be in peril and this was something else where he could be right. Had the girl watched whatever was the earlier part of that business in Chase Woods? She had been at the window. She talked to Harpur? She was a witness, the only one? It troubled Lamb that this girl and Helen saw so much of each other these days, here, around the town – especially around the town. Someone going for

Denise might easily get Helen by mistake, or as well, for convenience. Harpur should look after Denise. Lamb had to think of his girl. And at the party? As Harpur said, darkness, shadows, sudden chaos. There could be foul errors. This would be a very grown-up occasion.

'Denise,' he said. 'Great. You complete the picture. Look, why don't you move in here until after the big do? There's enough spare rooms, God knows. And people will be quitting the university flats now term's almost over, yes? You don't want to be down there alone.' At least then they needn't go off the grounds too often. And if she had someone tailing her a shift up here could confuse.

'Oh, yes, do,' Helen said.

'It's got points,' Mrs Lamb remarked. 'Jack foresees.'

Denise had the feeling this might somehow get in the way of things with Harpur. All right, perhaps it would become lonely in the flats. Mandy had had her results already and was leaving. But Denise liked the freedom. These days, she needed to give her whole attention to Harpur. He would talk about his wife sometimes – what she'd said, or what he'd said – and the relationship sounded all right: they would joke and rib each other. He did not seem to realise how much of an outsider Denise felt then, how far back. She still thought he had meant to drop her not long ago. It was a relationship that required a lot of looking after. Some more pressure could fall on it when he heard she had asked Stephen Patterson, one of her tutors, to take her to Lamb's party. In any case, there were shadows. She loved this place, and yet it did frighten her. She liked coming here, but needed to be able to leave.

'It would be great and thanks, Jack,' she said. 'Results aren't out yet and they like us to use university accommodation if we're still around. It could cause a panic.'

'Tell them where you'll be,' Mrs Lamb said.

'Kind, but I don't think I'd better,' she replied.

'Well, the offer's open, Denise,' Lamb said. He went into the house and up to his den. At the desk he wrote Harpur a note, something he had never done before.

One of my sources has been skilfully loaded with outright decoy lumber – a new boy, good, but bugger-all judgement yet. I'd say something big is going to happen at around 11 a.m. on July 10 but definitely not at the Nat West, Stipend Road, because that's what's named. Date and time spot on, locale elsewhere. Sorry this is a little vague.

He tore it up and felt enraged with himself. Christ, he had been seriously thinking of asking Denise to carry that to Harpur at their next meeting – in other words, turn her definitely into the kind of messenger Harpur feared she might be mistaken for. Gross. That letter – Harpur would have finished with him for keeps, and rightly. Lamb would have to go through the standard rigmarole for another meeting.

In the grounds, his mother said to Denise: 'Gives you a tremor, the thought of taking a room here, kid? You've got a feeling about this place.'

'I adore it. Please – what was in Chase Woods? Please.'

'Yes, you adore it, yet still a feeling – you can see it's not right somehow.' She had sat up again on the lounger, her face fierce, as before. 'Jack does his best, and he's wonderfully gifted. I love him, really love him for it. There's this garbage element in him, though. I can sympathise. He gets it from me.'

Chapter Fifteen

They had another meeting in the station buffet, and at the same table away from the window, as a matter of fact – Ralph Ember, Courtney Sanquhar-Perry and Doug Webb. Ember thought it was pushing their luck a bit, but apparently Courtney felt more comfortable here than anywhere, and on this job it was his say-so, up to date. You humoured people like Courtney. It kept them on an even keel. Breeding made them expect consideration.

They drank coffee and Courtney had a big Chelsea bun, to go with the boyish curls. He had not brought the suitcase this time, but often looked at his watch, like worried about a connection. You could see Courtney thought matters through and looked after details. He must have a powerful administrator somewhere in that fine Scottish lineage.

'Definitely the tenth, eleven a.m., boys,' he told them. 'That's a fortnight plus. We can put things nicely into shape. As agreed, I supply all weaponry. No extra charge.'

'You'll get a knighthood,' Webb said.

'I just follow a pattern, and wait for my information, Doug. It's confirmed now.'

'Sweet,' Ember remarked.

'And we'll be all right for a decoy, after all,' Sanquhar-Perry said.

'So, Towler's turned up again and done the necessary?' Doug Webb asked.

It was quick and natural, Ember had to give him that. The jail-wall face went into a nice show of relief and you could really believe Webby had no idea where Towler was, if you were a fucking zombie.

'Well, not quite, Doug,' Sanquhar-Perry answered.

'You're not telling us he's still missing?' Webb asked, as if this was beyond belief.

'How it looks,' Sanquhar-Perry replied.

'Giving you genuine problems, then,' Webb said with weight. 'We could have done without that. Responsibility – a word he's never heard of?'

'Right,' Sanquhar-Perry replied. To Ember, he sounded as mild and reasonable as Webby. Both stars in the Olivier class. If you'd come through a stack of interrogations you picked up all the deadpan skills. 'But Towler's not the be-all. I've got a substitute lad – in some ways even better. Younger, fatter in the face, sort of homely and convincing. He's another Lamb source, for certain.'

'Fall-back's always crucial,' Webb said.

'You'd be impressed by him, Doug. By now, he'll have taken the tale to Jack for us.'

'He believed you, this source?' Webb asked.

'I think so. Ralphy thinks so.'

'Yes, indeed,' Ember replied.

Angrily, Webb said: 'Ralphy knew about this?'

'Nothing secret, Doug,' Sanquhar-Perry replied. 'I wanted to do it so this kid, the source, would hear as if by accident? Look, I said sawn-offs, really to get Lamb going. So, Ralphy and I are talking about it, and, because I'm feeling so big and mighty at being asked into an operation by major folk, I forget this lad's in the room? Or don't care he's in the room – wanting to boast? You get the pageant?'

'It worked a treat,' Ember said. He had not liked this Gary getting a look at him, but Courtney reckoned he was safe. Of course, anyone could be safe until the heavy questioning.

'Well, I should have been informed,' Webb replied.

Jesus, he had balls. He knocks out one pillar of the planning, and then expects to be in on the repairs.

'We had to get things moving,' Sanquhar-Perry said. 'It's a matter of several stages, Doug – me to source, source to Lamb, Lamb to Harpur. Takes time. Of course, Tony Towler might have already spoken to Lamb, before the disappearance. So this boy would only be confirming what Jack's got. Same date, place and time, but official now – as to date and time, that is.'

'And place as far as he knows,' Ember remarked.

'Obviously,' Sanquhar-Perry said. 'So he can talk to Harpur. All their most talented stuff down to Stipend Street that day, for the ambush. And the best of luck! They can switch, yes, when they get the call. That takes time, too, though. Remember Planner Preston – he very nearly got away through a decoy. Only a freak snag and sodding Harpur. That won't happen with us. I think I can say I take care of all eventualities.'

'It's in-built with you, Courtney,' Ember remarked.

The buffet shook as an express passed without stopping. Webb said something, his face masonry again. 'How's that, Doug?' Sanquhar-Perry asked.

'I can't stop thinking about this bloody girl,' Webb said.

'Which girl?' Ember asked, as if he needed to.

'Harpur's girl, of course.'

'For Christ's sake, Doug,' Ember replied.

'She's still up at Lamb's place half her time.'

'So?' Ember asked.

'Who knows what she knows?' Webb replied.

'What's she going to know because she's at Lamb's place?' Ember asked.

'What? No, not because she's there,' Webb said. 'Obviously. I mean knows because she's carrying stuff between. What else?'

'How do you know she's there so much, Doug?' Sanquhar-Perry asked.

'I want to be in the picture on what she's up to,' Webb replied.

'You're dogging her even now?' Ember asked. 'Look, that's trouble.'

'She's of no consequence at all,' Sanquhar-Perry said.

'Got a half-daft son dead, his chest torn from point-blank, Courtney? Got a loved one in Long Lartin?'

'What's Long Lartin to do with it?' Ember asked.

'I'm saying, of no consequence at this point, Doug,' Sanquhar-Perry told him. Then, leaning across the Formica towards Webby, his teeth clogged with bun, Courtney did it again, in a kindly, spelling-out voice, slow, clear. 'At this point.'

Ember saw Sanquhar-Perry realised at last it was a mistake to have kept Webby in. Now, he could not change the personnel, though – only a fortnight off. And Doug would know that, too.

'Tell me the detail, Courtney,' Webb said.

'The battle plan?'

'That later. No – how you planted this stuff on the source. I'll love hearing how you worked it.'

'Well, he told you,' Ember replied. 'Done like an overheard conversation.'

'Yes, but where?' Webb said.

'Does it matter?' Sanquhar-Perry asked.

'Only so I can enjoy it. Visualise it. In your house, Courtney?'

'Am I going to take a mouth into my personal home?' Sanquhar-Perry said.

'Is he?' Ember remarked.

'Sorry,' Webb said. 'I don't know the procedures. So where, Courtney? You said a room?'

'This was a rendezvous. Like here,' Sanquhar-Perry said.

'You brought him here?' Webb asked. 'A room like this? Public?'

142

'I said like here. Similar.'

'A private room in a pub? Something of that sort?'

'A rendezvous.'

Webb said: 'I know I go on. So how do you get him there? What I'm curious about is how do you get him to some place where you can tell him something by accident? This is the bit, the talented bit, that intrigues me, see, Courtney?'

'This is a lad I meet up with now and then as ordinary routine. We've handled little jobs together – that's his league. We plan a small operation once in a while. We have meeting places. The usual drill.'

'What, the three of you – you, Ralphy and the source?'

'Sometimes, yes. Sometimes only him and me. Sometimes more. What's eating you, Doug?'

'Only it sounds good – it sounds a natural setting.'

'That's the whole point,' Ember said. 'Casual. He's not going to swallow it otherwise.'

'It's a treat to hear the ins and outs,' Webb replied.

Sanquhar-Perry left first today.

'What I feel when Courtney's doing the thinking is confidence, Ralphy,' Webb went on. 'I'd go through hell with that one.'

'He's a coming man. That hilarious house of his – only a launch pad. So, nerves make him gnash at a Chelsea bun. Nerves aren't always a drawback.'

'I ask the questions out of admiration – professional admiration.'

'He sees that, Doug. Oh, Courtney's big enough to take scrutiny.' Ember went next, and Webb watched that important-citizen's walk – very upright, very brisk, very world's-his-oyster. He lingered, considering. There was next to no chance Lamb would believe this mouth. They thought they were thinkers, these two, but you had to wonder. Didn't they know about Jack Lamb? Hadn't they heard he'd made a rich living for years and could not be touched by the law? Did he get there or a place like Darien by believing every tale that blew in off the street? Lamb would realise straight off that nobody with class was going to let some second-string source hear real intentions, not deliberately or by accident. Accidents like that did not happen or jails would be even fuller. Lamb would want the details of how it took place, and the details did not add up. So he would talk nicely to this lad and listen and know this lad brought him hand-tailored rubbish.

Except it was not all rubbish, of course. The date and the time were right and he would get in touch with Harpur and tell him to be ready with a maximum response at that moment, wherever the

143

call should come from. They would have cars on the road, full of armament and dislike, scouting for the scene. They would find out where cash deliveries were due that day and time and make a list of probables. It was a gift. Sanquhar-Perry, the coming man on his launch paid, had sent Harpur an invitation.

Webb bought himself another coffee and a Chelsea bun. He had liked the look of Courtney's but did without while the other two were there, not wanting to seem just an imitator. Those two would have been so quick to notice something like that, so destructive. He would have liked to drop out of this raid now. Suddenly there was a touch of the suicides about it, and he had two families to breadwin for, including possibly a shrink for Rodney, to convert him from fucking religion. But you could not drop out of a job, not when you had said you would do it. How did you face people afterwards – not just the people in the job, but family and all the rest who heard about it? And everyone who mattered would hear about it. Plus, he had to admit he had brought some of the snags by finishing the usual channel of communication, Tone Towler.

Worries persisted as Webb worked through the bun. He knew he might get things wrong. These people, Courtney and Ralph Ember, definitely had brains and successes, especially Ralphy. Yes, they thought they were thinkers but possibly they thought right most of the time. Maybe, after all, this lad they'd picked to carry the tidings really was good enough to get it past Jack Lamb. They were used to taking decisions, doing that balance of risks stuff, especially Ralphy. Look at Low Pastures. You judged people by what they had and held on to. Somewhere like Low Pastures came from knowing what you could get away with, the same as Darien. All the same, what he had to keep in mind was that Harpur might have seen off Martin and now might have a chance of seeing him off, too, or putting him out of action, anyway, for fifteen years. He had his duty to Sanquhar-Perry and Ralphy, but there was still the stronger duty – to make sure it was put right for Martin, and that people – people who counted – knew it was put right. Seeing to Towler helped put it right, but nobody knew about that, except, maybe, Lamb.

Doug Webb finished his snack and reasoned that if he had to go because of partners' mistakes he must make a good and clear mark first. To him, that still meant the girl, and the girl now, not after the job, as Sanquhar-Perry promised with all that slow talk, like D. Webb was simple. A definite duty to Courtney existed on certain things, but not family things. Those were private debts, the same as Tone. Christ, Lamb might have used the bitch student to carry the warning to Harpur that something was in the air for eleven a.m. on the tenth, but not at the bank in Stipend Road. She had to be dealt with. More than ever now.

Jesus, get out of this. Secure in his Rover, Ember drove away from the station and decided the raid was dead. Courtney alone did not realise it. Courtney alone believed in it, and he believed in it only because his breeding screamed at him to escape immediately from that rough hole on the Ernest Bevin and shame his ancestry no longer. Ember sympathised greatly with the motive, but it was not enough.

Webby? He could not go through with it. Although he made a show, you could see he had no faith in the substitute mouth. Ember himself had doubts over whether chubby Gary would do the trick with Lamb, but if you were big you looked at such big risks as standard. Webby was not big and big risks knocked him gutless. In any case, the sod couldn't seriously think about anything beyond hitting back for Martin. He had vengeance like a pox. This girl, Denise – he would get her somehow. It could even be at Lamb's famous summer wine-bibbing. Webby would love that for timing – a full expression of hate plus envy. Or it could be anywhere, at any time.

Ember was on his way to see Christine Tranter in the multi-storey. That would give him some comfort, and he felt the need. Although, in a vague, decent way, Ember still wanted to protect that girl, Denise, he did not see how he could, and, in any case, he was too occupied now with the need to step out of Courtney's dim project, but not turn Courtney vindictive or start a new avalanche of poison chat among acquaintances about Ember's unreliability. Maybe the thing to do was raise it as a topic, direct to Courtney – tell him to drop the raid and wait for another chance, because all the signs were poor, and Webby would not turn up on the day.

At the multi-storey he parked on one of the lower levels, then walked up a couple of floors until he found the dormobile with the curtains closed and light on. He climbed in. Chris was at the table in a white short-sleeved T-shirt and multi-coloured knee-length shorts, reading a thick book called *Possession*, which she had held up in front of her, supported by the table, like a vicar with the Bible. There was a picture on the front of a man and woman in long robes, the man with a rough old face recalling Webby's. Possession would be right to describe the way vengeance had hold of the bugger. 'Who's the pretty boy?' he asked.

She peered around the edge of the book at the dustjacket. 'Merlin. It's a picture by Burne-Jones. He's getting beguiled.'

145

'Lucky, looking like that.'

'The book's about wanting to possess and to be possessed. Something I never felt for poor old Les.'

'Me?'

'What do you think?'

Just the same, when they laid out the bed and made love he had the feeling she was not herself. Oh, her legs went up high in that lovely, happy way, nudging the light, and she whispered great and abiding things with her mouth touching his ear, so he would get them regardless of the vehicles revving and manoeuvring outside, and the bellowing voices of people leaving for a night on the town. 'What's wrong, love?' he said, when they were lying side by side later on. The light looked pretty steady, so dozy Les must have got around to the battery at last. Ember felt reasonably content now. The fact that Iles knew he came here had troubled him at first. Then he began to see it as a sort of safety: if the police kept an eye open for the dormobile, it amounted to a kind of protection. He was conscious of anxiety in her, though. It would not be the place: she never worried about that and, in fact, until now, had never seemed to worry about much at all – one of the things he prized in her. He could always hearten himself by seeing Christine.

'We might have to leave, Ralph,' she replied. 'Leslie and I and the children. Sell up. Look, this line of his, the damned dumb waiter for pets – he's in competition with all kinds of big organisations. You can imagine. Poor dear, he works himself thin, but it's all very near the dead-loss area. Then interest rates, mortgage, some trouble over patent for the invention. He's talking about a job in London. You're tied here. Your wife and daughters, the club and so on.'

'But Leslie created that thing, surely. Those bastards in offices. Men with gold-nibbed pens.'

She laughed for a moment.

'Yes, crazy to hear me defending him, I suppose,' Ember said.

'It's serious trouble, Ralph. I don't know if you can remember money problems, owning Low Pastures and so on. It's so degrading.'

'To London? I thought it was hit worst of all by recession.'

'He knows someone with a hi-tech factory.'

'That's here today and gone tomorrow stuff. Competing with the bloody Japs.'

He found it devastating to think she might go. In due course she might have the dormobile waiting for someone else at Brent Cross or Lewisham. Or, if Leslie was doing regular hours and home every evening, she would settle into a satisfied life. That prospect hurt him more still.

'Property's cheap in London now,' she said.

'And cheaper here. You'll take a loss. And to throw away all the work he's done on pets' behalf.'

'I suppose so. It's miserable,' she replied. 'I've got money of my own – something Leslie doesn't know about. A great-uncle's will. But it wouldn't come near even our immediate needs.'

'What would?'

'Oh, thousands, I think. Impossible. At least thousands.' She was almost in tears, staring up at the dormobile ceiling. 'Ralph, I don't want to go. Apparently, we've got arrears, and he can't finance his travel and accommodation any longer. If he can't travel he can't sell, not even as much as now. And lawyers for this patent dispute.'

'Don't talk to me about lawyers.'

'If we're going to fight. If we *were* going to fight.'

Ember said: 'I can see to this.'

'What?'

'Stop-gap.' Thank God, thank God, he hadn't told Courtney to kill the raid.

She turned on the bed and stared at him.

'A loan,' he told her. 'No difficulty.'

'Ralph, you can't, you mustn't.'

'I can't lose you. I'd fall to bits.'

She kissed his forehead. 'It wouldn't be a loan. You know that. It would be swallowed up and gone. I'm never going to be able to replace it, am I?'

'It's not important.' It would be chicken feed if the information about this cash load was right and the job worked.

'It's important to me. I can't – we can't, Leslie and I – allow ourselves to be financed by you, Ralph.'

'I said a loan. He wouldn't know, obviously.'

'Yes, but—'

'Tell Leslie it's a loan from you to him, from your legacy. You want it back, eventually – when the business is OK. That's a perfectly conventional financing deal. One's involved in that sort of thing in business all the time. London's a shit heap, crawling with foreigners and druggies. You can't go there.'

'You sound really jealous and, well, possessive. It's beautiful. I'd so grieve to lose you.'

'We've got to have faith in Leslie's work, Christine. He deserves that. We depend on him.' He would have to get hold of Webby again, urgently, and try to drag him on to the bright side about the project – persuade him away from mania over Denise. As Courtney said, Doug Webb was an out-and-out blot but he did know how to

147

pull his weight on a project, and he did have this photographic eye. Scarcity value. 'A couple of weeks, Christine,' he said. 'Just to realise a few assets. It can be quicker if you like.' Of course, he had a cash escape-and-emergency fund in boxes around Low Pastures and the Monty, money it would be tactless to put through a bank account, anyway, except in dribs and drabs. He felt suspicious about touching that, though, as if inviting crisis. Always, you had to keep an exit open.

'Ralph, this wasn't even remotely in my mind when I told you – you know that?'

'Of course, darling.'

'You're a saint.'

'I need you. How else?'

She bent over and kissed him on the mouth. In a while she said: 'Actually, I don't think you need anyone, not your wife, not me. Ralph Ember's on his own.'

'Wrong.'

'But it's so deep of you to say so.'

Chapter Sixteen

Harpur drove down in a different old car from the pool and had another look at Towler's place by night, to check if Tone had come back. This time, he went even more gingerly. Towler might be here and, if not Towler, Iles and the girl reporter reconsummating their tangled rapport. The house was empty, though, and apparently unchanged inside. Entering now lacked the gorgeous thrill of dissection he savoured last time. It had become just a break-in. His den had told him all it was going to about Towler.

Occasionally, he risked the flashlight, masking it with his fingers, and saw the three bills were as he had left them, with a couple of pieces of junk mail on top. Upstairs, the chair still stood against the wardrobe and Towler's shirt was where it had been flung back on the bed by the ACC. The small, professional hole Iles had made in a rear window remained unrepaired. RIP, was what this house said.

From the directory, Harpur had Towler's father's number and rang it now, sitting on the floor in the jumbled living-room. A precise, combative but weary male voice answered, the voice of a schoolmaster and amateur genealogist. Harpur did what he could with his own voice. 'Mr Towler? This is Courtney Sanquhar-Perry. You remember me – at Tony's? Scottish connections?'

'Why, of course. Nice of you to ring. How are you? And how is Tony? Is he there?'

So Tone was not in Devon. Harpur would have liked to cut the call. But he went on: 'No, I'm ringing from my home and Tony's not with me at the moment. We're both fine. He tells me you're investigating my family tree. Most kind.'

'An historian's obsession.'

'I wanted to thank you and say how much I look forward to the result.' Soon afterwards, Harpur ended the conversation and a few minutes later Towler's telephone rang. Harpur ignored it and left. This would be father wanting to tell Tony of Sanquhar-Perry's graciousness. It was why Harpur had used Towler's telephone – confirmation: Tone was expected to be here.

Harpur saw he ought to mount surveillance on Sanquhar-Perry, which would be tough. Old hands like Courtney knew the head-quarters faces, including, and especially, Harpur's. Even Erogynous Jones, a tailing genius, would find it hard with Courtney. He and lads like him were aware they had given up all rights to privacy and that off and on or oftener they would be watched. They stayed awake. Harpur had to choose between using people who were good, experienced and recognisable, and people whose faces were new, and who were gumshoe babes. He would think about it. That discreet trip without his car made by Panicking Ralph, which the tart Elvira reported to Garland, possibly began to mean more now. The taxi man had said Ember went to the Ernest Bevin. Courtney still lived there. Was a team job being put together? Who else? It might be an idea to put an eye on Ralphy, too, though the difficulties would be similar.

Soon after Harpur arrived at headquarters next morning, the Chief sent for him. Harpur went up and found Iles and the woman reporter, Wendy Sellick, already with Lane, plus Bob Tarr, the press officer. Looking persecuted and anti-suave, in some of his car-boot sale clothes, the Chief said, with brave buoyancy: 'Colin, Bob thought, and I've come to agree with him – in this specific instance – that it might be reasonable for me to see *Searchlight*' – he smiled and waved an arm in apology – 'I mean Wendy Sellick, personally, rather than expect her to deal only through the press office. There are times when a direct contact is appropriate. And, of course, that includes direct contact with my senior people. The ACC agrees.'

'Certainly,' Iles remarked. 'I believe wholly in trust between the media and ourselves.' Wearing an old-style ducal grey pin-striped suit, the ACC was seated on the arm of a leather easy chair, feet in gleaming black slip-ons crossed neatly before him. In the Chief's room, Iles hardly ever sat properly on a chair, probably hating Lane's scope to offer luxury.

'But I gather, Colin, that you and Desmond have already met Wendy.'

'A few words in the carpark, sir, and then a conversation at the Monty club,' Harpur replied. 'That's the lot.'

'Yes,' Iles remarked. 'Brief, though pleasant, in each case.'

'This is what I mean, you see, Colin,' the Chief went on. 'Scram-bled exchanges with senior men, or formal, sanitised statements from the press office – unsatisfactory either way. We are dealing with a major paper and a writer of repute. Things should be tackled prop-erly. That's how Bob sees it. I'm in his hands.'

'Everything's off the record,' Tarr replied. 'Guidance only.'

'I see no harm, sir,' Harpur said. He took a seat opposite Wendy Sellick, who had on a formal olive-green cotton suit today. Her face, which Harpur had thought of previously as cheerful and frank, looked more hostile now, ferociously sceptical: ready to deal with four heavies, even though she had been in bed with one of them.

Delightedly, Iles clapped his hands twice. 'Good, Harpur. What I said, sir?' he asked Lane, genially. 'Openness is one of Colin's bywords. I forget the other.'

'Openness subject to operational requirements,' the Chief replied.

Iles smiled and nodded. 'Thank you, sir. Always the Chief can put his finger on the crux, Wendy. Well, if I may say so, how people become Chiefs – fingering cruxes.' He leaned forward to look better at a framed picture of Lane's wife on the desk, then hurriedly turned away, as though having accidentally discovered the Chief in some foul act.

'Towler,' Lane announced. 'Colin, Wendy is still concerned to find one Anthony Towler of our parish. She's raised this with you already.'

'We couldn't understand her interest, sir, but, yes, he was mentioned,' Iles replied.

'She believes Towler might be concerned with informing,' Lane continued.

'We've still no grounds to declare the man missing, sir,' Harpur said.

'And does he inform?' Lane asked.

Iles said: 'I explained to Wendy, sir, that, in accord with your wishes – wise and progressive wishes, all agree – we have no truck with informers, whatever other Forces do.'

'Does he inform, Colin?' Lane asked.

Harpur said: 'We do like to operate without that kind of help.'

'Help!' Iles remarked. 'More trouble than it's worth, sir. Which is, I think, your own view. Witness the recurrent agonies of the Met.'

Wendy Sellick said: 'A newsboy can't just drop out of sight like this. Or, if he does, it signifies trouble.'

'Newsboy,' the Chief murmured, wonderingly. 'That's jargon, I gather. Apparently, Wendy is an expert in this kind of situation.'

'Which kind might that be, sir?' Iles asked.

'Grey areas?' the Chief replied. 'Contact on an informal basis with criminals?'

'Grassing,' Sellick said. '*Quid pro quo* commerce.'

Iles replied: '*Quid pro quo*. Yes, I've seen that phrase applied to police work, but elsewhere, very elsewhere. I suppose we could run

151

a quiet, unofficial inquiry or two on Towler, Col? As the Chief says, if Wendy's concerned it won't be trivial grounds.'

'Got an address for him?' Harpur asked.

'You mean you haven't?' Sellick replied.

'Why would I?'

She stared at Harpur for a second. 'Diamond Street.'

'I adore those precious-stone names, don't you, sir?' Iles remarked. 'Often for the least advantaged housing. Our city fathers' forefathers loved a sharp joke. Mind you, Castro Close isn't bad. This would he off Corporation Street, Wendy, near the new estate?'

'We could certainly ask around neighbours,' Harpur said.

'Obviously, you've been to the house, Wendy,' the Chief said. 'How does it look?'

'All right – as far as one can tell from outside. Dark at night.'

'Yes, we should get an inspection done, Colin,' Lane went on. 'Search for possible breakages. Vandalism.'

'Yes, sir.'

'And he might be travelling for his work,' Lane said. 'Do we know what he does? Or visiting relatives. Have we anything on that?'

'Now that's a hell of a point, sir,' Iles replied. He did what he often did, and made a slow, reverential performance out of pulling a silver pencil and notebook from his pocket and writing a reminder, then underlining it several times. Harpur could read 'Anthony Towler's granny?'

'I'll try to discover if he has any family,' Harpur told Lane.

'We like to help, you see, Wendy,' the Chief said. 'To you he seems important because — ?'

'Frankly, because he might be the way into the whole grassing structure here, which is what interests the paper and me.'

'We'll help look for him, but it won't turn out to be anything like that, rest assured,' Lane said.

'Hardly,' Iles remarked. 'No informers, but at the same time, Wendy mustn't think we're half-hearted about beating crime, sort of culpably neutral.'

'Simply, we are absolutely aware of which side we are on,' the Chief remarked. 'My God, anything but neutral!'

Iles grew reflective: control through drooling, a technique he excelled in. 'Neutral: sometimes a good word, sometimes *odious*. I see the film *Casablanca* as a brilliant onslaught on neutrality, don't you, Chief?'

Lane gave a small groan and for a second clutched at his throat, as if feeling stifled.

The ACC proceeded: 'Remember that contemptuous line to the

piano player by Bogart when his club's been crawling with Nazis: "If it's December 1941 in Casablanca, what time is it in New York? They're asleep all over America." This is just days before Pearl Harbor pitched the dreamy buggers into war. Yes, December the second. As you know, sir, we glimpse that date on the cash chitty Bogart signs, before he even appears. Pearl Harbor – the seventh. The film wasn't made till 1942, naturally: typical fucking Hollywood hindsight.'

With sympathy, Harpur watched the Chief trying to see past or through this Iles miasma. As almost ever, Lane would be striving to sort out what spoken by the ACC, and by Harpur himself, was relevant truth, what half truth, what a tenth truth and what pure net curtains. Mark Lane had been in this job long enough now not to be a total outsider, which meant just long enough to know he had not been there long enough to be generally considered to have been there long enough. As a Catholic, he might never be. Iles, and most of those Iles believed in and advanced, were Freemasons. Thus, the standard, great police gulf, in lights. Perhaps the powers had put Lane in over Iles hoping for balance. One day it might work. Harpur, in neither camp, hoped so. Lane did try.

But, in any case, even without the ideology, Lane used a different style from Iles and Harpur's, or attempted to. The Chief possessed grand, foursquare qualities and not all that long ago was a fine detective on the neighbouring patch. Harpur had worked with him then on inter-Force cases and found Lane brilliantly ruthless. Office gutted people, perfumed them, coshed and bureaucratised any bottle they had, and put them fatally out of touch with the living, winning evil. At Lane's rank some backslid so far they talked seriously, and even off public platforms, of policing by consent.

'Grassing *structure*, you say, Wendy,' the Chief remarked, yearning for a straight narrative. 'This really is very big talk.' Lane rose from his desk and paced awkwardly to the main window, as he frequently did when agitated. Iles said once he could have been doing the sum-up for 'flatfoot' in charades. Lane would gaze out across the yard, as though longing to be somewhere else: say, seconded to the Falklands. 'Wendy, I almost think you came here with your mind already made up, your article written.'

'Wish it were,' she said. 'I've got two names and that's about it. One of them you say you've never heard of, and, anyway, he disappears as soon as I talk about him – Towler. And then there's Jack Lamb.'

The Chief was obviously startled, and thank Christ. 'Do you mean Jack Lamb of Darien? The international art dealer?' Lane replied.

'How on earth would he be involved? You really must be careful what you're alleging, Wendy, even in privileged conditions like these.'

'Towler fed Lamb,' she told him. 'Grass's grass.'

'Grass is grass?' Lane said. 'What does that mean?'

'No, not quite like Gertrude Stein's *a rose is a rose is a rose*, sir,' Iles replied, smiling very benevolently. 'The grass *to* a grass. More "in" language, I'm afraid.'

The Chief said: 'Jack Lamb? An established informant? Is this absurd, Col?'

'Absurd, sir,' Harpur replied. 'As I understand it, he's in a position to entertain the Lord Lieutenant at his annual summer gathering.'

'So?' Sellick asked. She turned again to look straight at Harpur. 'Does he grass to you? An implied contract? Does his business depend on judicious blind-eyeing from you and yours? Neutral? No, I wouldn't ever call it that.'

'Lamb?' Harpur replied. 'Absurd.'

'Did he, for instance, tip you on the Link Street raid, so you were there to pull the trigger? Towler to Lamb to you?'

Harpur thought he had kept his face rigid but, still staring at him, Wendy Sellick seemed to soften for a moment, as if sensing she had done a bad injury. Harpur was surprised how bad. He thought he had been getting over Martin. Hurriedly, she went on: 'Look, I shouldn't say that. I've no information that you did, and even if you did, I don't know the circumstances. It could have been unavoidable. I accept that police work isn't all like Hendon training school. But it's the foreknowledge we're concerned about. Not just this job. How the grassing system works.'

'System, structure – it's all absurd,' Lane replied.

'You've pre-agreed "absurd" as a brick-wall reply?' she asked. 'My information is Lamb might talk to you, Harpur, directly, or via a girl I still haven't been able to identify. I'm slipping.'

'Information from where, Wendy?' Lane asked.

She pretended not to hear. Harpur was embarrassed: Jesus, had the Chief forgotten everything? Did he expect this woman to expose sources?

'Well, these supposed means of communication: I do see what you mean about a structure, even a system,' Lane said, 'that is, if it were all true. But this really is absur– nonsense. These are immensely grave imputations. What girl? Colin, are you in touch with any such girl?'

Iles declared: 'That kind of connection could scarcely be kept secret, I think, sir.'

154

Sellick brought a sheet of paper from her handbag and read from it, slowly. 'Two distinguished paintings, for instance: a Kees van Dongen nude, *Céleste*, and a Bronzino, *Portrait de Bertrand*. Both sold by Lamb within the last three years, we believe, prices unknown but massive, and both certainly stolen in the mid-1980s. I can give you all the details of where from, if you like. Yet, as I understand it, no inquiries. This kind of protected deal is said to be typical. Endemic.'

Iles chuckled for a time. He turned to the Chief: 'Of course, you'll know Kees van Dongen, sir – real names Cornelis T.M. but referred to in that way, as Ralphy Ember's called Panicking. Kees – one of the more genuine people to finish his life in Monaco and a demon for pudenda studies. For example, *Anita*? Correct me if I'm wrong, sir. Look, a bevy of provisos in what you say, Wendy. "We believe." "As I understand it." "Said to be." Journalistically, these are perfectly valid, well, "terms", as you put it. Meat and drink to reporting. They won't do for Colin, however. They won't do for any of us, and certainly not for our scrupulous Chief. I mean, "said to be" by whom? By you? We move in self-proving circles? Believe me, we all admire your tenacity and flair. Again, I'm sure I speak for the Chief in this. But I'm afraid we're not with you, not at all.'

'Do we know anything of these works, Colin?' Lane asked. His body looked unbearably tense, giving cruel strain to the weary, man-made fibre of his cardigan. He wore a 1967-type red and gold striped tie, open-toed sandals and possibly Army-surplus khaki socks, plus the beige cardigan, bearing up. Lane abhorred smartness. He abhorred the Army, even if he bought its surplus. Especially he abhorred the proposal that top police posts should be filled by retired senior Services officers, and he dressed to proclaim resistance. Iles had put around a tale that Lane owned a lot of gear after going undercover for at least three years as a wino and was too thrifty to waste it.

'I know nothing of those paintings, sir,' Harpur replied. That much was accurate, dismally accurate.

'As a matter of fact, I really feel we are not getting very far,' Iles remarked. 'Disappointing. Unnamed messenger girls around Col! Supposed filched art! An absconding "newsboy"! Fantasy?'

Lane said: 'Regrettably, I'm inclined to agree with the ACC. We'll probably find this Towler back at home tomorrow, after a few nights out in London's West End.'

'More than likely, sir,' Iles remarked.

'But I'd still like you to have someone take a look at the house, Col,' the Chief said. He edged back to his desk.

'We're more than keen to co-operate, you see, Wendy – if there is anything substantial to go on,' Iles remarked.

Bob Tarr stood up to make a formal declaration: 'Please remember all that's been disclosed today is entirely off the record, Miss Sellick.'

'Mrs,' she snarled, the teeth pushy. 'All what, for Christ's sake? Except by me.'

Iles went down in the lift with Harpur. 'She looks even more desirable when venomous, doesn't she, sir?' Harpur said.

'Who?'

'Sellick.'

'Oh, you find that attractive? Seen the legs?'

'Burlyish. Yes, but—'

'Who's the grass go-between girl she mentions, then, Harpur? This isn't connected with your teenage dipping, is it?'

'And I thought the more formal clothes did something for her. That unreachable, married woman allure.'

'Sellick as Madame Bovary?'

'She'd strip well, possibly.'

'A cop-hater,' Iles replied. 'Routine trite Press mind. I think Lane was taken, though. Is he likely to notice triteness? Be the making of him to swing his holy dick a bit.'

Chapter Seventeen

Ember said: 'The hit's going to be fine, Doug. Lamb's swallowed the tip – the second voice. This I've had hard from sources. If Lamb swallows it, Harpur will. Most probably Lamb never gave a dud all these years. We've got our decoy, just like Courtney said. Judgement, that boy. Look, I could see you had big doubts. All right, me too. But this changes it. We've got an operation, Doug, and a princely one.' He worked a juicy quota of passion in. Then he went back to quiet, respectful argument: 'All I'd say to you – say again, really – is forget about the messenger girl until afterwards. Tactical delay only. Yes, a sacrifice for you. I know about family and culture pressures. They matter. But again, like Courtney says, just a postponement.'

'It's a beautiful surprise to be discussing with you here, Ralphy. A privilege. Your call – well, out of the blue. I know you never talk trade in the Monty. Quite a club. Mahogany? Brass handles. Pictures. In frames.'

Ember glanced around, but nothing arrogant. 'Myself I see as custodian. You're the kind to appreciate things. And you're right, I think twice before asking work colleagues here. In rare cases, OK.'

'Thanks, Ralph.'

'And an emergency, needing to move fast to brief you. You seemed a bit down last time. This information – very recent.'

'Have you told Courtney?'

Ember leaned forward across their table. 'It's between you and me, Doug. At this stage. We're not cutting Courtney out, not in any way. Would I – the heart and soul of this project? The thing is, Courtney's never had doubts. He thought all along the new man would do the trick. I'd be ashamed now to show I worried. He'd see weakness? We've got to believe in one another, Doug. That's a team.'

'Yes.'

'For Courtney, this job has been proceeding, no problems at all – except when Tony Towler went absent without leave, of course.'

'A blow. A puzzle.'

'So, right. But it's been corrected, and now we don't do anything more to shake Courtney. He's leading, organising, providing firepower. He must keep his confidence.'

Ember watched Webb get behind the bumper brandy glass and sip. 'So, the decoy's as we hoped, Ralph. I won't ask you where this good information comes from.'

'I knew you wouldn't, Doug. Confidentiality.'

Christ, it hurt, bringing something rock-bottom like Webby into the club, feeding him the Kressmann Armagnac. The thing was, though, he knew Doug might need some softening up, and an invitation here would flatter. Ember could see the gratitude in that sad cow's-arse face. The Monty ambience, the Kressmann, the decently behaved members tonight, would make what Ember told him seem possible. And Margaret would be civil if she looked in. She could put on a friendly show.

'I'll be there, Ralph.'

'A fine old share-out session. I can feel the healthiness of it already, the way new fifties and twenties lie so sweetly flat, like true Bass in a glass.'

'Figures?'

'Just very, very heavy.'

'Meaning?'

'Meaning a lot of noughts on the end of a nice fat starting digit.'

'Excuse me, you saying hundreds of grand, Ralph? I only ask because I know you like being numerate.'

'I'm saying enough notes to give us carriage problems. But we'll cope, don't worry!' He let go a big laugh.

So, no figures, just sales flam. Webb had heard more facts from double-glaze reps. Ralphy opens the doors of the sacred Monty with its brilliant bits of old wood and thinks this will do every trick he wants to pull. Low Pastures is still off limits, though. Holy of holies. That's the kind of partner he was – curtaining you from his house and loved ones like you'd buzz about spreading malaria.

Anyway, why Ember's big switch – all at once, the sureness about this job? Why the extra extra pressure to leave that kid girl alone? Now and then he wondered about Ralphy Ember. Well, now and then he wondered about everyone – that was life – but he wondered more about Ralphy. Now and then everyone wondered about Ralphy Ember, but he wondered about him more than everyone else wondered. It was a thing with Webb – when he wondered he wondered and stayed with it. He did not claim mighty thought-power or a mention in *Burke's Peerage* but staying with it nobody beat him at.

Watching that girl, Denise Prior, and trying to work out her habits and pick what could be a likely location for the act, he had followed her a couple of times to the university. She seemed to idle there, the way students did in summer. It angered him. If Martin had been all right upstairs he might have gone to this sort of life, sitting around like the world was longing for them to come out and take whatever they wanted. Martin had tried to take the little bit he and the other boys wanted, and loses a chest.

He heard some students talk and gathered a lot were dawdling until exam results came out. Once, he had seen Ember down there, too, trying to look intelligent and young, idling the same gifted way. As far as Webb could make out, Ralphy never spoke to the girl, and might not know her, but could you be sure? He would be crafty enough to make no display, even here.

Ember had sprung up nearly as high as Lamb. Low Pastures was not in the Darien league, maybe, but nearly: definitely niftier than Courtney's place, and Webb's own – either of his own. So, did Ember have some intimate talks with police now and then? He collected special treatment, like Lamb? Christ, Ember was chipboard throughout, not mahogany, and famed in the whole uncivilised world as Panicking Ralph, yet he always finished so nicely, stuffed with cash and undamaged except for one old scar along his jaw, which some reckoned he'd got tripping over his Valium, anyway. Did Harpur look after him? Naturally, that would give Ember a duty to shield Harpur's girl.

The questions hounded Webb. Ember did his talking to Harpur via the girl? And Ember would go on this raid and somehow it would be arranged that he survived and got clear? His assignment might be to make sure it took place, make sure the sitting ducks sat. This would explain the sudden Monty gush treatment, the special bottle and smart label, the big promises. There was a time when Webb thought Ralphy and Sanquhar-Perry had a little sealed off understanding together. Now he wondered whether Ember was on his own – on his own except for this girl and Harpur, and behind Harpur, the sweet, garrotting eminence, ACC Iles.

'Yes, I can shelve the girl, I expect, Ralph. Marty can wait a few more days.' If they devoted themselves to you and warmed your gut with a top-quality import you said what they wanted to hear. It did not cost or mean anything.

'This makes sense, and I knew you'd see it, Doug.'

Ember went from their table in the corner to the bar to pour two more bulging Armagnacs. Webb took a slow look around. Jesus, this rancid club. Sometimes you could get a whiff of it off Ralphy's clothes and hair, even outside. He was supposed to look like Charlton Heston but smelled like an underpass. Webb would give his own suit a blow-through on the line as soon as he got home and have a shampoo. He did not recognise everyone in tonight but most of those he did had small-stuff records. Put all the Monty's grievous bodily harm lads end to end and they'd reach Wormwood Scrubs. Slabs of the antique woodwork had very up-to-date scars on it, where bodies were flung about in the club lately and someone's skull or teeth or boobs had made contact during a little difference.

Ember came back. 'How's the university, Ralph?'

'I get first-year results tomorrow. I can specialise from then on. Politics, I fancy.'

'These courses give you another dimension,' Webb said. 'How to talk – "princely" about a job. Who'd come out with that? You've got a store. I love education.' When they had their results these kids would disappear. The girl would go to Lamb's ball, probably, and afterwards home to wherever it was. Finding her and reaching her would be hellish then. People like Ember and Courtney did not think of detail when they said wait. All they cared about was their job, and getting him there to help and stop any spare bullets – plus needing to keep Harpur and the rest quiet until it was over. But when you were settling up you had to move when you could, the same as with Tony.

Would it put Ember in bad with Harpur if the girl got it? Tragic. Webb must try to find out whether Ralphy really was talking to Harpur, through the girl or otherwise. If he was, Webb would skip the cash raid, obviously, because Harpur would know not just that Stipend Street was wrong, but where was right. And who was going to volunteer into a sodding blue-beret ambush? Not D. Webb. They had very high-yield marksmen, like Sergeant Robert Cotton, whose big wife Harpur used to take comfort from. So, then, doubts about the project, none at all about dealing with the fink girl. No, he could not wait. Martin could not wait.

Webb chuckled and said: 'Harpur will be up to his eyes trying to solve this raid and then, wham, his bird gets it, so he won't know what to do first. Confusion. Yes, a little pause could be a sound idea. You're sharp, Ralph. Look, I'm not gross or savage, but now and then I get visions of that girl's body, torn all ways, like Martin. It keeps me well.'

Webb watched Ember's face go that humble shape again. 'Education can't change your real self, Doug. It tells you how to use knowledge and your mind for the best, that's all. You're in touch with great thought – through books, even some of the teachers. Yet I remain Ralph Ember, the one you've known from way, way back.'

What scared Webb shitless.

When he reached home just after midnight, he found a sealed envelope on the mantelpiece addressed in Kay's handwriting with his initials. He opened it.

Dear Doug,

I'm really sorry to say I have to leave you. But perhaps you have seen this coming for a while, that is, my awakening interest in Geoffrey, since the funeral and developing into wholehearted love on both sides. That makes it sound only recent, but I believe I had feelings for him even before that, from when I attended occasional services and he preached on many great topics, Redemption, for example. He is a good man, Doug, despite what is happening. I hope you can believe this, although I know it is a lot to ask. You have your other commitments, of course, and I have never really accepted that split of loyalties, as you know.

We have gone away, a great distance. Please do not try to find us. We hope to begin an entirely new life, and Geoffrey will try to find work outside the church. It is possible I am pregnant by him. I have to tell you that I hope so. I want a dear little girl. Nevertheless, in due course we might like Rodney to come and live with us, now he has a religious outlook. In a spirit of charity, Geoffrey has agreed to this. Don't be offended, but I think it is unsuitable where Rodney is now. However, we will have to wait and see what accommodation we find.

Goodbye, Doug. Take care. Please try to explain my decision in the best way possible to the boys, though this will be very hard for you, I appreciate.

Best wishes,
Kay

He moved a take-away Mexican meal carton out of his chair, sat down, folded over on himself and began to weep. Christ, yes, his nose was against his lapel and the smell of Ralphy's fucking club had spread all through the jacket, drowning even the afterglow of that old supper. He struggled out of the jacket, still crying, and threw it to the other side of the room, wallet, French letters and toothpicks scattering from his pockets. He tried to weep silently. The boys would be asleep upstairs and he did not want them down here now, and particularly not Rodney, heavy with the New Testament, and caring, and comforting the bereaved. Kay, Kay, how could you do it? 'Best wishes'. It was like something from a second cousin. Pregnant? At her age? But at her age she had had to stop the pill. What did she mean – she *thought* she might be pregnant or she knew she was but could not tell who by? So, a daughter. He would not have minded that. Why did she think it was that robed sod's and not his? Hadn't she been wearing her thing? Love with Geoffrey was too fierce and passionate, too pure and full of the future?

He could feel tears soaking through his shirt to his chest. Geoffrey? She called him Geoffrey as if he had been around her whole life, talking his bloody archaeology and Shakespeare and meditation and all the time thinking how long before he could get it in again. It was the sort of name vicars did have, Geoffrey, and you could not turn it into Geoff, unless they were one of those call-me-common, factory-gate vicars. A long time ago she used to adore oral, and it gave him agony to think of that smirking, pulpy, pulpit face rolling its lucky eyes until only the whites showed, and murmuring to egg her on when she was down on him, like prayer. It's better to give than to receive, he'd say, giving it to her.

One of your women go off with the Church: that would start real merriment all round. It deeply bruised the family, deeply bruised this household. Courtney Sanquhar-Perry would be so quick with sympathy, of course, and giggling himself speechless under those curls in private, or in bed with his bird, the two of them shaking. What he would think was, Webby could not handle anything that had a whisker of class to it, not even a wife.

Well, it did not matter what any of the buggers thought, and definitely not someone on the Ernest Bevin with lumpy-cheeked Scotch relatives. But he wanted Kay. There was nobody like Kay. Louise, in Preston, was nice, but not the same. Kay had fortitude and true beauty. She could look through things to what they were really about. Everyone who saw Kay could tell she was beyond unusual. Damn it, that's what got to the loving Rev, of course. Saying his piece at the funeral, he saw quality in black across the box. Webb had to bring her back. He wiped his eyes and face and looked at the letter again, trying to work out from it when exactly she had gone. It could not be very long, or the boys might have seen something and would have stayed up to meet him. He put on the jacket again and hurried out, making for the vicarage. Possibly they had a rendezvous near there. She would not bring that bastard to the house, surely. Not Kay. If he found them he would be reasonable. Who beat up vicars, except the bent ones with each other?

A woman was coming up the steps from the street. 'Mr Webb?' she said. 'Sorry to be so late. I called before.'

'What is it? Wanting help? You the vicar's wife?'

'Vicar? Wendy Sellick. I'm a journalist. I wish to say how sorry I was about Martin.'

'Yes, but what do you want?'

'The whole picture, Mr Webb.'

'What picture?'

'Police methods.'

'They shot a kid. I've got to go.'

'Why were they there?'

He ran to his Fiat and drove to the church but saw nothing of Kay, or Kay's car or Geoffrey. The vicarage was dark. For a couple of moments he thought of rousing the house and actually left his car and went in through the front garden gate. But it would not be right to hammer a vicar's door like police heavies in the middle of the night, especially not with rough news, if his wife did not know. Perhaps he had told her he was on a retreat or akin. *Your holy husband's a tearaway shag.* There were proper ways of behaving towards a woman in a vicarage so late, even in a crisis, and even when the vicarage was this vicarage and the vicar this vicar.

He went back to his car and found the journalist had followed him and was waiting. 'You still can't get the funeral out of your mind?' she said. 'You have to keep coming back to the church. Reliving the pain. God, this is heartbreaking.'

'I'll get over it in time.'

Despite the darkness he could see she had a very friendly, cheerful face, all kindness now. Be careful with these people. They switched on what they liked. They went on courses.

She said: 'Can I talk to you – informers, newsboys, the whole system? It's made you suffer, Douglas. Is still making you suffer. I want to help you. My paper wants to help you. And, if I could put it this way, we wish, in a sense, to help Martin and the other Martins – make sure there are no more unnecessary and cop-convenient deaths. Open the curtains around their deals. I need to know how it all works, and, of course, the police will say nothing. Between us, we could blow this apart. You'd be doing a public service.'

'Look, I have to—'

'There are people who tell the police and people who tell the people who tell the police. One of them's just dropped off the face of the earth. Another's a girl.'

163

'Kid, I've got other things to think about.'

'The scar of the death, the funeral. Yes, I see that. But – well, there's a newsboy called Anthony Towler. He was at the funeral. I saw him, perfectly all right then. I must find him. But utterly gone.'

'Tony gone? How do you mean, gone? He's a lovely lad.'

'I talk about him to top police, and straight afterwards he's missing.'

'Ah. It can happen here. You had any contact with one called Iles?'

'And there's a girl.'

'Which girl?'

'This is a go-between.'

'Who says that?'

'The local correspondent tells me it's a rumour among low-rank police.'

'Rumours. They come and go. I can't help you,' he said. 'Just a victim. Or victims – my family. We get used to it here. I must go. I'll sleep now – now I've been to the church again. Oh, listen, you're not writing this down?'

'It's moving, Mr Webb, unbelievably moving, these sad, irresistible visits, revisits. Grim therapies. It gives the story such feeling. And your wife, Kay – does she have to haunt the church, too? You said the family.'

He drove home. The reporter's car did not seem to follow. He took his suit off, discarded the damp shirt, then went into the back yard in his underpants and hung the jacket and trousers on the rotary. In the kitchen he thoroughly washed his hair. He lay on the bed thinking about Kay and the way her face had glowed when she was in discussion with gorgeous Geoffrey, even on the day her son was burned. Then he thought again for a time about the girl who had helped cause it all, and knew what he already knew: that she had to go. Briefly, that journalist and what she was discovering or suspected had seriously troubled him, turned him fearful that, if she dug around, everything would get into the open and make his move impossible. He had badly wavered then. But it had been smart to play dumb with her. Courtney and Ember considered him ignorant but he was not so ignorant that he could not spot it was better to seem ignorant sometimes. The Press would have printed her article and there in black and white would be a motive for seeing the messenger girl dead. Anyway, nobody ever talked to journalists, nobody wanting to stay free and undislocated.

Kay's desertion made it even more unavoidable to attend to the girl. Of course it did. It was not just that he blamed her and Lamb and Harpur for the loss of a superb woman, but now he felt that there was so little left of him. Squaring it with that girl would be self-expression. A necessity. He was alone and lonely in bed, in a soiled dump of a house, with one boy dead, another gone Biblical, and the other not pulling his weight at all yet. Some twinkle-voiced clergyman could talk his best woman away from him, give her things he hadn't got and would never know how to get. He wasn't going into any hairy black robe and tasselled hat. All he had left was to tend this family, patch it up if he could, and look after the memory of Martin in the only way he could look after it. These things were the guts of life, the centre, not like just skipping off by night for nationwide coitus. If he failed, he was nothing, an emptiness, something that used to be Doug Webb, husband of Kay, and so on. What he had told the reporter – a victim. You did not let that happen.

Towards dawn there was sudden loud yelling that went on and on, and Webb awoke terrified and incapable of movement. He thought first of Iles, then of Harpur, then of Iles again, then of Sergeant Robert Cotton, then of the woman journalist, all or any of them breaking in to get at him, and turn him into a victim. It was only Rodney, crying in his sleep. After a couple of minutes, Webb could get the words: 'Let down your nets on the other side. Let down your nets on the other side. I say unto you, fish swim on the left.' Webb heard Bernard get up eventually, shuffle to Rodney's bedroom in bare feet and murmur something soothing and patient, and the house went back to complete silence. Webb hated that – no small warm sound of breathing from Kay alongside him. He would forgive her if she came back, forgive her even for making Martin with only half a brain. Because of Rodney, Webb climbed out of bed a few minutes later, went downstairs and gathered up the possessions that had fallen from his jacket. Condoms all over the place like that would jar on the boy.

Chapter Eighteen

Ember was at the university early in the morning for his results and found he had done well. When he saw Big Vera, his professor, about the coming two years, he said immediately that he would do his dissertation on the decline of public standards of community support and how political parties in Britain were trying to deal with this.

'It's a real worry of yours, is it, Ralph? You'll do a good job, I know.' She was a nice double-helping, crumbling old thing, yet, once, life and sex must have been there.

'It should be everybody's worry,' he replied gravely. Then, suddenly, for a couple of seconds through her window, he glimpsed Doug Webb in the street, obviously obsessed by something or someone hidden from Ember.

'I'll write it on the card then, shall I?' Big Vera asked. 'Shall we say, "What happened to social responsibility?" '

Webb had disappeared. 'What?' Ember said. 'Oh, exactly.'

When he went down to Central Hall he saw Harpur's girl chortling and shouting and knew for certain what had interested Webby, if he had not known before. The sod said one thing and went on as he wanted, no real surprise. He would have to be coped with. Ember did not know the girl but in today's all-round excitement felt it would be fair enough to speak. 'How did things go?'

'OK,' she said. 'I passed.'

'Great. Me too. You'll be away home now?'

'Not quite yet.'

'Oh? I thought most out-of-town people had gone already – just came back for the results and so on today.'

'I've got a nice social thing locally in a couple of days.'

Friends drew her away into their group. Christ, why didn't she just vanish, get the protection of distance and family? Perhaps as long as she stayed with her chums, in a crowd, she would be reasonably safe. That was Webby's trouble: he did not know what reasonable meant.

Ember drove up to near the Ernest Bevin, then walked the last

166

mile to Courtney Sanquhar-Perry's place. Approaching quickly along a lane, he could see Courtney apparently at work in his garden. He had on shorts and a blue T-shirt and, as Ember came nearer, he could read 'Scotland the Brave' in gold lettering on the back. Sanquhar-Perry seemed to be re-arranging some of the debris and bits of machinery that lay about in the earth, maybe thinking of building one bicycle out of the three or four wrecks there. Ember opened the gate and joined him: 'Courtney, forgive my coming unannounced,' he said. Courtney's classy background was probably rubbish, like his garden, but Ember found it natural to give him a bit of *politesse*. 'Things are catastrophic. Webby's not going to do the raid.'

Courtney was holding the central piece of a lady's Raleigh and put it down carefully. Ember saw he wanted some time to take in the shock and stay composed. 'Zena's thinking of cycling as exercise,' he remarked. 'What the fuck are you talking about, Ralphy? What the hell are you doing here at all?'

'Don't worry. I'm not in the car.'

'If you were watched? If I'm watched.'

'We'd know, Courtney. Are we children? We can't believe anything Webby says. He'll leave us to fry alone. Get a replacement number three.'

'Now? A fortnight? You mad?'

'It's got to be. He can't see straight for vengeance.'

'Better call it off.'

Courtney was doing his instant, resolute act.

'No, save it,' Ember replied.

'The two of us can't handle this alone.'

'Why I want someone else, Courtney.'

'You didn't even believe in it. Anyone could see.'

'Yes, always. Would I have started?'

'Special needs all of a sudden? The piece in the dormobile costing?'

Courtney had grey matter. 'Find someone,' Ember replied. 'You've got great contacts. Famed for it.'

Zena came into the garden, a real improvement on the other: not just breasts, but friendliness, even delicacy. 'Have you met Ralph Ember of the Monty?'

'Heard so much,' she said.

He hated that, but she meant well, which the earlier one never did.

'Is this the place to be in discussion, Courtney?' she asked, passing her eyes with disdain over the crop of iron. 'We'd have this garden tidied, if we were staying, obviously, Ralph. It's been let go a little. We're expecting to leave, though.'

'I hate show-piece gardens,' Ember replied. 'This garden looks used. This garden is part of life.'

'Oh, the garden we had in my parents' home,' Courtney remarked. 'My word, yes!' He passed a hand lightly over his hair. 'Gardens, actually.'

'Sometimes, I do feel I'd like to look out on a mixed border,' Zena said. 'The tall ones at the back. That sort of thing.'

'Larkspur,' Courtney replied.

'Anything in that line,' Zena said. 'Are you fond of any special bloom, Ralph?'

'Spring's own flowers,' he replied. 'The newness. Primrose, bluebells. I go for the wild ones.'

She smiled and returned to the house.

'A lovely girl, Courtney,' Ember said.

'Keep your fucking hands off her. All that Charlton Heston drool,' he replied. 'Bluebells? Since when? She walks ten paces to the house and your eyes are on her arse every step. It's mine. This is a class person.'

'I show women respect, that's all. Look, just get someone, will you?' Ember stepped around a doorless fridge, preparing to leave by the lane.

Sanquhar-Perry said: '*Get someone. Get the weaponry. Get the information.* I'm carrying the whole thing? I'm the maid of all work? If Webby does this girl we're still in trouble, whether I find a third or not. Harpur and his people will go mad, everyone pulled in.'

'I'm thinking constructively about that.'

There was an around-the-pubs celebration in the afternoon and evening after results and Denise felt glad to be in a mob, even glad to be continually on the move from one bar to the next. The mob, though, dwindled towards evening as many people said goodbye until the next session and left to travel home. It troubled her. As Jack Lamb had said, the block where she stayed would be almost deserted.

Just after the lists went up this morning she was almost sure she caught sight briefly of the same hate-filled sad face that stared at her during the boy's funeral. She had wished Mandy was around to check with, but Mandy's results had come out a week earlier, and her flat opposite had been empty since then. There had been a rush of students towards the notice boards at the time, so her impressions were confused. She had been rushing herself, of course, eager to

168

spot her name. When she had a moment to look back to where the man had stood, just at the entrance to Central Hall, he was gone. After a few minutes she had walked to the door and gazed up and down the road, but could not see him.

Then a little later in the JCR there had been that strange encounter with the live-at-home mature student, the one who had a frightening scar along his jaw and looked a bit like Charlton Heston. There were wacky rumours about him: that he had run with gangs at one time, and that even now he might be into all sorts of shadiness. Apparently, he had a dubious club in Shield Terrace, a grim part of the city. Never before had he spoken to her, or even appeared aware of her. Yet today she had felt not just results comradeship but some sort of anxiety for her in his voice, a regret that she meant to stay. She would have liked to describe him to Colin and see whether he was known, but she was not seeing Colin today. Hadn't she already told him her results were good – in fact good enough for the non-existent Bell Prize? She had no special cause to make contact. In any case, if she had desribed this man, or either of them, to Colin he would have listened, stayed blank-faced, said nothing, or nothing to show he recognised them, in his impenetrable way.

Stephen Patterson, the post-graduate tutor who was taking Denise to Jack Lamb's party, had fixed on to her for the pub crawl. She could not object. She would have preferred to be somewhere private with Colin but he had said he was busy today, anyway. Something was on the move, though not something she could know about. It might get awkward with Stephen later. He would probably want to come back to the flat with her. Part of her would not have minded at all, but not the right part. The loneliness of the building did make her tense, and she knew she would feel worse there tonight after those two incidents. It might have been a comfort to know Stephen was in the flat – to know anyone was in the flat. He would not expect to be invited back simply as a companion, though.

Early in the evening, from one of the pubs, she rang her parents and then Helen to tell them the results. At Darien, Mrs Lamb answered and said Helen and Jack were in London at the opening exhibition of a new gallery. 'He loves going legit in between. Is it trouble, kid? Something caught up with you? I hear the background carnival sounds, but they might signify zilch.'

'I'm fine. I rang to say I passed my exams.'

'You sure?'

'My name's on the list, Alice.'

'You sure that's why you rang?'

'But what else, Alice?'

'People keep using my name, I always think something wrong here. To me you sound, is the word haunted? Probably not. I'm not much of a mot juster, but I've heard that tone before. It's something that happens to people in touch with Jack. There's plenty that's good about him, sure. Pain's in his wake?'

'I'll see you at the party then.'

'Don't ever let anyone tell you daughters are more fret than sons.'

By the end of the evening, Stephen had had plenty to drink and took some fending off. She managed it, though. This was not the 1960s, for God's sake, and she was not like her mother. You slept with the man you slept with, and that was it. Bad luck if he was married, but the rule held. She explained it all to Stephen, differently, though. 'We're not on a fuck basis,' she said. 'Close, but you know about fine points. Sorry.'

She went in past the porter's lodge. Although the light burned there, his glass-walled room was empty and locked. The porter looked after all the Jonson Court buildings and must be doing a patrol. She wished he had been there, found herself more nervous than before of the corridors, stairs and landings, and she would have liked to speak to someone sober, safe and reasonably old, whose job it was to look after her. Pathetic, really. She felt ashamed to realise she was thinking like a child.

In her flat on the third floor she locked the door and, before turning on the light, looked out of the window at the grounds and roadways of the flats complex. Beyond them, at one corner, she could make out a good stretch of the street, where a few people were still about, mostly in couples or groups. She saw nothing to bother her. It did bother her, though, that she could find only four or five rooms with lights burning in the whole of Jonson Court, and those in other blocks, some nearly a hundred yards off.

Closing the curtains, she switched on her light, took off her clothes and then, in a slow, stately way, brought out from the wardrobe the Katharine Hamnett evening dress she would wear at Darien. She wanted to make herself feel adult again, chic, and hummed a fanfare, to signal the glamour of the sequined moment. Putting on the shift, she fluffed out her hair and stood before the mirror. It was lovely. Her father had taste. To be immodest, her father also had a not-bad-looking daughter. She would take aboard some make-up for such a special do, naturally, and wear heels, not these dying desert boots. The bed-thwarted Stephen could be proud of her then.

Oh, God, she wished Colin could see her dressed up. Always student clobber, because they could never go anywhere smart and public, in case he was spotted. She wanted him to think of her as *soignée* and mature. Looking and being young had its points, yet she was afraid of coming to seem impossibly young to him, improperly young. He worried.

She would have liked to check outside again. It would be blatant now, though, if she opened the curtains and stood with the light behind her. She could not relax. Relax? Christ, what was that mad word of Mrs Lamb – that mad, worrying word: haunted. You saw a face and saw it again, and wondered when the next time would be, and hoped it was any time but now. There had to be a more sensible term than haunted. She had never felt less sensible.

In the middle of her corridor there was a big landing window giving a view of the street, and at the far end of the corridor another window from which you could see a big area of the grounds. The corridor lights were low-powered, and if she took care she should be able to look out unnoticed. This would involve unlocking the door, though, and leaving the safety of the room. Safety? The thought of venturing out terrified her. She glanced again in the mirror and saw that her face above the gorgeous pink dress had become suddenly pinched, hunted-looking – yes, haunted-looking. She realised she was thinking of Colin now not just as someone to show off the dress to, but someone to tell her weird fears. And that meant the fears were bad, because previously she would never have considered disclosing them, in case he blamed himself and decided she was better off without him. If she did tell him, he would certainly say nothing much in reply. He would know, though. He would not let anything happen to her. On the ground-floor at the other end of the building were two phone booths. Contact. But he had said he was working out of town today. Knowing he was away made her even more uneasy. He had to return some time, hadn't he, and it was late now?

Unlocking the door, she opened it and looked into the corridor. She felt like a scared animal peeping from its hole. Of course, the corridor was empty and silent. Almost silent. A small breeze coming up the stairs from an open door or window rustled old notices on a board next to Mandy's room opposite – announcements of a 'Forget Finals – Get Pissed' dance from April, a list of secondhand books for sale – 'Unopened', a warning against thieves and prowlers, advertisements for thesis-typing, degree-gown hire, a Chinese take-away. The normality of it all – the recollection of normality – consoled her for a minute or two. There was even a more up-to-date notice for an incoming summer school, but that was not until the day after tomorrow.

For another couple of minutes she considered going back into her room, locking the door and pushing the bed across it. And then she recalled that petrified, hounded appearance in the looking glass: it was all wrong for someone in such a brilliant dress, all wrong for a woman with a brain and an adult and adulterous love affair. Sod it, she would not cower. She might not even call Colin.

Cower from what, anyway? She had seen nothing to frighten her, heard nothing. That was the point – why she wanted to watch secretly again from a window for a while. She left the door of her room open and began to move slowly along the corridor.

The desert boots looked monstrous with her dress, but she was unlikely to meet anyone. That had to be true, surely? And, Jesus, if she did it would not be someone interested in fashion. She had worn these boots to the funeral. Would they identify her? She did not need identifying. She was the only student on this floor and conceivably the only one in this building. Whoever came looking would know he was looking for *her*, and would know her room. That ferocious, graveyard face had taken a fixed, a lasting picture of her in his head. The dress was no disguise.

And, standing at the edge of the landing window, she saw that face again now in the street. It was after 11 p.m. and dark, but she had a longer sight of him than at Central Hall, and no crowds of students jostled or got in the way. The street was well lit, after university complaints to the council.

Briefly, she found herself unable to move. It was the shock of seeing what her instincts told her to expect and which her thinking mind said was rubbish: there were no hauntings. Then she decided this sequin dress would send signals like neon, the bloody daft, super-bourgeois garment, and stepped back. As she did, she realised that it would not have mattered if she had stood square in view in the middle of the window. The man was looking up, but with his eyes fixed on her room, where the light still shone behind the curtains. When she moved back like that, she lost sight of him. Half a second later, she looked again and he had gone. That part of it, at least, was like Central Hall. She turned at once, as though he would emerge immediately from the stairs at the other end of the corridor, probably able to cut her off from her room. Such speed was impossible. She knew it, yet still peered that way, and still calculated the distance back to her room. It seemed too far. If he ran in through the main door and up the flights of stairs he would intercept her.

She could scream, but who would come? The lodge might be still empty. And scream about what? She had seen someone in the street and now he was gone. Infantile to make a fuss. She had to behave

172

like an intelligent woman, a grown-up woman – simply, like a woman.

Write off the room. Avoid getting cornered. Make for the far end of the building. As well as the phone booths, there was an emergency door there, operable by a push bar from inside. She longed again to speak to Colin. He would have to listen, even have to react, if she yelled her dreads at him on his private line. He could no longer pretend not to know or not to register what she spoke about. His number was in her memory, though she had never dared use it. That was recognised by both of them as being not on. To her surprise, she had found him listed in the book, as though he acknowledged no worries over publicising his address: *C. Harpur, 126 Arthur Street*. She saw it as a sort of feint: he was so secretive and devious he had to make a show of being open. By now he should be back from whatever he was supposed to be doing, surely.

She began to run – a real, flat-out, frantic gallop, her boots smacking hard and loud on the lino, the dress feeling tight across the chest and under her arms as she laboured for breath, part effort, bigger part terror. She wanted to listen for footsteps behind her – on the stairs or actually in the corridor – but was making too much noise herself. She began to sob. Saliva oozed from the side of her mouth and swung in a string down on to the skirt of her dress. So what? Spit didn't stain.

But did she deserve this? What had she done? She had gone to a crooked boy's funeral to spectate, wearing suede boots. That was a dark, unforgivable offence?

At the end of the corridor she quickly descended the stairs. From the ground floor there she could look through the big, dark, locked common-room to where the light of the lodge shone at the other end of the building. The lodge still seemed empty, but, as she looked, someone passed quickly in front of it towards the stairs. Although she could not make out the face, everything else was right for the man she had seen outside. He would go up to her room, see it was open and empty and guess she had spotted him and fled this way. Now, she did think of screaming. But now, also, she thought of going back up the stairs to meet him head-on and ask what in God's name it was all about. She wanted to believe people could see reason. If they could not and would not, life was a mess.

Life was a mess. She could not imagine arguing with that determined, hate-heavy face. Forget the call to Colin. Get out into the space of the grounds and, better still, into the street where there would be the protection of passers-by. Now, though, she saw that the common-room must have been cleared for cleaning or painting in the vacation and its chairs were stacked against the emergency doors, so she could not reach them or the push-bar. 'They shouldn't,' she muttered to herself, but they had. She tugged at one of the chairs, trying to reach the bar. The stack swayed and shifted, making what to her seemed an appalling, give-away din. It would take her minutes, a lot of minutes, to move the obstruction. If the sounds signalled her position he would not even bother to look in the room but come straight on. She had dreaded being cornered there and instead was cornered here, trapped between the stairs and two doors, this one and the common-room's. Outside seemed more than ever like salvation. She could not get to it.

Instead, she thought of the other outside: Colin Harpur, in his house, on the end of a telephone line, please God – 705141. She went into one of the boxes and dialled. It took three attempts, her fingers were so little under control and, for a vile second, she thought the digits were going to swim and tangle in her head, through panic. Once confusion started the right figures would be irrecoverable.

What seemed to be a girl answered. Colin had a daughter old enough to be up so late? 'Chief Superintendent C. Harpur, please,' she said.

'Not here. He's working. Can I take a message? I'm recording.' There was silence. It was as if this girl had been given set instructions on how to deal with calls from out of nowhere to her father. She would ask no questions, not even who was speaking. Perhaps especially who was speaking: many who phoned him would not want their names known. Well, she did not want hers known. But where was Harpur's wife? The girl spoke as if she had charge tonight while her father was out.

'Please don't go away,' Denise said. She stared out of the booth towards the stairs.

'No. The machine's running all right. Say what you like. Dad will get it.'

'No time.'

'So ring 999,' the girl replied at once. 'That's what I'm to say if it's bad.'

'It's bad.'

'They come. He says so, anyway.'

'Yes, but I don't want to put the phone down.'

There was a pause. 'I think I understand.'

When she looked again, he was there, gazing through the panes of the box at her, the face not so fierce now, almost miserable, worn-looking. She must have made some sound, though was not aware of it.

174

'What?' the girl asked. 'Say where you are. Say what it is. I'll do 999 for you. I'll mention dad's name. Clout? He's got it.'

'Don't go,' she whispered. It was child to child – child to helpless child.

'It's stupid,' the girl said. 'I can't help.'

He stood there, almost like someone waiting politely for use of the booth, but then she saw him put his hand inside his jacket.

'A knife,' she said.

'So, ring off, you silly cow. Where? I can't dial until you clear.'

He pulled open the door and said: 'Always working, aren't you?'

'What?' the girl said. 'Who's there?'

Car headlights from the delivery yard outside suddenly blazed in through windows to right and left of the emergency door, shining on him and the blade. A second afterwards, Denise heard loud braking and then someone leaned on the car horn and it blared and blared. For a second he turned when the beams first hit him and almost at once she struck down twice at his wrist with the receiver as hard as she could. On the second blow, the knife fell near her feet. Urgently, he bent for it, but she kicked hard and his knife skidded across the lino out of reach and under the stacked chairs. The horn stopped. He looked back at Denise once, then into the shadows for the weapon, then at the stairs. He must have feared that in a moment he would be trapped here by people coming down, as she had been trapped. He let the booth door swing shut and turned and ran up the stairs out of sight.

When she tried to speak again to the girl, Denise got only a deep, continuous howling on the line. Something had broken. All the same, she put the receiver back to her mouth and ear, as if she could still reach the world – child to child, child to anyone – in case he came back.

And in a couple of seconds, she was aware of someone descending the stairs again, slowly, very deliberately. Denise had been telling herself just then that she might not be such a child, after all. A child would not have recovered quickly enough to disarm him. Now, all her baby terrors hurtled back, even worse than before – to be safe, then safety taken away. This time she did scream – uselessly, into a dead telephone: perhaps even double dead, because Colin's would be disabled while still connected to her, even though there could be no message.

Mrs Lamb pulled the door open. 'Don't say I didn't warn you, kid. Who you talking to?'

'Oh, Alice. Wonderful. Did you see him?'

'Well, I saw him. If it wasn't him it would be another. This was

175

a Jack-type person? I knew it was trouble. I told you. I hear trouble in a voice. It's an old flair. Look, I've been around three student residences before this one. You dressed up for something – those boots?'

'We should get help.'

'Help? Jack's away.'

'No, but—'

'You're not saying police, are you? Is my Jack going to like that?'

'Isn't he?'

'My husband used to say, "Call the police, call me crazy." He was a prick, but pricks do penetrate. I reckon you should come to Darien now. A kind of balance of horrors?' Mrs Lamb took the receiver and put it back on the cradle. 'We get out. Maybe say nothing to Jack, either, not now, anyway. We'd only give him extra tremors, and the boy has enough. He looks strong, yet such frailty. That Mercedes klaxon, though – designed to scare them into surrender at Stalingrad, and never modified. We'll have well-wishers et cetera here.'

'Your Jack wouldn't like that?'

'You're Ivy League quality, Denise. You want to pick up some occidental heels and so on from your room?'

Harpur spent the afternoon and evening touring three outlying police stations, sounding out a few lads and girls recommended by Francis Garland or Erogynous Jones as possible tails for Courtney Sanquhar-Perry. Harpur had decided finally that not even Erogynous could hope to stay unobserved if he did the job, so find a new face. Garland spoke especially well of a young detective at Dobecross, Wayne Timberlake. The Waynes, Deans, Justins and even Chantelles would probably run the whole outfit one day, possibly the world.

Harpur could see why Timberlake would impress Garland – the boy had even more arrogance and push than Francis himself. He impressed Harpur, too, though. Thank God boys like this still wanted to join. Harpur arranged for him to start surveillance next day. He hid nothing in the briefing: 'People where Courtney lives feel it in the air as soon as a cop enters the estate, uniform, plain clothes, it's all the same. You've got a chance, but not much. If he moves, go with him and tell me when he gets there. By phone. Not radio. This is private.'

When Harpur reached home, Megan was there drinking a whisky before turning in, and he mixed himself a pint of gin and cider.

'Listen to the telephone tape, Col,' she said. 'Hazel took the call.

176

She's gone to bed very upset. Should she have to cope with things like that? She asked me to listen. It's unnerving.'

He played the conversation and heard Denise grow increasingly afraid. Then came some kind of interruption – perhaps a blow – and the tape began to whine.

'Who is it, Col?' Megan asked.

He replayed.

'There's a kind of familiarity when she asks for you,' she said.

'Detective Chief Superintendent C. Harpur, you mean?'

'Oh, that's a ploy.'

Yes. 'So where's the familiarity?'

'Tone. Do you know the voice?'

'No.'

She gazed at him. 'Someone nineteen, twenty?' she said. 'Faint Midlands accent.'

'Might be. I'll have to go out.'

'Why? Where – if you don't know who it is?'

'She might have done what Hazel told her and rung 999. We'd have a location.'

'Well, she'll be all right then, won't she? They'll have sent.'

'This is someone who asked for me.'

'So ring headquarters and find out where. You can go direct.'

'I'll ask them by radio when I'm on the road.'

'I see. It sounded to me as if the line at her end went dead. There'd be no 999.'

Yes, again, it was like that. 'Who knows?' he replied.

He drove fast to Jonson Court and left his car in the street. Her room was dark. So were all the rest. He would have to risk going in tonight. Approaching the entrance to her building carefully, he saw a light burning in the porter's lodge but nobody present. He entered quickly and went up the stairs to the third floor. He hoped they put names on their doors or he would have trouble locating her room. It was marked, but he found it locked. His magic keys probably would not cope here, so he knocked and called: 'Denise, it's Colin.' When she did not answer he raised his voice. God, but this was self-publicity. 'Denise, love, are you all right?' For a couple of seconds he stood there and knocked three times more. There was still no answer and he decided to look for the telephone. He had not passed a booth near the entrance and decided it must be at the other end of the building.

There were two and he looked thoroughly in both, finding no evidence of trouble – by which he meant blood. One telephone worked, the other howled. That booth he examined with special closeness, but still discovered nothing to frighten him. When he looked back through what seemed to be a long student common-room, he saw that the porter had returned to the lodge and was sitting there, reading a paperback book. Harpur decided he must leave by the emergency door and began to shift stacked chairs from it as noiselessly as he could. As he moved one group, he saw beneath it a long-bladed sheath knife. Setting down the chairs, he crouched over it. The light was poor and he wanted above all to see whether the blade was stained. His anxiety grew so great that he almost picked it up with his bare hand, to see better. The ingrained rules of detection stopped him, and he brought out a standard plastic container from his pocket and held the knife through that: not that he would be submitting this anywhere for official fingerprinting.

The blade looked blessedly unused. He put the knife into the container and then into his pocket. After he had worked on the chairs for a little longer, he could push the release bar. As Harpur operated it, he glanced back towards the lodge and knew that the porter had spotted him – maybe had heard something – and was staring at him through the length of the common-room and talking into a walkie-talkie. Harpur opened the door and ran into the grounds, looking for a way out that would not bring him near the lodge. All sorts were going to be here shortly. The porter himself emerged at his end of the building and the beam of a powerful flashlight fell on Harpur for a second. He turned his back, ducked and made for the shelter of a hedge. The porter yelled at him to stop, calling that he was surrounded, game old idiot.

Harpur ran fast between blocks of flats, knowing vaguely where he could get back to the road through the gardens of private houses on the west side of Jonson Court. He heard the two-tone of an approaching patrol vehicle, and possibly a second. Jesus, some rôle for a detective chief superintendent – dogged by his own people. Reaching the edge of the grounds, he met a ten-foot wall before the first garden. It was stone-built and gave footholds, but broken glass had been cemented along the top, perhaps to protect the residents from the students, perhaps vice versa. Here and there bits of it had been smashed down, possibly by kids, possibly by burglars, but he was grateful regardless. All the same, missed fragments of the glass tore his hands, his jacket and trousers, and his ankle as he prepared to jump.

He landed in what seemed to be an abandoned fish pool, water-filled, though not water capable of sustaining life. The smell as he disturbed the surface sickened him. That water, plus the cut on his ankle – septicaemia? It was a semi-detached house and he made his way up the drive to the street. He would be leaving a fairly unmissable trail, especially if they brought dogs, which the buggers would: blood and moribund pond weed. Not much to do about that. Although walking gave pain, he knew he had better keep going. The car was about two hundred yards away if he went back past the lodge, and about half a mile if he took the safer route. He went the half-mile. Another blue-lamp car passed the end of the street. For a second or two he paused in someone's porch, then moved on again.

At home, he did what he could about the cuts and put his jacket and trousers in a bag for disposal. Oh, great – that had been a suit with a few good years left in it. And he would not be able to claim. After clearing up the floor and carpet he ran the tape once more, in case he had missed anything. Another call had been recorded: 'I'm all right, Chief Superintendent,' Denise said. 'False alarm.' This time she sounded as if she were speaking from a room, not a public booth.

He went to bed. Megan stirred: 'Anything much from Miss Anon? The phone went again when I was in bed. I couldn't be bothered to get up, but there might be something else on the tape.'

'I'll listen tomorrow. Where the hell were you tonight, anyway, when the first call came?'

'Meeting of John Locke school governors. You know that.'

'So late?'

She snorted and slept.

Chapter Nineteen

Next evening Harpur had another call at home. It came from Wayne Timberlake. 'I've lost him, sir. But I don't think he's far away.'

'Where?'

'I was behind him to Grant Hill. He parked and had gone by the time I'd found a place and come back.'

It was one of the oldest and easiest dodges.

'He didn't know I was with him, sir. I'm almost sure. It was just his good luck.' Yes, this boy had plenty of confidence. But he also had the courage to ring and say he had lost the target.

'Stay there, Wayne. I'll come over. Where exactly are you? It could be all right.'

It was Jack Lamb's ball tonight and Harpur had meant to do a bit of a secret loiter at the edge of the grounds to make sure Denise stayed safe. That would have to be shelved, though, if he went to join Timberlake. Jack was bringing in private security, so there should not be too much risk. And she would have himself keeping an eye, plus the bright university lad who was escorting her. Harpur did not believe the part of her second call that said the cry for help had been unnecessary. He had to believe she was all right, though. Where? Had she moved in with the escort for the night, for more than the night? He did not want to think about it.

It was a Thursday and Megan was having one of her literary evenings. From the front room, Harpur could hear what might be a play-reading – rather gorgeous voices calling someone what sounded like Petulant, and bursts of poncy laughter to signal wit.

'Say your spot again, Wayne,' Harpur told him. 'There's an outbreak of badinage here.'

Timberlake was waiting near a bus shelter. 'He went into one of those four private apartment buildings. Cut your hands, sir?'

'He'll come out this way. We wait.'

'Unless he saw me.'

'You said he didn't.'

'Even if not, sir, he might use another exit. These people don't like repeating themselves.'

Garland was right. This boy might be wasted in Dobecross. 'Was he carrying anything, Wayne?'

'A briefcase.'

'Soft sided?'

'Sir?'

'One of those boxy, executive things, or the old type?'

'Old.'

'So you could see whether it was full.'

'Not full, I'd say. Only glimpses of him as he came out of his house and then when he left the car, but it seemed light. Papers? Money? He might be buying and collecting, sir?'

Definitely wasted in Dobecross. Harpur had an idea that somewhere in these parts lived Teddy Brinscombe, long-time suspected arms supplier to the trade, though never charged. They stood in the bus queue and waited, its only members hoping the bus would not come.

'I'll disappear as soon as he shows,' Harpur said. 'I just want to look at the case, and where exactly he comes from. If he spots me we're finished.'

'You could have been smaller, sir.'

Timberlake himself was built like Iles – slim, almost slight, under six feet, lean faced: hardly like a policeman at all.

'Do I get told what it's about, sir?'

'I'm not sure what it's about. No, you don't get told. Nobody does, so don't feel hard done by.'

Nobody. In the morning, at another meeting with Lane and Iles, he told the Chief he had taken a good look at Towler's house from outside and through the windows and seen nothing wrong. Iles listened and watched without a twitch. 'We've still no grounds to declare him a missing person, sir,' Harpur told Lane.

If they did, he feared the reporter might put her inquiries into a higher gear, might even publish. And if she did that, all sorts of other London Press would arrive. This could mean upset for the Courtney Sanquhar-Perry situation – whatever it was. And, much worse, the whole grassing edifice would be imperilled. They would all want to find out about that. At this stage he had not thought it necessary, either, to tell the Chief or Iles about the possible link between Courtney and Tony Towler. How was he supposed to know of it? He could not produce Towler senior's letter.

Harpur had gone from this careful conference to a short emergency meeting called by Jack Lamb in a supermarket carpark, Jack just back from what sounded like a passably clean art trip to London.

'Someone tried to feed me a dud tip about a Nat West bank raid in Stipend Road, July tenth at eleven a.m., Col. Deception nauseates me.'

'You think two-thirds right?'

'Spot on.'

'How do you know it's a plant?'

But Lamb did not answer that kind of question.

Timberlake said now: 'Sanquhar-Perry had a visitor today. I've got a note.' He began to pull out a book.

'Not here. Just give me what you remember.'

'Sorry. Yes. A man in his forties, decently dressed, scarred along the jaw. Craggy? Like a half-price Charlton Heston. Mean anything, sir?'

'Not to me. I'll ask around.'

'Then Courtney went out alone not long afterwards in his car to a house off Lichfield Square. I tried to reach you, but you were in a meeting.'

'You've got the exact address.'

'In the book.'

'I'll have it later.' Courtney, Panicking Ralph Ember and a third colleague from off Lichfield Square. Erogynous could work on the geography of that, too.

'Here's Sanquhar-Perry, sir,' Timberlake said.

'There's some bulk in that case.'

'It's different. Weapons?'

'He came out of Embard House?'

'I think so. That important, sir?'

'I'll go now. You've done a nice job, Wayne. I've got you in mind.' Was it Embard where Brinscombe traded? Erogynous would know.

Timberlake said: 'We could stop him and do a search.'

Young talent went only so far. 'And if it's a few works by Thomas Harris?'

'Is it?'

'Is it?' Harpur replied. 'He could complain of victimisation.'

'That would bother you, sir?'

'There are proper ways of doing things.'

'Oh, right, sir. You want him to go ahead, so you can take him and the rest actually using them?'

Timberlake was beginning to sound like the Chief.

182

Sanquhar-Perry went into a street telephone booth. 'Has to bring someone up to date with developments,' Harpur said.

'Who? The craggy visitor?'

'Might be.'

Chapter Twenty

Sanquhar-Perry said: 'I've picked up the equipment and I've got us a new Number Three. Able boy. He can do everything that's needed and agrees to a quarter – I mean, through coming in so late. So three-eighths, three-eighths, a quarter.'

'Grand,' Ember replied. 'Jesus, this job. Substitutes like a cup final. But you always come up with something.' He took care not to speak Courtney's name. They had worked out a way of keeping in contact which did not involve meeting or visiting each other, for the time being. Sanquhar-Perry telephoned the public box in the Monty from another public box. The arrangement said he would ring mid-morning, when the club was empty and Ember preparing the bar, but this was late evening, the Monty's busiest time. Ember could forgive him, though: Courtney obviously felt excited and wanted to tell all the news right away. Eventually, they would need another get-together, obviously. Ember had to meet this new recruit before the actual raid, the Quarter Man. And there was the matter of distributing the equipment. Ember never carried a weapon he had not done the checks on. For the moment, though, it was clever to keep apart.

Ember knew Sanquhar-Perry would have been content to use ordinary lines. He did not believe police did much tapping, and only when they suspected people were up to a job. They could have no idea about this one. All the same, Ember had insisted on basic precautions. Some habits came from too far back to break for a piece of the far-flung Caledonian gentry. If police did listen in it would be to the Monty's office line, and Ember's private number at Low Pastures. The club pay-phone was probably as safe as anything could be. Just in case it was not, he left Courtney's name out of things. This was basic consideration.

'So our original Number Three could get upset,' Sanquhar-Perry said. 'He's dropped.'

'He doesn't think about it, I tell you. His head's full of something else.'

'His interest might pick up again, Ralph. Or there's the other problem – he could stir the opposition by some sick behaviour.'

'He won't.'

'You just said that's all he's thinking about.'

'It is and he won't,' Ember replied.

'I—'

'Just count on me. All right?'

'I heard Kay's legged it with a priest.'

'Fact.'

'People hate priests fucking their women. Somehow against the grain. This is going to make him mad. Madder.'

'Just count on me.'

'I like the sound of that, Ralph.'

'This has to go through.'

'The spare growing pricey? Multi-storey fees gone up? I had a funny call.'

'Funny how?'

'This is Towler's father.'

Christ, names were spilling from Courtney's end.

'Called me at home, Ralph. My God, I mean – in my home.'

You'd think it was baronial or more.

'Wanting to know if I'd seen Tony lately. The dad's been ringing there. No reply.'

'Well, that's all right. You said, no. Nobody's seen him.'

'He said I'd called him earlier, saying Tony was OK.'

'Who did?'

'Old Towler.'

'*Did* you ring him?'

'Would I?'

'You told him you hadn't?'

'He got ratty. Thought I was pissed.'

'So, who called him?'

'This could be our former Number Three, couldn't it, Ralph?'

It was a bit late to go confidential on Webb's name after mentioning Kay. Ember said: 'Why would he?'

'He rings the dad to say Tony's fine, because he knows he isn't. Doesn't want any inquiries. It's selfish, Ralph. Now the old man's confused and worried.'

Christ, but Webb was a vast hazard.

'So he mocks up some cause to ring the dad, and slips in a clean bill of health for Tony. This was about my ancestry – the excuse for calling him.'

185

'He should never have been in with us. This bugger has to go,' Ember said.

And another reason: he had an idea that Webb believed he might talk to Harpur. That could turn Webby more savage yet. Self-preservation said from all sides that Webb had become too much of a peril, and at self-preservation Ember shone.

'Yes, I'm really pissed off,' Courtney continued. 'His using my family tree. Old Towler asked me if I knew my name was sometimes written S-A-N-Q-U-A-H-A-R and sometimes S-A-N-Q-U-H-A-R.'

You try to keep the sod anonymous and he gives it to them at dictation speed twice, with the alternative. 'What family tree is that?' Ember asked. 'How's your sexy companion?'

Sanquhar-Perry rang off. Ember had thought one question or the other would do it. He liked calls short, even on this line.

Chapter Twenty-One

Every year when his summer party was in full swing, Jack Lamb liked to retreat briefly to the house, go upstairs to his den and look out upon the scene. Normally, he saw something triumphal in it. The three big marquees gave a hearty, civilised glow and there was bright gaiety in the strings of multi-coloured fairy lights hung across their summits. Guests in fine gear strolled back and forth in happy, loud groups between the dancing and the bar and catering marquees. He had duckboard laid in case of the worst, and these pathways were lit by a line of handsome imitation Victorian-style street lamps. Occasionally, the dancing would spill out on to the lawns as people sought space and air. From his room upstairs, the sound would reach him as a delightfully genial mixture of music, chat, laughter, shouted greetings. He brought folk together in cheerful conditions. This had always been one of his aims. Naturally, some people, like poor Tone Towler and others who received the 'for refusal only' invitations, could not be asked and nor could police, like Harpur or Harpur's chiefs. Within such obvious limits, he could provide for all sorts, including this year – and perhaps from now on, regularly – the Queen's Lord Lieutenant of the County and his Lady.

And yet this year, as he gazed out, he suffered fierce uneasiness. Previously, it had always given him special satisfaction to see all this created light and high spirits because they were set in such a frame of darkness. Chase Woods and the fields all round his estate lay quiet and shadowy, even utterly black if, as in some years, cloud hung low and there was no moon. He used to feel he had contrived a little realm of style and good fellowship in the centre of this wide, sombre spread of ground, like a pleasure liner partying at night in an otherwise deserted sea.

Tonight, though, the contrast disturbed him: he saw this small patch of light, noise, ebullience, in the surrounding blankness. It was not a very dark night, but dark enough. Instead of feeling the usual pride at what he had put here, he thought only of how miniature it seemed and felt how much of the black other there was. He found himself thinking as he knew Colin Harpur did: that the darkness had a damn good chance of doing better than the light – might swamp it at any time, as a pleasure liner could be swamped in a storm, and was so powerful and intrusive that it might envelop even those who considered themselves on the side of the light. By that, Harpur presumably meant himself. Lamb had once heard him say he felt like one of those dirty white cars or vans where someone had finger-written, 'Also available in white.' Of course, Harpur would not regard Lamb as ever available in white. In fact, what Colin had been saying in his roundabout, gentle way was that his contact with Lamb brought much of the dirt. And the darkness.

Tonight, Lamb stared more at that than at the valiant outdoor lights, and tried to hear any sounds from that darkness above the wild, tame din in the grounds. How could he gaze out and not think above all of Tony Towler going from bad to worse in an oak and of the mystery that brought his body to the woods? Yes, the dirt and the darkness might have the real triumph, not this once-a-year, desperate beano, just as his mother as well as Harpur would probably always believe.

His mother knew something about Denise's sudden arrival in Darien overnight, but they seemed to have agreed to say nothing. That girl said nothing about a lot. No wonder Harpur felt suited to her. She had never mentioned what she must have seen on the edge of the woods the day Towler died. Tonight, she seemed very subdued, even scared. He wondered again whether Harpur realised the sort of strain he put on that kid.

Well, she would be all right tonight. On second thoughts late this afternoon, after his return from London and swift meeting with Harpur, he had doubled the security, telling his mother it was on account of a couple of paintings he had brought back from London – a Max Ernst and a John Dawson Watson. Denise had her escort, anyway, Stephen Something, and he looked the sort who would stay close – but not the sort who could do very much if things went bad suddenly. Lamb decided he would go back down himself. First, he opened his safe and took out a Mustang Colt automatic, small enough to cause no give-away bulge in his dinner-jacket pocket. He hardly ever carried a gun and had earlier decided not to tonight. These few minutes spent gazing out towards the woods had changed his thinking. He told himself, also, that the Mustang was because of the paintings, and to do with taking care of the Lord Lieutenant. He did not believe it, though.

Returning to the party, he saw Denise almost at once. She was with Helen and her university man and looked totally recovered –

bright with enjoyment, very pretty in her modish dress, some drink aboard, obviously, though nothing disastrous. As the three of them made their way towards the food, she took hold of the escort's arm and you could have read genuine fondness there. Perhaps one day she would be weaned away from Harpur and his attendant perils. That might be sad for him. He seemed genuinely attached. But he had a wife, and there had been other women Lamb knew of to whom Harpur had also been genuinely attached. He did not fall apart when affairs ended.

In the bar marquee, Sir Benjamin Lutton, the Lord Lieutenant, congratulated him on a wonderful party. His wife, Elaine, endorsed that. 'Could I drag you away for a few minutes, though, Jack?' Lutton asked. 'Elaine and I would love to take a turn with you around the grounds, and down towards the woods. Do you know that the house which stood on the Darien site previously – I mean twelfth or thirteenth century – might well have been the seat of some of Elaine's ancestors.' Lutton was small, with a glistening, birdy face, full of enthusiasm for his project now.

'It's vague,' Lady Lutton said. 'Records from that time are, but—'

'This would be the Fédin or possibly Ferdin family,' Lutton added. 'Norman, of course.'

'It's very dark away from the marquees,' Lamb replied.

'You're our admirable guide, Jack,' Lady Lutton cried.

As they were leaving the marquee, Mrs Lamb joined them. 'We're going to beat the bounds,' Sir Ben told her. 'Do you have that phrase in the States, Mrs Lamb? And maybe stir a few old ghosts. Do join us, if you will.' They carried their champagne glasses and Lamb brought a bottle from the bar.

Mrs Lamb said: 'We hear some sounds from those woods, but maybe a bit loud for ghosts.'

'These would be rather warlike, conquering ghosts, so possibly they would sound off,' Lady Lutton replied.

'Wouldn't it be easier in daylight?' Mrs Lamb asked. 'And not too easy in party shoes.'

'This is the time for true ghosts,' Sir Ben declared, laughing.

'I'll carry my heels if the going gets rough,' his wife said.

'And should the host leave his guests unprotected?' Mrs Lamb replied.

Lamb knew she meant one guest only.

'Unprotected? This is a strong word,' Sir Ben said.

'Oh, I don't know,' Mrs Lamb replied.

In the woods, the four of them stood in a clearing and Lamb

refilled the glasses, pouring carefully in the dark. He thought they might be very close to Tony Towler, but the foliage had thickened even during the last few days and in the dim light here there was no danger he would be seen. The music and laughter could still be heard, at that distance as the same mellow mix which had reached him in the den.

Lutton talked effortlessly about local history, including the rôle of Darien in the Civil War, when he thought some sort of Royalist–Roundhead skirmish might actually have taken place in Chase Woods.

'I never knew who really won that damn war,' Mrs Lamb said.

'Who wins any war?' Sir Ben replied.

'The Viet Cong?' Mrs Lamb said.

Lamb thought he saw something small, whitish, fat, perhaps alive, perhaps lethargically wriggling, drop from the oak under which they stood and into Lady Lutton's champagne. It did not seem to be a swimming creature and sank. Lamb could no longer discern it in the glass.

'A toast!' Lutton cried. 'Not to the past or to history or to ghosts, but to the present occupants of this lovely house.'

'Kind,' Lamb said.

The three raised their glasses to him. 'You drink, too, Jack,' his mother said. 'Toast yourself, son. While it's all still yours.'

'Ah, you take the perspective of history, Mrs Lamb,' Sir Ben said. 'Long term.'

'I wouldn't say so,' she replied.

A shaft of moonlight broke through the trees. 'Don't we look impressive?' Lady Lutton cried.

When Lamb bent over to refill her empty glass again he could see nothing untoward left in it. Presently, they made their way back to the party. As they approached the dance marquee, Stephen, the escort, came to meet them. 'Oh, Denise is not with you? I seem to have lost track of her.'

Chapter Twenty-Two

A newspaper cutting in his hand, the Chief said: 'Wendy Sellick's taken advantage of the Summer Ball murder to go a bundle on everything.' He read silently for a while. 'Damn me, it sounds as if she's actually got into Towler's place at some stage. A reference to turquoise sheets and a wardrobe full of silk trousers. Silk?' Lane glanced down at his own hard-done-by-looking serge.

'They're keen on such touches, sir,' Iles replied. 'A couple of accurate details of no importance, and then they feel entitled to give whatever slant they want to their articles.'

Lane said: 'Yes, Desmond, but how did she—?'

'Towler's father has come from Devon, I believe, sir, looking for his son,' Harpur replied. 'He may have run into Sellick hanging about Towler's house, waiting for him. She could have talked him into showing her around the place. Perhaps he has a key.'

'I gather he's a schoolmaster,' Iles said. 'He'd be no match for her.'

'Towler senior has reported Tony officially missing now, sir,' Harpur told Lane. 'We are searching.'

'Am I right in thinking, Col, that he also reported evidence of a break-in at Tony's house?' Iles asked.

'He did, sir.'

'There you are, then,' the Chief exclaimed. 'This was probably the journalist.'

'We've had a look at the damage, sir,' Iles replied, 'and it's Col's view that this was the work of a professional.'

'Exceptionally neat,' Harpur said.

'So, who?' Lane asked.

'We're finding Towler was into all kinds of dubious areas, sir,' Harpur replied. 'There could be fifty people wanting to get at him, many of them accomplished burglars.'

'Is it your suggestion that the break-in took place while Towler was in the house?' Lane asked.

'This has to be a possibility, sir,' Iles replied.

191

'He was abducted from there?' Lane asked. 'Perhaps even—?'

'I think Col still has an open mind on what happened, sir.'

Harpur said: 'There was no evidence of actual violence. But the rooms seemed disarranged and untidy – a tie thrown down on a living-room chair, a bedroom chair in a strange situation, a shirt dropped anyhow on a bed. Towler was a very organised, house-proud person.'

At his desk, Lane silently read a little further into the *This Morning's Searchlight* article. 'Is she right, Colin, that the last sightings of Towler were on the day of Martin Webb's funeral – at the funeral itself, and then the gathering in Doug Webb's home?'

'One of his homes,' Iles remarked.

'We've nothing afterwards,' Harpur said.

'My God,' the Chief whispered.

'Yes, there are tasty implications, sir,' Iles said.

Lane had taken his jacket off. He was in quite a spruce white shirt and what could be a new tie, silver and rose stripes, so he might be attending a lunch function later somewhere. The press office had put about a dozen newspaper clippings ready for him when he arrived first thing. It was the big Wendy Sellick article that preoccupied him. He would pick it up, read a little or stare at one of the pictures in it, then put it down and turn to one of the other clippings, as if seeking solace, even contradiction of what *Searchlight* said. After a while, he would return to Sellick.

'It's clever and, of course, it will have been gone over with a toothcomb by *This Morning*'s lawyers, sir,' Iles remarked. 'As far as Col and I can see, there is nothing factually wrong – nothing where we can demand retraction or, better still, on which one of us could sue. That's what I meant, sir, about peppering the thing with irrelevant, truthful background fact. Their deductions, their underlying thesis, may be grossly awry, but if we protest they say, "Does he or does he not live in Diamond Street? Are his sheets turquoise?" '

'It's devilish,' the Chief replied, glancing across to the window, as though he would have to take a walk to it in a minute, and as though he again longed to open it and fly free and far.

'Precisely the word, if I may say, sir,' Iles said. 'Devilish.'

'And the rest she says about this Towler, Colin?' Lane asked. 'You mentioned activities "in dubious areas". This article is more specific. She says he was feeding a major police informant.'

'Her and her paper's obsession, sir, as you know,' Iles replied. 'Grassing.'

Lane said: 'She doesn't actually use the term supergrass, does she, but—?'

192

'It's a quality paper, so to speak, sir,' Iles replied.

'And she doesn't name him, this "major informant",' Lane said.

'My point, sir. We're supposed to make do with the name of Towler's street.'

Harpur said: 'I think she may have been forced to go early with this article, sir. Events accelerated. Her editors knew all the other papers would today carry stories of the murder, and possibly send people here for deeper inquiries. They'd order her to write as much as she had. They have to be first.'

'This is people's lives and deaths we're talking about,' Lane replied, his plump, kindly face appalled. 'Have you hurt your hand, Colin?'

'Lives and deaths, so right, sir,' Iles said. 'Again. It's a childish, win-at-all-costs game, journalism.'

'And yet in some ways essential, even admirable,' Lane replied.

'They get the soccer results right usually,' Iles said. 'After they've been on TV.'

Lane tried to smile. 'Newspapers do have a legitimate, important role, Desmond. We cannot take them lightly.'

'If you say so, sir. I know that's the standard wisdom for senior officers.' Iles was in a close-fitting cream lightweight single-breasted suit, which was open to feature his waistcoat. Lately, he had told Harpur that he admired pictures of an American author named Tom Wolfe – 'this is Wolfe with an E and by no stretch a double 0, Harpur' – who always appeared in white or cream suits, apparently, and came over as brilliantly thoughtful and ironic. Iles did prize irony, frequently spotting it in events where most might see only pain.

'I'm going to read this from the beginning,' the Chief said sadly.

'Oh, would you, sir?' Iles remarked.

'Perhaps we could discuss it bit by bit,' Lane said.

'This will be productive, I know it,' Iles replied, 'as long as we don't mistake the fucking rot for gospel.'

An elaborate system of reciprocal deals between police and criminals is believed to lie behind a seemingly routine gangland murder in the early hours of yesterday morning.

This killing throws back into prominence the controversial issue of use by police of criminal informants and the protection and/or favours detectives may give some criminals in return for 'grassing', as passing information is known.

The overnight shooting yesterday is already being referred to as 'the quid pro quo' murder. In this context, the Latin phrase, meaning 'something for something', does not refer merely to the repayment of a gangland death. The whole grassing structure is referred to as 'the quid pro quo' system. Put in basic language it is policing reduced to you scratch my back, I'll scratch yours.

Lane stopped reading and looked up. To Harpur he appeared hurt – sickened by the allegations. '*System, structure*,' he muttered.

'Words she brought with her, sir, before any inquiries,' Iles replied. 'As you know. They must have really frog-marched her into writing this. She's obviously not ready. High wool-quotient.'

'I had the impression when the girl came to see us that – having found what we were like – she might have shown us some consideration, even affection,' Lane said.

'Possibly she can dispense both, sir,' Iles remarked. 'But she is not her own master.'

'Mistress,' Harpur said.

The Chief continued to read:

The grim details about the murder of 51-year-old ex-convict Douglas Alfred Webb are given in our news columns on p. 3. *Searchlight* was already investigating matters which may be connected with his death and has established:

1 That Douglas Webb believed underworld informants had made possible the ambush in which police shot dead Webb's son Martin during a post-office raid earlier this month.

2 That Webb believed certain informants, and particularly a rich and all-powerful one, enjoyed complete police protection, and were allowed to carry on their own borderline or frankly illegal businesses as *quid pro quo*.

3 That after the death of his son – a death due to police haste or malice, he believed – Douglas Webb became determined to destroy the grassing infrastructure responsible, and if possible expose police connivance at informants' law-breaking.

4 That Webb, a man who never denied a long criminal record, including convictions for armed robbery himself, had lately reformed and wanted no further part in criminal ventures. But the brutal shooting of his son (as he saw it – Martin was mentally retarded) forced him to contemplate violence once more.

5 That Douglas Webb was so desolated by the death of his son that he had to pay continual late-night grieving visits to the church from which his funeral left before he could sleep.

6 That the sudden disappearance of a young local man, Anthony Towler, known as Tony or Tone, is in some way connected with the Webb family tragedy.

Laughing, Iles said: 'She has to go gingerly now. She can tell us safely enough that dear Webby had made a bid for canonisation late in life, and nobody can gainsay it. But Towler could turn up again this afternoon. She daren't suggest he's crooked, or even connected with crooks, or a grass, or – what was that term, Col, a "newsboy"? – because he could slam her paper for libel.'

'These are all very grave suggestions, Desmond,' Lane said, waving the article.

'Once more, sir, the perfect word: suggestions.'

The Chief read again:

Webb's body was found in a lane near the country home, Darien, of prosperous international art-dealer Mr Jack Lamb. He had been shot with two bullets in the chest from a .38 Spanish Astra Modelo revolver. The glittering annual summer party and ball given by Mr Lamb and his nineteen-year-old companion, Helen Surtees, was taking place in the grounds of Darien on the night before last, attended by the Lord Lieutenant of the county, Sir Benjamin Lutton, and Lady Lutton. Police believe Webb may have been making for the party, or had already been there and was leaving, though not an invited guest.

'We've spoken to her, Colin – since Webb was found?' the Chief asked.

'Bob Tarr might have given her a general briefing.'

'Is what she says right?'

'Astra? Two wounds? Yes.'

'But as to why it happened where it did?' Lane replied.

'He might have been en route to or from Darien, yes, sir.'

'Remind me: who saw the body first?' Lane asked.

'It was found by a farmhand on his way to work.'

'No, I mean of our people.'

'Myself, sir,' Harpur replied. 'I had a call at home just after dawn yesterday from the Control Room. The whole murder crew arrived a few minutes after me.'

Iles remarked: 'You see, sir, in a way the death was a Godsend to her – if you'll forgive the term.'

The Chief winced, as if he found it wholly unforgivable. 'In what way, Desmond?'

'We know she thinks Lamb is the supergrass, don't we, sir? She came right out and said so to us. She can't risk publishing that, though. The body enables her to hint as much, without saying it. One of those code things, isn't it: "prosperous" signifying "criminally successful". She has to be even more careful about libel with Lamb.'

'Because it's so unlikely – Jack Lamb a grass?' Lane asked.

'I believe you may have used the word "absurd" about the suggestion earlier, Chief. That seems to me unmatchably apt.'

'Yes, absurd,' Lane said.

'Absurd,' Harpur replied.

Iles said: 'And, of course, Lamb is in a position to pay for a libel case, if she put a foot wrong.'

'Skilful,' Lane remarked.

Iles said: 'It's a skill all right, sir. Not a very elevated one, possibly – smearing without being actually seen to smear.'

The Chief continued his reading aloud:

It is believed that two knives were found on the body of Douglas Webb and that his purpose was to avenge the death of his son on the informant or on one of the informant's sources. Vengeance had become as much a burden and duty in Webb as it was in *Hamlet*.

'That's the quality touch,' Iles said. 'Webby did have a princely flavour to him, don't you think, sir?'

'Two knives?' Lane replied. 'Is that right?'

'It is, sir,' Harpur said. 'I did a quick search of his clothes when I arrived, of course. A flick knife and a long-bladed sheath job. I don't know who told Sellick about them, though. She might have cornered and quizzed one of our younger lads. Or possibly Bob Tarr gave her that, too, off the record. That's what "it is believed" usually covers. No damage is done.'

'Why two, though?' Lane demanded.

'People like Webb in his state are very determined, sir,' Iles replied. 'Not a bit like shilly-shallying Hamlet, in fact. Manic, possibly. To that sort of frantic mind, a pair of knives might seem twice as likely to work.'

'I agree,' Harpur said.

The Chief read on but little else of importance came. There was the description of Towler's house and sheets and a vague reference to 'grasses' grasses, one possibly a woman or girl'. The Chief, Iles

196

and Harpur were named, but in neutral, very guarded terms. Stock pictures of all three had been used plus a large *Home and Gardens* type shot of Darien and some of the grounds. *Searchlight* was saying police ran a racket, but not necessarily the particular police on show. Of course not, m'lud. All the same, Harpur felt he had got away lightly.

'I take it we're talking to Lamb,' Lane said. 'This does not mean I attach the slightest credence to this article, or to any implication that Lamb is a protected informer, you understand. I think we should ask whether he knows of any reason why Webb might have visited the party, or wished to visit it.'

'We got a guest list yesterday, sir, and have been interviewing people non-stop since. I'm going up there myself immediately after this meeting,' Harpur replied.

'Perhaps I'll come, Col,' Iles said. 'I love old properties and art, sir.'

Jesus. 'Of course,' Harpur replied.

Lane abandoned the article and did now walk to his window. He had shoes on today. Speaking half over his shoulder, as he looked out, he said: 'It occurs to me we might be reading more into that piece of writing than there is. As Desmond points out, it is not a Gospel. Perhaps she's not trying to tell the reader about Jack Lamb. Isn't it conceivable there was someone else at the party who would interest Webb? A big cross-section of people. Ample opportunity, I imagine.'

'This had occurred to me, sir, yes,' Harpur said.

'So, back to our muttons,' Lane went on. 'Who did Webb?'

Iles exhaled noisily in congratulation. '"Back to our muttons": that's a really old down-to-earth injunction, sir. Yes, let's get away from all these distractions. Col will come up with something, don't doubt it. And it will be something to end all this tiresome speculation.'

As the ACC and Harpur were returning to their rooms, Iles said: 'Two knives? Did you put an extra egg in that pudding?'

'He did think in doubles. Two homes, two murder weapons.'

'And do we really not know whether he was going to or coming from Darien?'

'No, sir.'

'But Lamb's all right?'

'Yes, and his bird and mother.'

'So, Webb must surely have been on his way there.'

'I have to keep an open mind, sir.'

'Don't give me that in-front-of-camera, senior-cop recitation, Harpur.'

Mrs Lamb called up the stairs at Darien: 'Police again, Jack. Big boys this time, I'd say. Harpur one. Any particular lies you want told?'

Lamb looked from the den window and saw Harpur in a new Scorpio approaching from the gates – a change from one of his customary clapped-out, supposedly anonymous vehicles, so the call must be official. Of course it was official. Alongside him, Harpur had someone who might be ACC Desmond Iles. And, in any case, Harpur did not make visits here in the normal way of business. That would be good for nobody.

Lamb went down. 'What about Denise?' Mrs Lamb asked. 'We say what? Jack, where is the kid?'

'Helen's still trying to find her. Say nothing, unless we're asked. We won't be.'

It was not a subject Harpur would raise, especially with Iles present. At least, it was not a subject he would raise unless they had found her.

'I said we should never have left the guests,' Mrs Lamb went on. 'The Sir and Lady. Who the hell cares? Well, you do – you butter them, jump for them.'

Lamb went out to greet the policemen. Harpur said: 'I'm Detective Chief Superintendent Harpur. This is the Assistant Chief Constable, Mr Iles.'

'Ah, the party's over and the caravan moves on,' Iles remarked. Two marquees had been taken down yeterday and now men were dismantling the last. 'I believe, as ever, a splendid occasion.'

'Thank you,' Lamb said. They went in. 'This is my mother.'

'It's about this thug shot near by the other night?' she asked.

'Even to thugs we've a duty, Mrs Lamb,' Iles said.

'What we're trying to discover is whether the dead man had any reason to come to Darien,' Harpur remarked.

'That *Searchlight* make-believe you mean?' Mrs Lamb said.

'No reason I know of,' Lamb replied.

'That's a Max Ernst, isn't it?' Iles said, moving to a picture that stood resting against the wall. 'Very *cavalier polonais* style.'

'You don't know Webb?' Harpur asked.

'No.'

'How would Jack know someone like that, for God's sake?' Mrs Lamb said.

'So, among the guests might there be anyone who would draw him here?' Harpur asked.

'Draw him here with two knives, you mean?' Mrs Lamb replied.

'Draw him here,' Harpur said.

Lamb saw what answer was needed. 'Not that I know of.'

'Assassination of the Lord Lieutenant?' Mrs Lamb suggested.

Iles had a giggle. 'Quite, Mrs Lamb. I wonder the crazy newspaper article didn't propose that.' He came back from examining the painting and gazed around at Darien's long drawing-room. 'You know, I feel restored just by being in this property. Sixteenth century, most of it, Jack? I look at slipshod ephemera like the *Searchlight* thing and know that real values will prevail, prevail untroubled.'

There was a moment as Lamb took them back out to their car when Iles stopped in the hall to look at another painting and Lamb whispered to Harpur: 'Is Denise all right?'

Iles rejoined them and Harpur did not reply. Lamb saw, though, that he looked appalled, looked as if he thought he should have been asking Lamb the question.

In the Scorpio, Iles said: 'We've taken care of him extremely well, then. He's worth his salt?'

'I hear he goes from strength to strength in the art game, sir, even though prices took such a terrible beating in the recession.'

Harpur was due to meet Denise in the afternoon. They had planned for a few hours in the Tenbury, before she left for the vacation. It was to have been a farewell for at least several weeks, until, maybe, they could see each other at some halfway point. He knew she had been working on maps and would probably have it all sorted out by now. Or perhaps it would be a farewell for longer than that. It might die now. It might be dead.

He went to the usual rendezvous-point they used for Tenbury visits, though there was now no question of going to the hotel today. He could hardly disappear for a few hours so early in a murder inquiry, not even for Denise. It had been difficult enough getting to the street rendezvous at all.

But he could not possibly have stayed away from that. He had to know she was all right. There had been the small, dubious comfort of her second call on the tape, but then the revival of all his terrors by the death of Webb and, above all, by Lamb's anxious inquiry. The memory of Webb's embittered, staring face on the funeral video had come back to him, and with it had come the memory of seeing Denise in the same video standing near the hearse. It was not clear whom or what Webb had been looking at, but could it have been Denise? Had he gone up to Darien, searching for her? Had he reached Darien and found her? Where was she? She had been missing for thirty-six hours. He could not risk reentering Jonson Court, but had done his street patrol there last evening and seen no light in her window. Why was she late now? His mind should have been focused on finding who killed Webby. He could not bother with that. Only one aspect of this mystery concerned him: had Webb been going or coming back?

When Denise had still not arrived after half an hour he found he was trembling. He had left the car at a distance, as always, but now wished he had brought it, for somewhere to sit down. Even before this crisis, his legs were not too good after damage on the wall glass. He wanted to grip the steering-wheel and steady his hands. Instead, he went into a shop doorway and leaned against the wall, trying to slow his breathing. God, he must look like a heart attack. Some well-wisher might call an ambulance.

He forced himself to move out and walk a few steps in the street, still working on his breathing, still unsure of his legs, still unable to think properly. Even supposing Webb had reached Darien, he could not possibly have hurt her, or it would be known by now, surely. Surely. Although there were dark woods and open countryside around Lamb's grounds, Denise would not have gone there, would she? Might she have looked for somewhere away from the crowd to take her friend and escort? Had things moved on between those two? Harpur wondered whether he should get in touch with him. And say what? *Denise's lover, here, sonny. You two get into the woods the night before last? I ask not as a cop, obviously. As a rival. What the hell were you doing there, and didn't you realise she was in peril?* He did not know the escort's name, anyway. Perhaps Lamb did. It might come to that.

He turned and saw Denise. He could not remember a time when he felt more relief. Relief? Feeble word. Joy. He shouted her name, waved, tried to start to run towards her, but his legs would not respond too well, and he staggered, bumping into an old lady with a terrier, almost falling over its lead. She raised an umbrella to him, perhaps thinking it was an attack. He apologised, and kept going. It was not an attack, but it was an accidental display. Denise was waving, too. It occurred to him suddenly that, if Wendy Sellick, or other reporters who must have arrived by now, were keeping an eye on him, this would be some declaration. He could not care. For the first time ever in daylight he kissed her in the street. For the first time, he felt he might have been wrong to let his training dominate him, and keep that careful distance between him and her, that

200

habitual barrier. The distance and the barrier did not count. The near-breakdown he had just suffered proved that.

'Colin, I'm sorry to be late,' she said, 'but I've been home.'

'To Stafford?'

'I panicked – like some child wanting mummy. Suddenly, things became too much for me.'

'I heard the tape.'

'Yes. That man – he's the one who was murdered? I read about it in the paper today.'

'What was your connection with him, Denise?'

'Connection? No connection at all,' she said. 'I saw him at a funeral. The dead boy's father? Can we go to the Tenbury? I suppose you're much too busy. I understand, Col.'

Yes, he was. 'An hour,' he said.

'And pay for the room for all night. Is it worth it?'

'It's worth it,' he said. 'You drove back just to see me?'

'Of course.'

'What will your parents think – motorwaying non-stop like that?'

'I shan't ask them, or tell them. I'm back to being an adult again.' She took his hand. 'I found just the place where we can meet in the vacation. Spotted it today. Sweetly rural.'

When their hour had gone and he was dressing, she remained in bed for a few minutes. 'Col, I recovered all right after that business – the thing on the tape – and went to the party. But there came a moment up there when I got fed up with it all – so many people having a fine time, me with a nice man but one I didn't want, and you, God knew where. I had to be in touch with you somehow. Phones didn't work. Then I thought that during the attack, he had dropped a knife. I decided I'd go back to my room in Jonson. To hell with being terrorised. I also thought that if I could get that knife and give it to you it would be – it would bring us together better. Not just Denise with Colin Harpur, lovers, but Denise helping Colin Harpur, chief of detectives. I'd be supplying a clue, wouldn't I? It would take me inside that wall you put around yourself and your job.'

'You were inside already.'

'Yes? Anyway, the knife wasn't there.'

'No.'

'What do you mean?'

'No.'

She thought about that: 'You knew?' she said. 'This dead man had two knives on him.'

'I read that.'

'True?'

'True.'

'I see. Yes, I think I see. Well, when I couldn't find the knife I was afraid he had been back for it, and might still be around. And that's when my nerve went again. I couldn't face staying in Jonson Court after all and I drove home overnight. Pathetic.'

'I don't think so.'

'Oh, yes.' She got out of bed and started to dress. 'Will you find who did it?'

'It's tough. Gangland crimes – nobody talks.'

'Am I part of the inquiries, Col? The attack?'

'We don't mention that.'

'Why come after me? I saw him at university, too. Hellish, Col. And then, straight afterwards, I get a warning something terrible might happen. As if I was on the edge of – oh, I don't know what.'

Yes, again. 'Warning? Who from?'

'A student.'

'How would he, she, know?'

'A mature student – supposed to have a rough past. Nasty scar along his jaw. He looks like Charlton Heston. Do you recognise that?'

'No.' Perhaps a little distance and a small barrier were still needed, after all. Ralphy Ember had wanted to look after Denise? Why? Varsity solidarity? There might be more to it: some job connection between Webb, Sanquhar-Perry and Ember? Harpur could not see exactly how it worked, but contact between the second two he had heard of from Timberlake. Towler had seemed to know the first pair. Was Courtney the centrepiece with Towler providing some sort of accidental linkage? A trio? The three were in a project? Had something turned evil between them, as things in projects would, and forced Ember to take out Webb? It was a bit rosy for Panicking Ralph, but you could never tell when people felt pushed.

And if he had done it, and saved Denise – possibly saved Lamb and Harpur himself, too – didn't Ember merit anonymity, some kindly curtains? 'Never come across anyone to fit that description, love. Most mature-age villains I know look like Godzilla.'

'Now, honestly, Col?'

Chapter Twenty-Three

'What we have, sir, is strong indications of an armed raid on July tenth at eleven a.m. somewhere on our ground,' Harpur told Lane.

'I don't understand that imprecision when the rest is so exact.'

'We've been fed a decoy location, for obvious reasons, sir.'

'Are we certain it's a decoy?'

'That's my information, sir.'

'From?'

Iles said: 'This is some of Col's special material. The kind we are not supposed to ask about?'

'The kind the Sellick woman wrote about, and these other Press people badger us over now?' Lane asked. 'In short, grasses. My God.'

'I think I can name two of the people who will do it, sir,' Harpur replied. 'There's been some very bright work by a young detective constable, Wayne Timberlake. We believe the governor is Courtney Sanquhar-Perry and that a light-weight called Clive Bowling is an assistant. Timberlake brilliantly tailed Courtney to Bowling's place and also to their armourer. There would be at least one other, but I can't name him.'

Iles said: 'It's not as vague as seems, sir. Col and I have itemised all known heavy movements of cash around that date and time and Col thinks the most likely target is a collection by Larch Security from the Barclays in Borough Walk.'

'God, I hate these situations,' Lane said. They were in Iles's room today and the Chief had simply drifted in, as he often did, for an impromptu talk. Lane felt most at ease in such a setting, and Harpur and Iles had waited for one to arise: it meant a better chance of persuading the Chief to approve an ambush than if asked formally.

'These situations, sir?' Iles inquired.

'Where we have to decide whether to thwart the raid by picking up the people in advance, or letting it go ahead, so we have a better case and graver offence, but with all the attendant hazards. Old people, babies, other mushrooms in the street, not to mention our own lads and the security van team.'

'That often *is* a most horrible dilemma, sir,' Iles replied, 'but not in this instance, I think. We really haven't enough to act on until the hit happens. And Col says we know only two of the three. Sloppy to miss one. Plus, we'd be going entirely on "information received" I'm afraid, which would be virtually to endorse all the hysterical allegations in the Sellick article – especially if anything went wrong.'

Lane said: 'It's the prospect of things going wrong that—'

'Col has provided us with ample time to prepare, sir.'

'Yes, but Colin above all will know that even with good information and preparedness things can still come unstuck.'

'You mean Martin Webb? With respect, sir, I don't see that as "coming unstuck". Not in the least: we knocked over a villain in the act. He knocked none of ours over and would have. Story closed.'

'But it was not closed, was it, Desmond? We had what appears to be repercussions in the death of the father. And then the body of Anthony Towler washed ashore miles away, apparently having been roped after death by knifing, God knows where.'

'God knows is right, I fear. We've really no idea how either of these deaths happened, sir, though Colin is doing all he can,' Iles replied.

'You say there are weapons, Colin,' Lane asked. 'We know where they are? Couldn't we get them for possession?'

'We believe Sanquhar-Perry picked up hand-guns from Teddy Brinscombe, yes, sir,' Harpur said. 'We haven't seen them.'

'Courtney's too smart to have weapons where we might find them, sir,' Iles told the Chief. 'What Col would like is to have a reception ready at Borough Walk, plus some touring tooled-up cars, in case our deductions about the Barclays are wrong.'

'It's all so damnably iffy, Desmond.'

'The nature of our trade, sir.'

Chapter Twenty-Four

Harpur decided to bring in Wayne Timberlake for the ambush. It was a risk, but he tried to help bright people develop, and it would do Timberlake good to see the heavy side of the craft after the ladylike skills of watching and tailing.

In some ways this job was not the best introduction because things went so nicely, at least until almost the end. Timberlake must not expect it always to be like this. These occasions could be very messy. Today, though, the ambush was properly placed, the van turned up on time and so did the raid. Timberlake would probably never see a better wedding of sound information, deduction and power. Harpur had twenty men there, six armed, including Cotton and Sid Synott, superlative marksmen with almost anything. Harpur did not carry a gun himself. The Post Office memories were too raw.

They came out of hiding in the shops and cars around the bank as Sanquhar-Perry and the other two drove up hard to the rear of the parked Larch van and jumped out carrying what looked to Harpur as he ran like King Cobra Colt revolvers, glistening new. Harpur was intent mainly on yelling his customary, stipulated, throaty lines, 'Stop, armed police. Put down your weapons.' He gave the whole lot twice, because there was a lot of the summer sales public listening, and that woman, Sellick, might still be around the city. The Chief had remained uncommitted to the ambush and would want all the protocol double done.

As could happen in these outings, it was the novice in the raid gang who gave most trouble, poor young sod. People like that had more to prove and had not seen enough to recognise disaster, even when it hit them head-on. The three were all balaclavaed, but Harpur could identify each easily enough. Clive Bowling stood close to the van doors and with his arm locked hard around the neck of one of its crew, held the man's body as a shield. Bowling raised the Colt, pointing it at Harpur who led, also as stipulated. Bowling was shouting something, too – something full of curses and promises, something routine for this situation, something terrifying and credible, until Sid or Robert Cotton hit him in the fraction of his boiler-suited chest that showed for a second as the guard struggled to break free. Only Sid or Cotton could have managed something so final and classic, given the microscopic chance. Or possibly both. The postmortem would say. Bowling slipped down behind the guard and seemed to curl slowly in the gutter around his feet, like smoke from a subsiding fire.

Sanquhar-Perry shouted, too, but his King Cobra was on the ground and his hands in the air. He had a ringing, masterful, well-bred voice and the words came clearly to Harpur, who by now was very close: 'All right, all right, we're fucking sold. Don't fucking shoot.'

Harpur grew aware of Timberlake sprinting easily by his side. 'The other's run around the front and through the traffic,' he said.

Harpur kept going, Timberlake with him. The heavy lines of mid-morning buses and cars obstructed them, and obstructed the right-hand segment of the ambush arc, which should have blocked this escape. But you could not shut down a street if you wanted surprise.

'Christ, he's clear,' Harpur said.

'No, we'll get him,' Timberlake grunted.

It was why Harpur had known it a risk including him. 'He's gone into the crowd, Wayne.'

'I think I recognise him, anyway, mask or not. His build,' Timberlake said. 'We can pick him up later. The Charlton Heston type who called on Sanquhar-Perry.'

'Means nothing,' Harpur told him.

'Sir, if we—'

Harpur had stopped. 'Gone. I asked around after you mentioned that the other day. Nobody knows anyone like Charlton Heston. He'll have taken the mask off now and merged with the shoppers. Hopeless.'

'We could easily—'

'He's clear, Wayne. Forget it. No cash went.'

Timberlake considered, then nodded. 'Yes, I see, sir. Sanquhar-Perry will point us?'

'Courtney never talks. He considers us déclassé.'

'And the other's dead.'

'One man is clear, Wayne,' he told him once more.

Timberlake considered again, nodded again. 'Right, sir.'

'You'll probably grow up fast here.'